PRODIGAL SON

By Danielle Steel

PEGASUS • A PERFECT LIFE • POWER PLAY
WINNERS • FIRST SIGHT • UNTIL THE END OF TIME
SINS OF THE MOTHER • FRIENDS FOREVER
BETRAYAL • HOTEL VENDÔME • HAPPY BIRTHDAY
44 CHARLES STREET • LEGACY • FAMILY TIES
BIG GIRL • SOUTHERN LIGHTS
MATTERS OF THE HEART • ONE DAY AT A TIME
A GOOD WOMAN • ROGUE • HONOR THYSELF
AMAZING GRACE • BUNGALOW 2
SISTERS • H.R.H. • COMING OUT
THE HOUSE • TOXIC BACHELORS • MIRACLE
IMPOSSIBLE • ECHOES • SECOND CHANCE
RANSOM • SAFE HARBOUR • JOHNNY ANGEL
DATING GAME • ANSWERED PRAYERS
SUNSET IN ST. TROPEZ • THE COTTAGE • THE KISS
LEAP OF FAITH • LONE EAGLE • JOURNEY
THE HOUSE ON HOPE STREET • THE WEDDING
IRRESISTIBLE FORCES • GRANNY DAN
BITTERSWEET • MIRROR IMAGE • THE KLONE AND I
THE LONG ROAD HOME • THE GHOST
SPECIAL DELIVERY • THE RANCH
SILENT HONOR • MALICE • FIVE DAYS IN PARIS
LIGHTNING • WINGS • THE GIFT • ACCIDENT
VANISHED • MIXED BLESSINGS • JEWELS
NO GREATER LOVE • HEARTBEAT
MESSAGE FROM NAM • DADDY • STAR
ZOYA • KALEIDOSCOPE • FINE THINGS
WANDERLUST • SECRETS • FAMILY ALBUM
FULL CIRCLE • CHANGES • THURSTON HOUSE

DANIELLE STEEL

PRODIGAL SON

A Novel

**Doubleday Large Print
Home Library Edition**

Delacorte Press | New York

This Large Print Edition, prepared especially for Doubleday Large Print Home Library, contains the complete, unabridged text of the original Publisher's Edition.

Published in the United States by Delacorte Press, an imprint of Random House, a division of Random House LLC, a Penguin Random House Company, New York.

DELACORTE PRESS and the HOUSE colophon are registered trademarks of Random House LLC.

ISBN 978-1-62953-394-0

Printed in the United States of America

This Large Print Book carries the Seal of Approval of N.A.V.H.

To my beloved children,
Beatie, Trevor, Todd, Nick, Sam,
Victoria, Vanessa, Maxx, and Zara:

Sadly, there is evil in the world,
unseen, unheard, often undetected,
but nonetheless still there,
a powerful force to be reckoned with.

May you always be protected from harm,
in all its forms. May you be wise, safe,
and shielded from all those who wish you ill.
May only goodness and kindness touch
you for all of your days. May goodness
always prevail in your lives. Good is
more powerful than evil.

And may my love for you, beyond measure,
warm you on dark days.

With all my love,
Mommy/d.s

"... for this thy brother was dead, and is alive again; and was lost and is found."

—**Luke** 15:32

PRODIGAL SON

Chapter 1

Peter McDowell sat in his office, surrounded by cardboard bankers' boxes after what had been the worst week of his life. The last month had been a nightmare, not just for him but for everyone on Wall Street. Peter stared at the screen on his desk, which he had been doing since early that morning, and for the past five days. It was Friday, the tenth of October, 2008, and stock prices had been plummeting since Monday. It was the worst stock market crash since the Great Depression.

Landmark events had taken place in recent weeks that had heralded the collapse

of the house of cards. Twenty-six days earlier, Lehman Brothers, one of the oldest
and most respected investment banks, had
filed for bankruptcy, stunning the financial
world. Even more stunning was the govern-
ment's refusal to bail them out, although
six months before they had done so for
Bear Stearns, which had been bought by
JPMorgan Chase. Just before Lehman
Brothers' historic announcement, Bank of
America had announced that it was acquir-
ing equally venerable and respected Mer-
rill Lynch. Investment banks and financial
institutions were staggering like drunks all
over Wall Street, and several smaller banks
had already closed. And the day after
Lehman Brothers declared bankruptcy, the
largest insurer in the nation lost 95 percent
of its value, and six days later was removed
from the Dow Jones.

And with everyone reeling over alarming
daily announcements, Whitman Broadbank, the investment bank where Peter
McDowell worked and had established his
meteoric career, announced that they were
folding as well. Peter had been told three
days before, as the stock market continued
to plunge. It was hard to wrap his mind

around it, as he leaned his head against the boxes on his desk. That afternoon at six o'clock, they were closing their doors. Peter's golden career, and famously high-risk investments, with previously outstanding results, were no more. He was putting whatever he had left in his office in boxes. He had told his wife, Alana, and their boys, Ryan and Ben, the night before.

"What does that mean, Dad?" Ryan had asked him with a look of panic. He was fourteen years old. Peter didn't dare read off the litany of things that were about to change for them all. Everything had to be sold. The firm had been leveraged to the hilt. The stock that Peter had gladly acquired in lieu of profits or salary on many occasions, and that comprised most of his personal fortune, was worthless paper now. The house in the Hamptons was history, the time share of a plane, their penthouse on Fifth Avenue, private schools, credit cards, the Ferrari he played with on the weekends and the boys loved to ride in, Alana's Bentley, and the brand-new Rolls. All were expensive unimportant toys and symbols of his success. More important, all of their security and way of life had evaporated into thin air. His money and investments were all in Whitman Broadbank, and whatever else he had had gone down the drain with the stock market collapse in the past five days. There was virtually nothing left, or so little that it hardly counted. Peter couldn't think of a single area of his life that wouldn't be affected by what had just happened to the economy, except his marriage and his boys. Alana had been painfully silent and watched him, as he explained it all to them. But even Peter didn't fully understand it yet. No one did. The day before, Iceland had declared the country bankrupt and closed its stock market, and other countries around the world were watching in panic, as they saw the American stock market fall and implode.

Peter finally managed to tear his eyes from the screen that had mesmerized him all week. His secretary had already left that morning, and there was silence in the halls. Others were doing what he was, loading a few personal things into boxes, and carrying them downstairs. All of them were facing the demise of their careers and radically changed lives as a result.

Peter stood up and dropped one of the boxes in the doorway. It was hard to imagine now what he was going to do about work. People were getting fired left and right, and there were hundreds of overqualified candidates for whatever jobs remained. In the musical chairs of the financial game, thousands had wound up without a seat, and Peter was no better off than the rest. His success had been extraordinary for the past twenty-one years, since he hitched his wagon to the star of Whitman Broadbank fresh out of business school when he was twenty-five. Now he was forty-six, virtually broke, and out of a job, and so was almost everyone he knew, with the exception of the lucky few who had survived the tidal wave of the past month. No one he knew had been untouched.

Peter had been famous for years, with almost every deal he made, but not this time. This time he had taken a fall with all the rest. His luck had finally run out. This wasn't the way he had expected his career to end, but it wasn't over yet; he wasn't about to give up. He was ready to do whatever it took to clean up the mess, tighten his belt, and he knew that sooner or later he'd be back. He just didn't know when, or how to accomplish it yet. And for now things were going to be tough. He had warned Alana and the boys of that. They were putting both the house in the Hamptons and the apartment in New York on the market that weekend, although real estate prices had already been hit, and were going to experience a severe drop. He would take whatever they could get. And as soon as the New York apartment sold, he was going to have to figure out where they were going to live. He knew that as long as the family stuck together, they'd be all right.

They had to get past this terrifying time and figure out what to do, and where to go from here. He'd been thinking that he could get a job in a small local bank, somewhere outside New York, and make a comeback on Wall Street when the economy was healthy again. He had grown up in a small Massachusetts town, and realized he might have to leave New York for a while and start from scratch. He had lain awake every night all week, thinking about it. All he had left now was a lot of worthless stock, and whatever cash they had on hand, which wasn't much.

He had insisted that Alana let their live-in couple go earlier that week. They didn't have a penny to spare. The couple had been nice about it and said they understood, several of their friends were in the same situation. And they'd been smart enough to keep their savings liquid in the bank. He smiled to himself, thinking that their housekeeping couple were probably in better financial shape than he was right now. He had tried to get them to invest their money, and they'd said they didn't trust any bank or investment service. Everything they had was in cash. And cash was king right now.

Peter rode down in the elevator carrying two of his boxes, with two junior partners, one of whom looked as though he were about to cry. Like most of them, he had been wiped out. Partners and employees who had been on top of the world only a few months before were now back to square one. Peter called it the Chutes and Ladders of life. One minute you're way up at the top, in the stratosphere, and the next minute you're down at the bottom, flat on your ass. It had never happened to Peter before.

"Don't give up, Marshall," Peter said to one of the men. "We'll be back."

"I'm going back to Ohio," the junior partner said, looking depressed, "to work for my dad at his factory. All I had was Broadbank stock." It was the situation that most of them were in. And even those who had other stocks knew they were worthless now.

"We're all in the same boat," Peter said, determined to be positive about it, although he had given in to panic himself many times in the last week, in the dark of night. But there had to be a light at the end of the tunnel eventually, even if they were going down the tubes right now. He refused to be beaten by this. It was bad, but it had to get better again at some point.

Peter left them with a nod on the ground floor. He put the two boxes in the back of the car he had parked outside. He was using the Volvo station wagon that their couple used to drive to do errands for them. He was planning to take his other cars to a fancy used-car lot for high-end cars that weekend. There was going to be a glut of fancy cars on the market, but whatever he got for them was good enough. He had listed his Ferrari on the Internet that week.

And Alana had cried when he told her she had to give up her Bentley. There was no room in their life for luxuries right now.

He brought down four more boxes, and looked at his office for a last time, wondering when he would have a palatial office like this again. Maybe never. Maybe he'd never be back. Maybe it really was all over, as everyone feared. He felt a wave of terror wash over him and then turned around and walked out. He stopped to see two of his partners, but everyone he wanted to say goodbye to was already gone. There would be meetings in the coming weeks about their bankruptcy proceedings, but for now, everyone was leaving the sinking ship and worrying about themselves.

Peter was silent as he rode down the elevator for the last time. He was a tall, athletic-looking man, who appeared younger than his years. He played a lot of tennis on the weekends, worked out with a trainer in the gym he had had built in the apartment, and he was slim and fit. There were a few strands of gray in his sandy blond hair, but it didn't show. He looked like the perfect all-American boy next door. All his life, or at least in recent years, he had been the image of the Golden Boy. For years now, he had embodied success. That hadn't been the case in his youth, when he felt like a screw-up, and had been treated like one. He had been labeled the family black sheep, compared to his perfect fraternal twin brother, whom his parents had revered.

Peter had been every parent's nightmare, a bright, handsome boy who did abysmally at school and was constantly in trouble, suspended or on probation, either for his behavior or for his appalling grades. Undiagnosed dyslexia had nearly destroyed his youth. His classmates called him stupid, teachers got frustrated with him and eventually gave up, and neither Peter nor his parents could understand his difficulties at school. His parents were educated and intelligent, and Peter appeared to be smart, but he was always accused of not trying, being lazy, and was punished for homework assignments he didn't complete. And even he couldn't explain why the letters on the page and the directions he was given made no sense. He punished the boys who made fun of him, with his fists. It was common for him to come home from school with a torn shirt and a black eye, and having delivered worse, while in the lower grades. In high school he took on an attitude of indifference, hostility, and arrogance to cover the sense of failure and incompetence he felt.

And all the while, his brother Michael was exemplary in every way. He wasn't as good looking as Peter, or as dazzling in some ways. He was shorter, stockier, quieter, and didn't have Peter's looks. Their mother always said that Peter could have been a star if he would just do his homework and behave himself. Michael was always solid and polite, dedicated to his schoolwork, and got outstanding grades. They never had to worry about Michael. It was Peter who nearly broke their hearts every time he failed again. And Michael was always quietly on the sidelines, pointing out Peter's inability to do what was expected of him, or control himself. Michael goaded Peter to lose his temper, whenever no one was watching, and on the rare occasions when Michael did something he shouldn't have, he saw to it that Peter got the blame. It was easy for their parents and teachers to believe that Michael was innocent and

Peter the guilty party. By the time they finished high school, Peter's parents were in despair over him. His childhood tantrums had turned into adolescent rages, based on the intolerable frustration he had lived with for eighteen years. He couldn't win his parents' approval, or anyone else's, so he had given up trying to win it or do anything he should. He and his brother were staunch enemies by then, and Peter saw him as the cause of many of the ills that plagued him, or even most of them. Peter could never measure up to him. And all of them were astonished when Peter got into college. He had one dedicated high school teacher who had written an extraordinary recommendation for him, insisting that beyond his poor grades and checkered school career was a remarkably bright, creative young man who would one day overcome his problems. He called him a "late bloomer," which was the kindest thing anyone had ever said about him, and assured the college that had accepted him that he would make them proud one day.

And once in college, Peter's entire life had changed. An English professor had taken a profound interest in him, sensed that his earlier poor grades were not due to laziness, and had sent him for sophisticated testing at the learning center. Like a specter in the mists that no one had previously suspected or seen, the dyslexia that had caused him so much pain emerged and was diagnosed. The English professor who had sent him for testing became his mentor and tutored him personally for all four years. The results had been remarkable, and Peter himself was astounded at what he was able to accomplish.

More than anything, Peter had wanted to impress his parents and win all the approval that had belonged only to his brother for so many years. But by then, all his parents were capable of, when it concerned Peter, was relief. And Michael had been threatened by Peter's new-found skills and quick to point out that all his success in college did was confirm how lazy Peter had been for all the years before. If he was able to win good grades now in college, why hadn't he in high school? The crippling effect of the dyslexia on his early life was more than his parents could absorb, and Peter found them no warmer and no happier with him than they had been before. With his wild, aggressive behavior and frequent rages, he had burned too many bridges when he was a boy. Their lack of faith in him made him even more determined to succeed once he graduated from college, and show them once and for all what he was capable of. Suddenly he burned with the desire to show everyone and be a "star," just as his mother had believed he could be, as a boy. But those days were long gone, along with her faith in him.

His success in business school afterward and meteoric rise on Wall Street came as no surprise to those who had mentored him in college. They had found him to have overwhelming motivation and drive. It only came as a surprise to his brother and parents, who still acted as though they expected him to revert at any moment to the headache he had been as a boy. There was no winning their confidence anymore, and Peter remained convinced that Michael exacerbated their fears about him, and kept the memories alive in their minds of how much trouble he had caused them for so long. "People don't change," Michael had often assured them, and although his parents wanted him to do well, their faith in Peter had been too badly shaken, and their relationship with him too strained by the time he moved to New York. Their life with Michael had always been so much easier, ever since he was born. Peter had become identified forever as their problem, and Michael as the perfect son. It was more than Peter could cope with, and too hurtful, and he rarely went home after college, once he realized how little faith they had in him, even then. It was Michael they always believed, and always had, and why wouldn't they? He had been the perfectly behaved little boy, doing everything they expected of him, not the one coming home from school every day with a detention slip and a bloody nose. Michael supported their beliefs about Peter, reminding them that people don't change, and they believed him. Michael had the stronger relationship with their parents once they were grown up, and he was so much more like them.

He went to medical school like their father, which was a powerful bond between them. And after a brief career as an anesthesiologist in Boston, he had ultimately stepped into their father's shoes. "Dr. Pat," their father, was a lovable country doctor, adored by all. And giving up his dream of anesthesiology in a big city, Michael had returned to the fold, to work with his father and eventually take over his practice, and he became as beloved as his father had been, in their general practice, tending to everyone's needs in a small Massachusetts town. In the end, it turned out to be a role that suited Michael well too. Patients thought he was even more lovable than his father; he had a wonderful way with children and old people, showed immeasurable patience and compassion to all his patients, and was a giver in every way.

By the time Michael joined their father in his practice, Peter was already a whiz on Wall Street, and rarely went home. He had given up trying to sway his parents' opinion of him, and his relationship with his twin brother was a lost cause. Michael had caused him too much grief, they had shared too many bad times, and Peter blamed him in great part for his parents' poor opinion of him. Michael had put too much energy into it for too long. The chasm between Peter and his family was too wide by then, and he put his energy into other things, like

making money and becoming a legend on
Wall Street, not for them, but for himself.
He told himself that what they thought of
him no longer mattered to him, and he no
longer cared. Appearing indifferent to them
and seeing them as seldom as possible put
balm on years of hurt. It irritated him even
further that when he did go home to see
them, it was Michael who pretended to
have been the injured party of their youth,
when the truth was the reverse. Peter had
been blamed for everything, even when it
was undeserved. Michael had seen to that.

One of the worst incidents Peter remembered of his childhood happened when
they were twelve. The boys had shared a
beloved dog, a shaggy mongrel that was
part husky and part golden retriever. He
was mostly white and looked like a wolf,
and he had been Peter's devoted compan-
ion much of the time. He had taken him
camping to a river with friends of the family
the summer they were twelve. Scout, as
he was called, had followed Peter into
the river, and been swept away by the cur-
rents, while swimming only a few feet from
them. Michael had been nearest the dog
in a small inflatable boat, and Peter had

screamed to him to grab Scout's collar and stop him, and Michael let the dog sweep past and never held out a hand. Scout was killed going over a waterfall, despite Peter's frantic efforts to reach him in time, to no avail. Peter had been heartbroken over it, and when they went home, Michael told their parents that it was Peter's fault the dog had drowned. Peter had been too devastated to counter what he said or try to explain it. They never listened to him anyway, only to Michael, even then. Peter had never forgiven him, and for their parents, it was just one more on Peter's list of sins at the time. The family had mourned the dog for months, and Peter had never wanted another dog after that. Whatever Michael said to their parents, both boys knew the truth. Their parents were all too willing to believe Michael a saint, and Peter the devil in their midst. Michael had appeared to be heartbroken over the lost dog, but it was Peter's heart that had ached for months, over that and so many other things.

The experiences of Peter's childhood had made him determined to make it on his own, with no help from anyone. And he had succeeded remarkably, until his whole world had just come tumbling down. Until then, Peter had been a star in his field for two decades. He had made more money than he'd ever dreamed of. His mother had followed his achievements in the business press. She was happy for him, although sometimes even she found it hard to believe. And given what they read of his immense good fortune, his parents had quietly decided that it made no sense to leave Peter the little they had saved. Michael needed what they had far more than his fabulously successful twin. Michael was a country doctor like his father, with a wife and two children, barely eking out a living. Peter had not yet married by then, and had more money than he could possibly need. As a token gesture, they left Peter their small summer cottage on a nearby lake.

His father explained in a long letter written shortly before he died that it would have been coals to Newcastle to leave Peter any money, and they didn't have a lot anyway. And Michael needed it far more than his twin. In response to that, they were leaving Michael their house in Ware, Pat's medical practice, and whatever they had managed to save. They were pleased and proud, the letter said, that Peter needed nothing from them. They hoped he'd be happy with the cottage on the lake as a token of their love.

There had been unpleasant words exchanged between the brothers after their father died, and again when their mother died the following year, when Peter accused his brother of manipulating them and turning them against him all his life. He had done it right to the end.

Peter had never gone to see the cottage after he inherited it, and paid a small fee to have it maintained by a local realtor. It was where he had spent his boyhood summers. He had never had the heart to sell it, and it was worth very little. Its value was mostly sentimental. His only pleasant memories of his childhood had happened there. But in the years since, Peter had nothing more to say to his brother. By now, the two men were enemies and strangers. His brother's constant lies and manipulations when they were children, always to implicate Peter as the one committing the crimes, however menial, had ultimately destroyed Peter's desire to remain involved with his family, and had destroyed his parents' faith in him.

He had been to see his mother on her
deathbed only once before she died. He
felt guilty about it now, feeling he should
have done more to repair the damage. But
Michael had been entrenched, too determined to cut Peter out of everything, and
most particularly out of their parents' hearts,
not just their wills, and he had succeeded.
Peter had never been able to win them
back after the failures in his youth. His
mother had been upset by him, and his father had never tried to understand him.
Sharing a career in medicine with Michael,
they had so much in common, and Peter
had never succeeded in forming a bond
with his father. All Peter had ever been was
a disappointment to him, and a problem.

Peter hadn't been home, nor had contact
with his brother, in fifteen years, and he
didn't miss it. It was a part of his life, and a
painful history, he never wanted to revisit.
And surely not now that he was suddenly
a failure all over again. Now once again, it
was Michael with the steady small-town life
who was a success, the beloved country
doctor whom everyone adored. Anytime
Peter ran into someone he grew up with
who had moved to New York in recent

years, he heard all about it. Saint Michael, who had been the nemesis of Peter's youth, since the day they were born. He had been the permanent wedge between their parents and Peter. It was embarrassing to admit now, but for years Peter had hated him, and he had no desire to ever see him again.

Michael had seen to it that Peter was viewed as the "bad guy" by everyone who knew them, and even by their parents. Michael had put a lot of energy into it, and God only knew what he would say about him now, if he heard about Whitman Broadbank folding and Peter's life dissolving into nothing—probably that he deserved it. Michael had compassion and empathy for everyone in the world, except his twin brother. Michael had been consumed by jealousy of Peter. When they were young, their father had called them Cain and Abel, and said he wouldn't have been surprised if they killed each other. They didn't. Peter just took off, and made his way in an entirely different world. A world that had just collapsed around everyone's ears, like a hovel in an underdeveloped country during an earthquake.

Peter parked the car in front of their build-

ing on Fifth Avenue, opened the trunk, and
showed the doorman the boxes. He said
he would send them upstairs with a porter,
as Peter slipped a twenty-dollar bill into his
hand and strode inside. The doorman had
already heard rumors that the apartment
was going to be put on the market shortly—
the housekeeping couple who had left had
told him. He was sorry for the McDowells.
There were people like them whose lives
would be changing all over the city, and in
the suburbs. All the hotshots in the financial world had been instantly ruined. Some
had made better investments than others,
or were with firms that were holding on or
had been rescued. But for the partners and
employees of Lehman Brothers, Whitman
Broadbank, and the firms, banks, and institutions that had closed, life as they had
known it was over.

Peter let himself into the apartment and
went to look for Alana. It was still warm outside, and she was lying on a deck chair on
the terrace, talking on her cell phone. She
ended the call the minute she saw him. She
hated to look into his eyes now, there was
so much pain there, and the acrid smell of
defeat seemed to hang all around them.

She dreaded seeing him now, and was terrified of what new horrifying announcement he would make. She looked at him
with terror as he gently put a hand on her
head. They had been married for fifteen
years. He had met her right after his parents' deaths, and married her a few months
later, dazzled by her beauty. And he had
already been a huge success at thirty-one
when they married.

Alana had been twenty-three years old,
fresh out of USC, and the most beautiful
girl he had ever seen when he met her. She
was the only child of Gary Tallon, one of
the biggest music producers in Hollywood.
Her father's career had started with the
Beatles, and he had been vocal and unhappy when Alana moved to New York
and married Peter. He had spent years trying to convince his son-in-law to move to
L.A. and come to work for him. But it was
a world and city that didn't appeal to Peter.
The thrill of the financial world was a drug
to him, and he was addicted to it. Peter
knew nothing about the music business.
The tinsel of Hollywood and her father's
scene was entirely foreign to him, although
he was well aware that Alana always missed

it. She flew out to see her father regularly in L.A. and took the boys with her. Her mother had died when she was fifteen, and she was unusually close to her father because of it. Gary liked Peter, but Peter was an unfamiliar breed of animal to him, and over the years, Gary had always acted slightly suspicious of him.

Peter appeared to be conservative in his looks and demeanor, but his father-in-law was also well aware of the enormous risks he took in business. They had always paid off for him and his investors. His father-in-law had placed a few million dollars with him over the years, and had done well with the investments. Until now. He had lost all of it when Whitman Broadbank declared bankruptcy. It had been only play money to him, so it was going to have no impact on his life, but he had been calling his daughter every day to ask what Peter's plans were. All she had been able to tell him so far was that Peter was planning to sell everything, which didn't surprise her father. He knew how heavily Peter's fortune was involved in the stock of the firm. When that went, Peter would have almost nothing. It was no mystery to him or anyone who knew their business. And no one expected this to happen. Peter had almost no liquidity as a cushion and too few other investments. He had taken better care of his clients.

"Well, that's it. It's over," Peter said as he sat down in a deck chair next to her, looking grim. "I brought all my stuff home. Twenty-one years in six boxes." He looked pained as he said it. It was an ignominious end to a brilliant career, for now at least. He wanted to go down fighting, but there was no fight here. "I've got to go out to Southampton and meet the realtor tomorrow. I'll leave my car on the lot there. You can follow me in the Bentley and drive me home. I'm going to sell that next week too." The Ferrari was at the house in the Hamptons, and he was planning to give that up to the dealer too. He had released his time share in the plane earlier in the week, at a huge penalty, which was still better than the expense they could no longer afford.

Alana's breath caught as she looked at her husband. At thirty-eight, she was just as beautiful as she had been at twenty-three, maybe more so. She knew everything about her father's business, but very little about Peter's. And she thought the world of finance was boring. It was a lot more fun being in L.A., when Stevie Wonder or Mick Jagger came to have dinner with her father. She had grown up around all of them. And Peter had always known what his parents would have thought about her, she was spoiled, and she had grown up in a rarified glitzy atmosphere light-years from their conservative small-town world. But Peter knew that there was more to her than his parents would have noticed. She was intelligent as well as beautiful, and she was a good mother to their boys, and had been a good wife to him. She had always been willing to meet his investors and put on a good show when they entertained them. Her father had sent her to boarding school in Europe for two years, and she spoke French and Spanish fluently. She had enrolled their boys at the Lycée, so they spoke French too. And she was on the boards of Juilliard and the Metropolitan Museum of Art. Before she had married Peter, she had wanted to become a dramatic agent, but had become Peter's wife instead. And after fifteen years, he was still in love with her.

Alana was a spectacular-looking woman,

immaculately groomed, with a model's body, and always expensively dressed, thanks to him. Alana was no stranger to luxury or money, and had never been denied anything. All the love Gary had once lavished on his wife before she died, he poured into Alana once he was alone with her. And before Peter had married her, her father had informed him that if Peter ever broke her heart, he would kill him. Peter had no doubt that he meant it, he was a little rough around the edges, but a brilliant businessman, and he had an incredible talent for and insight into the music business, of which he was the indisputable king.

"I'm sorry," Alana said sadly, as she looked at her husband. She knew how hard all this was for him, but it was for her and the boys too, or it would be, once all the changes in their life became evident. She had no idea where they were going to live, and neither did Peter, which was frightening for all of them. Being poor in New York didn't sound like fun to her. Alana had never been poor for an instant of her life, and her father had a Midas touch in business. He had never been through anything like what had just happened to Peter. She reached out and touched his hand, and he smiled ruefully at her.

"I'm sorry too. We'll put Humpty Dumpty back together again sooner or later. I promise. It's just going to be a little rocky for a while." He was trying to wrap his mind around it too. "At least we have each other." That was still what mattered most to him. Alana and their children. This was tough, but it wasn't a tragedy, just a very trying period to get through, and a whole life to rebuild.

She looked deep into Peter's eyes then. "I was talking to Daddy today, and I think he had a pretty good idea," she said, trying to look hopeful. She knew it wasn't going to be easy to convince Peter. He was a proud man, this was a hard blow for him, and he had never been crazy about L.A. It was a foreign land to him, too far from New York, which had always been the hub of his career. But now everything had changed. And she didn't want their sons living in poverty while Peter struggled. "He thinks we should come out and stay with him for a while. He says we can have the guest house." It was a house bigger than most family homes in the Hamptons, and Peter knew what came with it. An army of servants, every luxury imaginable, and a fleet of expensive cars.

Her father had always been very generous with them, but Peter didn't want to be beholden to him, and never had been. The only way to survive with a man like Gary Tallon was to be independent of him, and Peter no longer was. That was a very dangerous position to be in, and he didn't want to hurt Alana's feelings when he said no, but she could already see it in his eyes. Peter had no desire to move to L.A., and stay in her father's guest house, or worse, be supported by him while he was out of a job. For a long moment, Peter said nothing, while Alana went on. Her long blond hair fell heavily past her shoulders while she lay on the deck chair in short white shorts with a pink T-shirt. He could see her nipples through the shirt, and her long legs on the deck chair. She flew to L.A. every three weeks to get her hair colored, and every three months, they wove in extensions to thicken her mane of silky blond hair. After fifteen years in New York, she was still deeply attached to L.A., and everything about it.

"Daddy says you can work for him, if you want to. Or you can just take it easy for a few months. He's going to call you about it. And there's a Lycée in L.A., so the boys will hardly notice the change, and they love Grampa Gary," she pleaded. He was the only grandparent they had, and their grandfather doted on them. They were the sons he had never had, and they loved meeting all the rock stars in his business. He arranged backstage passes at every concert they wanted to go to. For them, it would be like moving to Disneyland. But for Peter, it sounded like moving to hell, and selling his soul to Alana's father, which was something he was determined to avoid at all costs. He was going to extricate himself from this mess. He didn't want her father's help, however well intended.

"I appreciate it, sweetheart," Peter said calmly, "but I need to stick around here while everything gets settled. I can't just run off to California, and live off your father. And I need to see what opportunities open up here."

"Daddy says there won't be any decent jobs for you here for the next year or two. We might as well be in L.A. until things get better. He says there's nothing for you here. Why not work for him? He'll find something for you to do."

"I don't want a mercy job, Alana. I want a real one, in my business. I don't know a damn thing about the music business. I have nothing to offer your father."

"You can help him with his investments," she said, still pleading, but she could see she wasn't winning.

"I'm sure he'd be thrilled," Peter said cynically. "I just lost him a bunch of money when Whitman folded. He doesn't need me for his investments."

"He wants to help us," she said quietly, with a look of determination in her eyes. This was a battle she didn't intend to lose. "We're not going to be able to afford a decent place to live, once you sell the apartment," she said with a tone of desperation. "What are we going to do?"

"I'll figure out something," he said softly. He felt beaten as he sat watching her. He was beginning to realize just how unhappy she was going to be without money, and he didn't want to be on the dole to her father. Peter had no idea how long it would take him to get back on his feet. And her father was right, it might take him a year or two to find something in his line of work. People were being fired at all levels in the financial world. "I want us to stay here," he said firmly, as Alana looked at him with sorrow in her eyes.

"I want to go home," she said quietly, and just as firmly. "I told my father we would. You can't support us here, and I don't want to move to some shit place where we'll all be miserable. They boys will hate it, and so would I. That's not fair to them when my father wants to help us."

"I grew up simply in a small town. It didn't kill me," Peter said, feeling frantic and as though he were about to drown. He knew that if he let him, his father-in-law would swallow him whole and own him, and Alana was setting him up for that.

"We could move to the country for a year or two," Peter said, sounding desperate.

"You hated growing up in a small town," she reminded him unkindly.

"For very different reasons. I had trouble in school, I was dyslexic, and I had a brother who made my life miserable. And I didn't get along with him or my parents. Our kids might be happy in a small town. It might be good for them. There's more to the world than just New York, L.A., and Southampton. Maybe this would be a good time for them to see that. At least for a little while."

Alana's eyes turned to steel then. She was still a daddy's girl, her father was rescuing her, and she wasn't going to let Peter stop him. Peter could see that it was what she wanted, even more than she wanted her life with him.

"I'm going home, Peter, and I'm taking the boys with me. We don't need to be poor. They don't need to discover what it's like not to have anything they're used to. My father wants to be there for us, and take care of us, and you too."

"I'm a grown man, Alana. I wouldn't do it even if he were my father. I can't live in L.A. like a gigolo, while your father pays the bills. I'll take care of us, and we'll work it out."

"I'm not going to live in poverty, and deprive our kids, to feed your ego. We have no other choice. You're telling me we're dead broke. My father isn't. He can afford to support all of us, so our life won't be affected. I want to go home." There was iron in her voice.

"What happened to 'for better or worse,

for richer or poorer'?" Peter asked her bleakly. "Or did I miss something? Was it 'for richer or richer'? Why can't we just suck it up for a while till I get back on my feet?"

"Why should our kids suffer because you lost your job, if they don't have to? The kids love L.A., and the Lycée out there is just like the one here. I called them this week, and they've got room for both boys. Ben and Ryan will be happy there, happier than they'd be in some mythical small town, or living in poverty here. I won't do that to them."

"Or yourself. Is that what you're saying?" He was starting to look angry, as defeat and frustration welled up in him. He wanted her to stay. "If you have to give up the Bentley, you're going home to Daddy? That's pathetic, Alana. No, actually, it's disgusting. Fuck the Bentley. We need to stay together right now."

"Then come with us, and forget New York for a while." Or forever, if she got her way, Peter thought to himself. She had wanted to move back to L.A. for years, and Peter never agreed. Even with his back to the wall now, he didn't want to. His life was here. But the life she wanted, under her father's wing, was there. This was the opportunity she had been waiting for, and she didn't want to miss it. It was now or never.

"I will **not** be supported by your father," he said in a voice quavering with emotion. This was a loaded subject for him. It made him feel like an even bigger failure to go to L.A. with her, and have her father take care of them financially. Peter would rather starve. But Alana wouldn't, and she was also thinking of the boys and their comfort. She didn't want them deprived, if there was no need for it. Her father had offered to pay for everything. It was the opportunity Gary had been waiting for too, to get his little girl to come home, and even bring her boys. And he was more than willing to support Peter in the bargain. Her father's fortune hadn't been impacted by the upheaval on Wall Street, and he had sound investments and an enormous business, owned several oil wells in Southern California, and had huge real estate holdings. The only one who didn't want to benefit from any of it was Peter, who felt completely emasculated by Alana's deal with her father, and humiliated to go out to California with his tail between his legs.

"You don't have any choice," Alana said as she stood up, and looked at him. "I'm not staying here in these conditions, with no money, nowhere to live, no prospects, and you out of a job, maybe for a hell of a long time."

"What are you saying?" Peter asked her harshly. This was beginning to sound ugly to him, and he could hear a veiled threat in her voice.

"I'm saying that I'm going back to L.A. You can sell everything you want. My father made us a good offer to live with him, and take care of us. If you're too stubborn or too proud to take him up on it, I'm not. The boys and I are going out next week, so they can start school there before it gets any later in the school year. I've already told them. They're happy about it. They want to go. I won't let you stop us."

"And if I won't go?" Peter asked her with narrowed eyes, wondering just how far she would take this and what she was really saying.

"Then we'll go anyway. I'm getting off the **Titanic**. I've watched your whole life, and ours, collapse for the last week. The ship is going down. It already has. If you won't get in the lifeboat, that's your decision. But I'm getting off. You can come or not, that's up to you."

"Are you leaving me?" Peter asked her bluntly, wanting to get clear on her implication.

"I'm leaving New York and the mess we're in here. My father offered us a safe haven. I'm going there. We're already starting to drift apart. You don't have time to think about us right now, you're too busy trying to keep your head above water, and I understand that. You're drowning, Peter. But I'm not going to let you drown me too. I'm getting the hell out. What happens to our marriage after this is up to you and what you do now."

"Are you saying that if I don't move to L.A. and become your father's minion, you'll divorce me?" He was pushing her, and she was more than willing to push back.

"You're not going to have a job here for a long time. You might as well go too." She didn't answer his question.

"What if I find a job somewhere else, like Boston or Chicago?" He was testing the waters to see how far she would go.

She hesitated for a long moment, as their

eyes met, and then she answered him at last. "I'm going home, Peter. To L.A. I've lived here for fifteen years, for you. It hasn't worked out. Figure out what you want to do," she said quietly, and then left the terrace, as he sat there alone, staring into space. He had heard her message loud and clear. If he wanted to save their marriage, which was about all he had left now that he cared about, he had to move to L.A., on her terms. And he could see what would happen if he didn't. He laid his head back against the deck chair and closed his eyes as he thought about it, and silent tears rolled slowly down his cheeks. He had never been so miserable in his life. It reminded him of the days when he could barely read, when it seemed as though everyone else knew the answers except him. It was a terrible helpless sensation. But this time he didn't strike out at anyone. He just felt like he was dying inside, and losing everything that mattered to him. His career, his wife, and his boys. She had delivered a hell of an ultimatum, and her message to him was clear.

Chapter 2

The weekend was as awful as they both expected. It was the undoing of a life, like a movie in reverse. They put the house in the Hamptons on the market, at a painfully low price. But Peter wanted to sell it soon. He photographed all their artwork, and planned to call their art dealer on Monday. He was also going to contact Sotheby's and Christie's to see about auctioning whatever he could. He was willing to sell to whomever would pay the highest price. All the art and objects they had collected over time were being dispensed with. The beach house they had loved and where they had

had such good times would belong to someone else.

Peter left the Rolls and the Ferrari at the
car dealership and was startled when Alana refused to give up the Bentley. She
said she was sending it to L.A. Her father
was paying for the transport, and offered to
buy the car from Peter, which he wouldn't
agree to. He didn't want her father paying
for anything, so he said she could keep
it, which was a hardship for him since
they needed the money. She wanted it in
California, and Peter didn't argue with her.
He hated making her unhappy. The atmosphere between them had grown chilly,
and had been ever since their conversation
on Friday, when Alana had made her position clear. She was on the phone with her
father every five minutes now, and she was
planning to leave for L.A. the following
weekend with the boys. She didn't ask Peter
how he felt about it—she announced it to
him as a fait accompli.

They had left Ben and Ryan in the city,
to play at their friends' houses, while Alana
and Peter went out to Southampton to deal
with the house and cars. They didn't want
to use the beach house since it was being

shown for a broker's open on Tuesday, so they went home, and Peter drove them back to the city in silence. He was feeling defeated by the decisions she was making. It was a painful process, and they kept to themselves in separate rooms on Sunday, and then took the boys out to dinner. Ben, their nine-year-old, was excited about living with Grampa Gary in his guest house. At fourteen, Ryan was unhappy to leave his friends, since he had just started high school at the Lycée. And Ryan was visibly worried about his father. After dinner, they played a game of pool in the game room while Ben went to watch a movie in their projection room with his mother.

Ryan startled his father with a painful question halfway through the game. "Are you and Mom getting divorced?" Peter didn't know what to answer but put a good face on it for his son's sake. He had been asking himself the same question for two days, since Alana told him she was leaving and taking the boys to L.A., and he could sense that she had no intention of coming back to New York anytime soon, if ever.

"Not that I know of," Peter said honestly,

not totally reassuring him. "Your mom's probably right. Things are going to be a little tough here for a while, and you'll be comfortable with Grampa Gary."

"What about you, Dad?" Ryan looked worried. "Where are you going to be? Will you come out after you do everything here?"

"Of course." Peter smiled at him and put an arm around his shoulders, but Ryan wasn't fooled. "I just can't come to L.A. yet. There's too much for me to take care of here right now. And I feel a little weird letting your grampa take care of us. That's my job. I just have to figure out how I'm going to do it. But I'll be there as soon as I can."

"I want to stay with you," Ryan said stubbornly, as much to support his father as to be with his friends.

"You need to be with your mom and Ben. I'll be there soon," Peter said quietly. He knew how much he was going to miss them. "I'll try to wrap things up here quickly." Ryan nodded, but they both looked distracted and unhappy while they finished the game.

Peter hated what the upheaval was doing to all of them, and he was worried that

their marriage wouldn't survive it. He knew
Ryan wasn't wrong to be concerned about
it too. He had picked up the same nuances
Peter had. Alana was making moves she
had wanted to make for a long time, but
had had no excuse to. Now she did. Peter
wondered if her loyalty was greater to her
father or to him. He didn't know if he wanted
the answer to that question right now. It was
clear to him that she missed her old life,
even more so now that theirs was about to
disappear, and in her mind, she had nothing to stay for. It made Peter feel lonely
thinking about it. And he hated the worried
look in his son's eyes too.

Peter met with realtors, attorneys, and
art dealers all week. And Alana packed.
The four of them had dinner together every night, and Ryan got quiet whenever his
mother and Ben talked about L.A. He asked
his father again if he could stay in New York
with him, but Peter thought it was best
if Ryan went to L.A. with his mother and
brother. And he promised Alana he would
come to L.A. as soon as he could, for a
while anyway, but he was not promising to
stay. It satisfied her for now, and she knew
how persuasive her father was, and in his

current circumstances, Peter had no other options. If he wanted to be with his wife and sons, he would have to accept her father's offer on his terms.

Alana and the boys left New York on October 18, eight days after Peter had walked out of his office for the last time. And their departure was wrenching for Peter. He was depressed as soon as they left. Several journalists had called him, wanting interviews, and he declined them. He had nothing to say, and there were to be hearings and investigations in the coming months, about why the business had gone down, just as there were about Lehman Brothers.

A week after Alana and the boys left, the stock market took another plunge and sank even lower. People were panicked, several more smaller banks folded, and customers began to doubt the stability of even the largest banks. Everyone wanted either liquidity or Treasury bills, and no one felt safe with the investments they had left. It was a terrible time. And so far there had been no offer on either the house or the apartment. It was a good time to buy, if you had any money, and a terrible time to sell.

Peter was asking considerably less than he had paid for either of their homes.

And every time he called Alana and the boys, they sounded happy in California. Her father was seeing to it that they had a wonderful time, and even Ryan seemed to be adjusting. The boys liked their new school and were making friends after only three weeks there. Peter had never felt so lonely in his life. He agreed to fly out to L.A. for Thanksgiving, a month after they had left, and to stay as long as he could. He had done all he was able to for now in New York. The art dealer had photographs of all their paintings and sculptures. Both homes were on the market. And his cars had sold for a fraction of what they were worth. Peter didn't even care. All he could think of now was where they would live if the apartment sold. He wanted to provide an alternate solution to L.A., one that would appeal to Alana, but he had none. And she was already saying that the boys needed to at least finish the school year in L.A. It was obvious that she had no desire to come back to New York, and Peter could see it in her eyes when he got to L.A.

Alana was excited to pick up the threads

of her old life, seeing her old friends and getting involved with the local scene. She had volunteered at two charities people had suggested. She was busier than she'd been in years. Her father was lavishing love and attention on her and the boys, and couldn't do enough for them, and she looked happier in his guest house than she ever had in their palatial penthouse in New York. Alana had come home.

The boys seemed happy too, and were constantly out, visiting new friends and staying with them. Peter felt more than ever that this was a fight he couldn't win. And he felt out of place here. He was an easterner to the core, and had been a New Yorker for more than two decades. L.A. still felt foreign to him, and his father-in-law's booming business even more so. The financial crisis in New York, and around the world, seemed to have had almost no effect on Gary. He took Peter to the Polo Lounge at the Beverly Hills Hotel for lunch two days after he'd arrived. Important deals were being made at almost every table. It was the favorite haunt of movie stars, agents, producers, and Hollywood moguls.

"It sounds pretty bad in New York these

days," Gary said after they had ordered. The stock market plunge had affected everyone who was invested in it, and the country's economy seemed shaky, but in L.A. the primary industries were show business and music. New York was the epicenter of the financial world, and more visibly affected. Life appeared relatively normal in L.A., although financing for a number of upcoming movies had been canceled. But restaurants were booming, stores were full. New York had looked like a ghost town when he left, and holiday shopping was reported to be nearly nonexistent. Life seemed more normal here.

"It's been tough," Peter admitted. He looked tired these days, and he felt ancient after sleepless nights, worrying about how to take care of his family. Gary wanted nothing more than to solve the problem for him, but Peter did not want to be owned by Gary Tallon. As loving as he was to his daughter, he was known to be ruthless in business, and it was not the industry Peter wanted to work in. He wanted to go back into finance, on Wall Street, as soon as he could. But it didn't look like that would be anytime soon, as Gary reminded him over lunch.

"I'd like to make a place for you in my business," Gary said generously, as a waiter served them coffee. He waited until the end of lunch to make an offer. Until then, all his offers had come through Alana. "Alana and the boys are happy here," he reminded his son-in-law.

"I can see that," Peter said politely. Gary Tallon was a powerful man and a force to be reckoned with, and Peter didn't want to offend him, but he didn't want to work for him either. Nor take a job that was being offered out of charity, and not for what he could bring to it. Peter knew his talents wouldn't shine there. "But I don't think it would be fair to either of us if I took you up on it. I don't have the right skills to really be of use to you, you'd get the short end of the deal on that, and I'd be wasting what talents I do have, working in an industry I have no feeling for, and know nothing about. My whole life has been geared to Wall Street, not the music business."

"You could learn the business," Gary said quietly, observing his son-in-law from across the table. The older man's eyes were hard and steely. He was a good judge of character and knew that Peter was a good man. And Gary's only goal was to make his daughter happy and get her what she wanted, and she wanted to live in L.A., not New York. He wanted Peter to agree to her wishes, no matter what he had to offer him to do so. Gary threw out a number of what he would give Peter if he took the job, and Peter's eyes widened when he heard it. It was a ridiculous amount of money, and pure philanthropy on his father-in-law's part. There was nothing he could do for Gary to earn that.

"That's an incredibly generous offer," Peter said honestly, "but I'd be robbing you if I took it. There isn't a damn thing I could do for you to be worth it." He would have loved the money, but Peter knew it would be wrong, and almost like bribery, if he took it.

"You don't have to be worth it," Gary said bluntly. "All you have to do is live here and make Alana happy." Peter felt more like a gigolo than ever.

"I can't be on your payroll just to make

Alana happy. I need to earn my keep," Peter said, looking sad.

"You could be out of a job for a long time," Gary said somberly, as Peter nodded and knew it was true. "You'll have nowhere to live when you sell the apartment, and no money to speak of, from what Alana tells me. You can't just live like nomads, with two boys to consider. I don't think you have much choice here," Gary pointed out, looking confident that he'd convince him.

"I need to figure out something when I go back," Peter said. He had been sending his résumé around, but it was pointless. Partners in investment banking firms were an unsalable commodity at the moment.

Gary didn't press the point, but he knew that Peter was cornered. His daughter had already told him that she wouldn't leave L.A. again. If Peter wanted his marriage, he had no choice but to live here, and he was too proud and responsible a man to stay unemployed. Gary was sure he would give in sooner or later. And as the days went by, from Thanksgiving to Christmas, Peter was well aware that if he wanted to be with Alana, he would have to stay in L.A. She was developing a full life here, with old friends and new ones. She was invited everywhere, and Peter felt like a boy toy following her around, or trying to spend time with his sons, who were busy now too. Only Peter had no life here, and nothing to do.

In an effort to be reasonable, and occupied, he agreed to spend a few days at his father-in-law's company, sitting in on meetings, and observing what they did. And he felt utterly lost and useless while he was there. Contrary to what he had promised, his father-in-law included him in no meetings. Gary gave him an enormous office, one of the most impressive in the building, and expected him to just sit there. It was obvious that he expected nothing of him. He told him he could come in as late as he wanted, and leave early if he had something to do, and that lunches as long as Peter wanted were fine with him. The only thing Peter knew, after three days, was that he would be entirely superfluous and useless if he went to work for him. If he took Gary's offer, Peter's career would be over. All he would be was Alana's husband and escort to Hollywood parties and events. It was an impossible and humiliating life for him. He didn't mention it through the holidays, and waited until after Christmas to talk to Alana about it. The boys were in Bear Valley, skiing for the weekend with their school, and Gary had gone to Las Vegas to watch one of his artists perform on New Year's Eve. Peter and Alana had the whole property to themselves, and Peter was looking forward to a few days alone with her. He felt as though he hadn't spent a moment of quiet time with her since he'd arrived a month before.

"It's a nice life out here, isn't it?" Alana asked him, as they relaxed on the patio of the guest house in the winter sunshine. The weather had been balmy since he'd arrived, but he needed more than warm weather to keep him happy. He needed a real life, and he knew he would never have one here. He felt like arm candy for Alana.

"It's a nice life," he agreed, "if you have nothing else to do and can enjoy that. Or if you run an empire like your father. I feel totally useless here," Peter said uncomfortably. He couldn't lie to her about it and didn't want to.

"I have a lot more fun here than I did in New York, and so do you," she said stubbornly, and in her case he knew it was true, but not in his.

"I need more in my life than just parties," he said honestly. "I want to go back to work. I want to go back to New York after New Year's, and see what I can turn up." And they had begun negotiating with a potential buyer for the apartment that week. Peter was crawling out of his skin with boredom in L.A.

"You can work for my father here," Alana said, looking at him with a serious expression.

"I can't. I have nothing to offer him, and he has no real use for me. I can't take an enormous salary from him and do nothing. That's not me, Alana. I need a real job. I can't just be your lapdog out here, or his lackey."

"What are you saying to me?" she said coldly.

"That I want to find a real job in New York, on Wall Street, where I've worked for twenty-one years, or at least something like it. I'll find a place for us to live, and then I want you and the boys to come home."

"I am home," she said simply, and he could see she meant it. "I'm not going back, Peter. I like it here. And so do the boys."

"I can't do this. I don't want to be a kept man, Alana. That's not who you married, or who I am. The bottom fell out of our life three months ago. I want to put it back together again, not be your boy toy out here." He felt like a gigolo most of the time, or even all the time now.

"There are no jobs for you right now, and it sounds like there won't be for ages."

"I'll find something. It may not be as comfortable as what we had before, for a while anyway, but it will happen. Things will settle down again. But this isn't a life for me in L.A." He was being as honest with her as he could, but Alana was no longer willing to negotiate with him.

"I'm staying, Peter. If you don't want to live here, then maybe we have a decision to make. My father is getting older, I want to be out here with him. We're all he has." She looked at Peter, and he saw something different in her eyes. She was no longer the woman he had married. She was her father's daughter. Hard times had hit them, and she was bailing. He could see that clearly now, and she didn't deny it.

"You're all I have too," Peter said quietly. "I love you, Alana, and the boys. I don't want to lose you because I can't live here."

"Then stay. My father made you a good offer. Take it." But she didn't ask him to stay because she loved him. She didn't say it. And he wondered now if she did love him, or had stopped loving him somewhere along the way, and he hadn't noticed. What Alana wanted was a lifestyle more than she wanted him. It was a brutal reality for Peter, but possibly true. It looked that way to him.

"I need to go back to New York next week anyway," he said unhappily. "We'll talk." She nodded, and answered her cell phone when it rang. It was her father calling from Las Vegas. She sounded closer to him now than she did to Peter. She was no longer interested in building a world with Peter. All she wanted was to share her father's. As Peter listened to them talk, he got up and went inside. There were tears in his eyes, but she didn't see them. He couldn't kid himself anymore. It was one of those de-fining moments when you know that a life you have shared is over, and the person you thought you lost temporarily is never coming back the way it was before. Peter knew it at that instant. Whether he chose to acknowledge it now or not, it was over. Alana preferred her own city to her husband. It was a bitter pill for Peter to swallow and a heartbreaking disappointment for him.

They went to a New Year's Eve party together, and Alana ran into several old friends, who were thrilled to see her back. She even ran into an old boyfriend who used to work for her father and had become an important Hollywood agent. She introduced him to Peter, and the three of them chatted for a few minutes, although he clearly had no interest in Peter, who drifted away and went back to the bar to get himself a stiff scotch on the rocks. He was tired of Los Angeles and the people he met there, and couldn't wait to go back to New York—unlike Alana, who was thriving in her old familiar world, and loved being her father's daughter in it.

They were both quiet when they drove home that night. Her father's driver had driven them to the party, and when they got out at the guest house, Peter told her he was leaving for New York in a few days. Alana nodded and said nothing. It felt like there was nothing left to say. He had lost.

They spent the next few days avoiding each other. He didn't want to bring things to a head, or come to any more painful conclusions than they already had. He waited until the boys got back from Bear Valley, told them he was leaving, and promised to come back as soon as he could.

Peter and Alana shared breakfast the morning he left. She was going to a luncheon that day, given by a Hollywood celebrity, and a party that night, to celebrate the premiere of a film. Nothing in her life had changed. She was still the spoiled little girl she had always been, and he had kept her that way all the years of their marriage. He could see that now. And everything in his world had changed since October. He felt as though he were totally alone. All sense of partnership seemed to have vanished between them. She was thoroughly enjoying her new life and he was mourning their old one.

She kissed him goodbye as though he would be back that afternoon, and when he went to kiss the boys goodbye, he saw her watching him from the doorway, as though he were someone she had never seen before. He turned to look at her, and their eyes met. There was no hiding from it anymore. They had become strangers overnight. She closed the door on their existence in New York and seemed to be moving on without him. And just as she had said two months before, she had abandoned ship. Alana was off and running. And there was no place in her world for him, unless he played by her father's rules.

Peter sat in silence as her father's driver took him to the airport in Gary's Rolls. The ride was smooth and the car perfect in every way, but Peter had never felt as uncomfortable in his life.

His cell phone rang as he was boarding the plane. It was Ryan, not Alana. She hadn't called.

"See you soon, Dad. Fly safe."

"I will, son. I'll call you from New York."

"I love you, Dad."

"I love you too, Ry," Peter said softly with a lump in his throat. Peter didn't say it, but they both knew that everything had changed, and it would never be the same again.

Chapter 3

When Peter returned to New York, he had the feeling that the entire city, and everyone he knew, had sunk into depression. Restaurants were deserted, stores were empty. People who still had jobs were terrified of losing them. No one felt secure, people were worried about the safety of their money in banks, and those with funds were hastening to buy T-bills with whatever cash they had on hand. And small banks continued to close all over the nation. A country that had symbolized success and security was no longer one they

could count on. The whole financial community was upside down.

And yet another shocker had occurred
while Peter was in California. A man
named Bernard Madoff was arrested for
investor fraud, in the largest crime of its
kind committed in history. He was accused
of cheating 4,800 clients out of $64.8 bil-
lion. He had wiped out entire communities
of investors, destroyed savings and re-
tirement funds and entire fortunes. The
homes of his investors were being put on
the market as a result, and his trusting
investors around the world had been
decimated.

It was a time like no other Peter could
remember in his twenty-one years in the
business. And his own situation was no
better than that of Madoff's unwitting victims. Peter was desperate to sell their city
apartment, and the house in Southampton.
They needed the money, although Alana's
father was providing generously for her and
the boys. But Peter wanted to resume taking care of his family himself. He had both
places listed with several realtors, and the
one serious prospect for the apartment was

driving a hard bargain, trying to take full advantage of Peter's plight.

Peter received yet another offer from the same buyer the day after he got home, and it was only minimally higher than the one before. The buyer knew just how desperate he was. He called Alana about it late that night and asked her advice, but she was vague. It was obvious that she was no longer interested in their problems in New York. Protected by her father now, they had less impact on her, and she told Peter to sell it for whatever he could get, since she knew he wanted the money, and had to have it.

Peter called the realtor back the next morning and sounded grim when he told her he would take the offer. It was for less than half what he paid for the apartment ten years ago, right before Ben was born. Four months earlier, before the market crash, the apartment would have been worth twice what he had paid for it, but not anymore. Those who still had money were preying on those who no longer did, and Peter was now one of the latter, a victim of the crisis.

"I'll take it," he told the realtor through

clenched teeth. "I'm selling it as is, and I want the fastest closing possible." She promised to arrange it, and then he called their realtor in the Hamptons. There had been no offers on the beach house so far, although it was spectacular, had been recently redone, and sat on several acres of property, on adjoining beachfront lots. But no one was buying second homes right now. The bottom had fallen out of that market, along with everything else.

"What about renting it?" the realtor suggested cautiously. Peter was about to decline, and then thought better of it, if they could get a decent rental price.

"How much would it go for?"

"Normally, an astronomical amount. It's a gorgeous house. Right now, maybe half of what it usually would, or less, and this is the wrong time of year to rent out here, but you never know. I can list it as a rental and see what happens."

The offer on the city place was presented the next day, pending due diligence, inspections, and the approval of the co-op board, all of which were standard procedures, but could take time. Peter signed his acceptance of the offer, and called the realtor to have it picked up. At least that was done.

He spent the rest of the week sending out his résumé, and he called the boys in California every night. Whenever he did, and asked to speak to Alana, they told him their mother was out. She was having a fine time in L.A. Peter was devastated by what was happening to their marriage. He kept hoping she'd want to stay with him after all. It made him even more anxious to solve their financial problems as quickly as possible, but he wasn't a magician. And he was doing all he could. He still had a small though waning hope that the damage between them could be repaired. He said nothing about their problems to the boys.

They were excited about going on a ski trip again with their school when Peter talked to them. Like their mother, they were busy with their activities in L.A.

He'd been back in New York for two weeks when they got a rental offer on the Southampton house. It was pathetically little, but it was money, enough to make Peter decide to take it. He was renting the place furnished, with everything in it, unlike the apartment in the city, which he had to empty now. He asked Alana to come to New York to help him, and she said she didn't want to leave the boys alone with her father.

"Just hire someone to do it," she said blithely, as he felt tears sting his eyes. He was exhausted and discouraged, and Alana wasn't making it any easier for him. He had spent an entire day opening e-mails that told him there were no jobs for someone of his qualifications and stature. He was willing to do damn near anything he had to, and now he had to empty their apartment on his own. Alana was acting as though she had never lived there. The buyers were offering to purchase some of their furniture, mostly the antiques, which was good news. Alana and Peter couldn't afford to be sentimental right now, about anything except each other, and Alana didn't seem inclined to do that.

"What do you want me to do with the furniture that they don't buy?" Peter asked Alana in a flat voice.

"I don't know," she said vaguely. "Put it in storage? Give it away? Do whatever you want." She obviously didn't care, about the furniture, or even him.

"Are we planning to live in your father's guest house forever?" he asked miserably. "Some of this is good stuff, and it would be nice to use it when we get another place of our own." He was trying to hold on to that belief, with no help from her.

"I'm not in love with it, especially if they're buying the antiques." Alana had made a full-time job of filling their apartment with expensive things for several years, and now she cared about none of it. It was as though she wanted nothing to remind her of her years in New York, and his recent failure there. Peter was feeling crushed by feelings of inadequacy, it was reminding him more and more of his youth, when he couldn't do anything right, and his parents blamed him for everything. Alana wasn't blaming him, but she didn't have to. Her actions and refusal to come to New York even for a visit, to help him, said it all. And she acted like she was in denial about the situation they were in, and wanted no part of it. Her father had given her the opportunity to dodge it entirely, and she had seized it gladly. Now it was all Peter's problem, not hers. He got that message loud and clear.

He spent the next two weeks packing up

everything he wanted to keep from the apartment. He got wardrobe boxes from the moving company for Alana's clothes, which she wanted in L.A. She was turning her childhood room in her father's house into a closet to store what she wouldn't wear, like fur and winter coats, and there were plenty of walk-in closets in the guest house for the rest of her clothes. Peter boxed it all up for L.A., along with the boys' clothes and toys. He didn't know what to do with his own things, and felt odd sending them to L.A. If he did, he would be tacitly agreeing to move there, and he hadn't done that yet. He wanted to stay in New York, even if they went back and forth for a while, until he found a job. In the end, he sent most of his things to storage, along with some books and furniture, and all he kept out were two suitcases of clothes, which were all he needed at the moment. He was living in jeans and sweaters while he packed up the apartment, and he had kept out several business suits for interviews and meetings. He sent his summer clothes and his tuxedo to California with Alana's things—he was more likely to use the dinner jacket there, escorting Alana to social events. For the moment, he had no social life in New York and felt like he was in mourning for his career and their lost life. He had hardly spoken to anyone in the past three months—he was too deeply ashamed over the demise of his career. He hadn't done anything wrong, but it seemed that way. He had advised the firm about some of their riskier investments. Peter had always been willing to walk the edge and take high risks, which was also why they had had big wins. And some of their high-risk investments had been very good for a while, although like everyone else, their real estate investments had proven to be disastrous for them. It was part of what had brought Lehman Brothers down too, and several banks. They weren't alone in their mistakes, and finally it had caught up with them.

The New York apartment closed within thirty days. The buyers tried to knock another two hundred thousand off the price, for things they claimed needed to be repaired, and Peter split the difference with them. He was grateful for the money, although much of it went to pay taxes, the mortgage, and some debts. There wasn't much left afterward, but it was at least a small cushion, along with the rental of the house in the Hamptons.

It was a depressing day for Peter when he left the apartment for the last time. He stopped in the doorway of the boys' wing of the apartment, and saw a book and a game forgotten in their playroom and tucked them under his arm. He drifted past the suite he'd shared with Alana, the projection room, and the gym with all the equipment still in it, purchased by the new owners since it was nearly brand new and state of the art. They had also bought the heavy silk curtains Alana had spent a fortune on, and much of the furniture in the reception rooms, and beautiful antique Persian rugs, and an Aubusson in their bedroom that Alana had purchased at a Christie's auction in Paris. They were all symbols of a lost life, and Peter couldn't help but wonder if they would ever live like that again, if he would be able to even come close to it, and if the world as they knew it would ever be the same. These had been golden years. They had taken a lot for granted, and Peter knew he never would again. But he had also never lost sight of

what was most important to him, Alana and
the boys. They were the only family he
cared about. Alana and the boys were all
of Peter's world, and more than ever now.

Peter moved to a small residential hotel
in the East Seventies after he vacated the
apartment. He had promised the boys he'd
come back to California as soon as possible, and he'd been in New York for a month,
selling the apartment and packing up their
things, sending out résumés and contact-
ing people about jobs. He could do that
from L.A., but he wanted to be in New York
in case someone wanted to meet with him.
So far no one had; they were too busy with
their own problems to think about hiring
anyone. But just as Peter was planning to
book a flight to L.A., he got a call from an
investment bank in Boston. They were impressed by his résumé, and Peter had met
the head of the bank several times over the
years. It was a solid, reputable firm, and
they had taken none of the risks Whitman
Broadbank had, so they were still on solid
ground. They wanted him to come up and
see them, and Peter readily agreed. He
was willing to go anywhere for a job. Chicago was on his list of possibilities too, as

well as San Francisco and L.A. But he would have preferred an eastern firm. He had gone to business school in Boston, so it was a familiar city for him.

It was snowing when he got there, in the second week of February. He had a long meeting with the board of directors, and they invited him to lunch in the firm's dining room afterward. It looked like a men's club, with somber portraits of their founders on the walls, and wood paneling, and his meeting with them went well, although he was severely disappointed to be told at the end of lunch that they were unable to hire anyone at the moment, in light of the current crisis, but he would be at the top of their list when they began hiring again. It was why they had wanted to meet him, but they had no idea when their hiring policies would loosen up, just as no one knew how long the economic crisis would last. So for all intents and purposes, and to meet Peter's immediate needs, the meeting had been in vain. It was a crushing blow to him.

Peter had driven to Boston, to avoid canceled flights in bad weather, and he was about to head south toward the freeway, when he saw the familiar signs he used to take to go home from school when he was younger. It brought a wave of nostalgia as he thought about his parents. He was tired after the wild-goose chase that had brought him to Boston, to satisfy the bank's curiosity, but not to offer him a job. He was bone tired, and then as though of its own volition, his car turned toward the highway that would take him home. The only thing he had there now was a lake house he had inherited fifteen years before, and hadn't been to since, although he had done yearly maintenance on it to keep it sound, and a brother he never wanted to see again. There was no reason on earth for him to go back to his hometown, but he was heading in that direction, whether he wanted to or not. It was almost like a **Twilight Zone** experience as he started to see familiar signs drift by.

He called the boys from the car, as he drove north toward his hometown of Ware, but neither of them answered, and when he called the house in L.A., he was told that they weren't home from school yet and Alana was out, no surprise. Peter was lost in his own thoughts and memories as he drove north. He realized, when he finally saw the turnoff, that he wasn't going to Ware, as he continued on the narrowed highway toward the house at Lake Wickaboag. At the moment, it was the only house that he still could call his own. It suddenly occurred to him that he might want to stay there for a few days, if it was habitable, before he went back to New York. He had nothing to rush back for, no appointments and no one waiting for him. At least he could take a look at it, and maybe sell that too. It had been foolish and nostalgic of him to hang on to it for this long, when he never used it, but it was the only place where he had pleasant memories of his youth.

The scene that came to mind immediately was a summer day when he had gone fishing with his father and Michael, on one of the rare days his father had taken off to just fool around with them. His mother had packed them a picnic basket, and they had sat in the boat all day, catching one fish after another. Peter figured he must have been about eight at the time. It had been a real victory when he had caught more fish than Michael, who was usually the better fisherman, but when they got home

Michael had claimed the larger number for himself. Peter had tried to correct him, and his father winked at him, giving him the message that the truth was their little secret and to let Michael have his day of glory, yet again. It had been a crushing disappointment to Peter. It was always Michael who was protected and never Peter. Their father had always had a soft spot for Michael and talked about what a "good boy" he was, with the implication that Peter was the "bad boy," and often enough he was. And Michael knew just how to play their father, saying he wanted to be a doctor just like him, which fed their father's ego.

Peter had been assigned the role of younger brother, although Michael was only twelve minutes older, but he treated it more like twelve years. Michael was so well behaved that he got all the dignity and praise, and privileges that went with the older brother's role, and took it seriously when he called Peter his kid brother. And after all, Peter was the screw-up, the "baby" who had tantrums and couldn't read. Their parents bought into it, and treated Michael like the responsible mature one, and Peter's inability to read for a long time gave credence to the myth that he was younger. Their treating him that way just made him act out more, and angrier at Michael. But until they got home and Michael lied about how many fish he had caught, and their father let him, it had been a golden day for Peter. He had loved fishing with their father and basked in the warmth of his attention. It was rare for him to take a day off from work.

Peter could still remember the crickets and the sounds of summer, whenever they were at the lake house. It had been one of his favorite places to be, swimming, fishing, playing in the woods. And being there in the summer meant that he didn't have to go to school.

Peter saw the signs leading toward the lake, an hour after he left Boston, and he took a turnoff he didn't recognize onto a familiar road. The trees lining it looked bigger than he remembered, and when he reached the narrow driveway, with a rusted mailbox at its entrance, he turned onto the dirt and gravel road. He could feel his heart beat in his chest as though he expected to see someone there, and as he squinted past the light from his headlights, he saw it, the house where he had spent his summers as a boy. It was dark and deserted, and if he closed his eyes, he could hear his mother calling his name as he hid in the trees playing games with Michael. For him, this was a trip back in time to a place filled with dangerous memories and people who had disappointed him, but his earliest memories here were those of any ordinary boy. Peter could feel his heart beating faster in his chest as he got out of the car and walked slowly toward the house.

Chapter 4

Michael McDowell hurried up the steps of the small tidy house on the other side of town from his home and office. He had been there before. There was a neat picket fence surrounding the property, rose bushes in front of it, and a deep rose garden on the way to the house. The fence was freshly painted, and the house was not imposing, but in good repair. He had come to see an elderly man with bronchitis. Seth and his wife, Hannah, had been patients of his father's, and their only daughter had come up from Boston. She owned her own business and had done well, and she was

as attentive as she could be to her parents,
while leading a busy life, running a business by herself, with three nearly grown
children of her own, and living three hours
away. Hannah had recently died of pneumonia after a long battle with cancer, and
now Barbara was concerned that her father
was so ill. She had driven up from Boston,
and called Michael on the way. They were
old friends, although they didn't see each
other often. But she counted on him to
check on her parents whenever they were
ill. And he had been wonderful to her mother
before she died—they often told their
daughter that he was like the son they'd
never had.

It was a relief to Barbara, living farther
away, to know that someone like Michael
was nearby. She trusted him implicitly, had
always liked him, and there was no question in anyone's mind, he was the resident
saint. He had taken over where his father
had left off, taking care of all the sick people
in town. He had given up a potentially great
career in Boston in anesthesiology, to come
back and take on his father's general practice in a less exciting small town. But he
seemed to love it, and always said he

had no regrets about the career he had
given up. Everyone could tell by the way he
spoke to his patients that this was where
his heart was. Both Barbara and the doctor were concerned that her father had lost
his will to live since his wife died six months
before.

Seth was sitting huddled on the couch
with a blanket over his shoulders, and a
wracking cough. He had refused to have
anyone care for him in the months he'd
been alone, and insisted he could do it himself. The house was in good order, but the
old man on the couch looked very, very
sick. He was eighty-five years old. His wife
had been eighty-seven when she died.
They had been married for sixty-seven
years, and had been childhood sweet-
hearts. Michael knew only too well that a
loss like that was tough for a man his age
to survive, and he didn't like what he saw
now.

"How are you feeling, Seth?" Michael
asked gently as he sat down next to him
on the couch and opened his bag. He could
see from the old man's eyes, without touching him, that he was feverish, and he shiv-
ered as though he were cold.

"I'm feeling all right," the old man said politely, as Michael took his stethoscope out of his bag. "All I have is a cold." He glanced at his daughter in annoyance, and she smiled. "There's no need to make a fuss over it. A couple of days, and I'll be fine. Barbara made some soup for me, that's all I need. She shouldn't have called you." He scolded his daughter, and the doctor smiled.

"If she didn't call me, how do you expect me to feed my family?" Michael said, teasing him. He had an easygoing, friendly style that went over well with his patients, especially the elderly and the children. He was one of the few doctors in town and by far the most popular, and everybody trusted him. He handled all their ailments, and if they needed specialists for serious problems, he sent them to Boston. But most of the time, they preferred to just see him. "I have to make a living somehow, you know. It's a good thing Barbara called me." The old man guffawed and looked a little less ill as he relaxed. No matter how sick a patient was, there was never anything ominous about Michael's home visits. He made even bad situations seem less frightening, with his reassurance. And Seth would never forget how wonderful he had been to his late wife. Michael had kept her comfortable until the end. Michael had recommended a nurse at the house for her, during her final days, but he came out twice a day himself. Seth's late wife had been so grateful to him that she had left Michael a small bequest, nothing important, they didn't have a lot of money. But she had told her husband before she died that she wanted to do that for him. It was only ten thousand dollars, but it was a lot to them, and a gesture of a lifetime of respect. Michael had been embarrassed and grateful when he received it, and told Seth that he was putting it toward his daughter's college fund, since she wanted to enter a premed program when she graduated from high school in two years, and every penny helped.

Michael had a solid, lucrative practice, but he also had an invalid wife and two children. His wife had been sick for all the years they'd been married. He had married her when he was in medical school. Like everyone else, he had responsibilities and financial burdens, and he had been surprised and grateful for the gift.

Michael listened to the old man's chest, and nodded with a smile. Nothing he did or said was alarming. He was all kindness and knew just how to calm his patients' fears.

"I'm happy to confirm your heart is beating nicely," he said in a joking manner and the old man laughed.

"I'm not sure if that's good news or bad news now that Hannah's gone," Seth said with a wistful look. Michael knew how much he missed her, and he and Barbara both worried that Seth would die of a broken heart, or just stop eating and let himself starve. He had lost a lot of weight since his wife died.

"The good news is that you don't have pneumonia. Yet," Michael said seriously. "But you will if you don't take care of yourself. I don't want you going outside until you get rid of that cough. I'm going to give you some antibiotics, and you have to take them until they're gone, not just until you feel better. I'm giving you some cough syrup too. You can take aspirin for your fever, and that's good for your heart." Seth had had a mild heart condition for several years, which had been aggravated by his wife's death.

"I'd say this is a good time for you to sit on the couch and watch TV, stay warm, and get lots of rest, and drink Barbara's soup. Have you got enough food in the house?" Michael asked him with a look of concern, and Seth just shrugged.

"I'm going to pick up some groceries now," Barbara said in a low voice. Neighbors had been bringing him casseroles and roasts for months, but he ate very little, and was getting thinner. She had tried to talk her father into moving to Boston, so she could be near him, but he said he wasn't leaving his house.

"I'll come by with your medicines later today," Michael informed him reassuringly. "I want you to promise me you'll take them," he said as his patient growled. Barbara was equally impressed that Michael would bring the medicines to the house. He always went out of his way to make the extra gestures for his patients, and go the extra mile. It was why everyone loved him so much.

Michael sat and chatted with them for a few more minutes before he left. He never gave his patients or their families the impression that he was in a rush. He always appeared to have all the time in the world to listen to their problems, especially if they were lonely or old. He had a particular gift with his geriatric patients, and sometimes he admitted that he loved them best of all. They were the forgotten ones most of the time.

Barbara inquired about his wife as she walked him to the front door. "How's Maggie doing?" she asked with a look of compassionate concern. Barbara had been two classes ahead of her in college when Maggie had the fall on the skating pond that changed her life. She hadn't seen her now in a long time, Maggie rarely ventured out, and her husband and daughter cared for her at home.

"Some days are better than others, but she's a good sport about it. We're lucky we have Lisa to take care of her. It's going to be tough when she goes to college." Both her parents were hoping she'd stay nearby. It would be a sacrifice for Lisa, but she was devoted to both her parents, and said she wouldn't mind.

Michael waved as he hurried down the front steps. He had four more home visits to make before he brought Seth his medicines and then went home. He had a new-born to see, and three of his older patients. The able-bodied usually came to his office, but he was always willing to make house calls, even on weekends or late at night. This was his life. The only other thing he cared about was his family. He had never wanted a flashy career, financial success, or an important life. He was a country doctor, faithfully serving his patients. That had always been enough for him—unlike his twin brother, who had gone after fame and fortune in New York and only came back for his parents' funerals and never since.

The two brothers couldn't have been more different, even though they were twins. Their mother had said that about them since they were born. Even as a toddler, Peter had been hot-headed, and given to rages as he grew up. Michael was quiet and patient. Peter constantly had to be punished. Michael rarely needed discipline. He had been gentle and even tempered, caring and thoughtful of his parents. As a teenager, he was always doing errands for his mother, and favors for people in the neighborhood. He was loved by all, while Peter was at war with the world.

Peter had been regarded as a bully at school, particularly when the other children teased him about not being able to read until he was nearly twelve years old, and awkwardly even after that. Anyone who dared mention it to him was sure to get a black eye or bloody nose. His parents were constantly apologizing for him. They were always embarrassed by Peter, and praised for Michael's behavior.

Michael had been at the top of his class from first grade to last. He won every award in school, and lorded it over his younger twin whenever he could, usually out of earshot of their parents. Peter reported it to them frequently, and when they didn't believe him, he took care of it himself. He grew taller than Michael as he got older, and had beaten him up more than once, which inevitably got him punished too. It had been a relief to their father when he finally left home. He couldn't stand the fighting anymore. Their mother insisted that underneath it all, Peter was a good boy, but given his obstreperous, rebellious nature, and the physical fights with his twin and the boys in school, by the end of high school, there was no one who believed in Peter's good heart except his mother. Michael was so much easier to love.

And he stayed close to them once he grew up. Although he loved his work as an anesthesiologist in Boston, Michael couldn't wait to come back to Ware once his father invited him into his practice. He had abandoned his dreams to come home. And once there, he loved working in a small town, and having patients who truly depended on him. And he had loved sharing an office with his father. He always said it was what he had always hoped for. Dr. Pat, his father, had quickly observed Michael's talent with the elderly, and had passed on all his geriatric patients to him. They all adored young Dr. Mike even more than his father. He had a compassionate nature and made the transition into the next world easier for them, and their loved ones. Everyone felt safer with Dr. Mike around. Not only did he live by his Hippocratic oath to do no harm, he did more good than any doctor they had ever known, even his father, who had gotten a little cantankerous and less patient as he got old. Michael was infinitely patient, endlessly caring, a skilled doctor, and beloved by all.

Michael pulled into his driveway just after eight o'clock. He was living in the home that had been his parents', and had moved into it fifteen years before, when his mother died, and she left it to him. It was a big, rambling old house, and had been wonderful for him and Maggie and their children. Bill had been seven when they moved in, and Lisa a year old.

Michael had married Maggie twenty-three years before. They had known each other growing up, though he hadn't paid much attention to her, she'd been closer to Peter. But a skating accident she had at twenty brought them together. She had been in a coma for several months. He'd been in medical school then, and once she began to recover, he had visited her whenever he came home. He evidenced deep concern for her and surprised everyone when he married her a year later, despite her fragile health. It contributed even further to people's high opinion of him, and still did. After her accident, Maggie had been an invalid for all of their married life. Michael had kept her alive, and they were grateful to have been blessed with two children.

A third baby had been conceived two years after Lisa, their second-born, but Maggie was so frail by then that Michael had insisted that she have a medically recommended abortion. They had two healthy children, miraculously, and he told her he didn't want to lose the wife he adored to a third. He was certain she wasn't strong enough to carry another child to term. And she had been heartbroken, but agreed. She trusted Michael implicitly with her medical treatment. She had total faith that he always knew what was best for her. When their children had been born, he had cared for her during her pregnancies, and only brought an obstetrician in to assist at the delivery. He didn't trust anyone with her care except himself. She knew that no one loved her as he did, or knew her as well.

Michael had kept her alive despite the catastrophic effects of her accident. Maggie was only twenty then, and a talented ice skater. She had been skating with friends on the pond when a piece of bark frozen in the ice had caught the picks on her figure skates. She had gone flying, and landed backward on her head. She had fractured her skull, and seeing her unconscious on the ice, everyone thought she was dead. She was airlifted to Boston, and lay in a coma for five months. She had surgery to relieve the pressure on her brain, and the doctors had been unable to predict how severe the consequences would be if she survived. Her parents had been over-whelmed with gratitude when she came out of the coma. She was their only child, and they doted on her.

Her mother had nursed her back to health, and worked hard on her rehabilita-tion with her. Maggie had been unable to walk at first, and eventually therapists got her walking again, although unsteadily, and stiff legged on one side. Although young and beautiful, she walked like someone who had had a stroke, but she was back on her feet. Her dream had been to walk and dance and wear high heels again, but that was not to be. She was able to walk, but never steadily, and frequently her bad leg gave out. She was good humored and brave about it, but frustrated that she was never able to progress further than that.

And the other most noticeable effect of the accident was slurred speech for a long time. She had had to learn to talk all over again, as well as walk. Her speech finally recovered, but her leg never did. She was a beautiful girl, just as she had been before the accident. But at first she had difficultly speaking, and remembering words some-times. It made people think that she was slow of mind now as well as speech, which was not the case, but it seemed that way.

And friends who felt sorry for her and were busy with their own activities visited her less and less. It was Michael who came to visit her regularly once she came home from the hospital, and began to realize what a remarkable young woman she was. He brought her books and magazines and lit-tle gifts. He always comforted her about her condition, and praised her for her progress. He took her out walking sometimes, and held her arm in his firm, steady grip. And he reassured her about her nerves. He told her that she would always be delicate now, and easy prey for infections and diseases since her system had been so weakened. His greatest concern was for some kind of paralysis to set in later, and he insisted that it was best for her to stay away from people and not to risk infection that could cost her her life.

He kept her company at home when no one else would. Michael made her feel protected. He didn't care how awkward her speech was, or how unsteady she was on her feet. He was there for her whenever he could be, despite the demands of medical school. And he was an extraordinary support and solace to her when her mother died in a car crash the year after Maggie's accident. It was a devastating loss to her and her father, and Michael impressed everyone shortly after when he proposed. It was obvious to everyone that Maggie would always be frail. Maggie herself had been convinced that no man would ever want her now, with her clumsy speech and awkward gait. Instead Michael made her feel like the most loved woman alive, and she felt so lucky to have him. Her father had been enormously relieved as well. He had been even more worried about Maggie now that her mother was gone. He had been busy with his lumber mill, and didn't have time to take care of her. He knew Michael always would. It was an enormous comfort to him. He couldn't wish for better for his injured daughter than to be married to a devoted doctor.

Michael and Maggie were married in a small private ceremony. She didn't want a big wedding since she couldn't glide smoothly down the aisle. She was afraid she might stumble or fall, and she was afraid that she might stammer or slur when she spoke up to say her vows. Michael didn't mind the small ceremony, nor having a handicapped wife. Her own doctor, who had seen her through the aftereffects of the accident, in Boston, said she was entirely normal, except for the awkward gait, and he felt sure that with speech therapy, she would speak more easily in time. He thought her leg would improve as well. He didn't agree with Michael about her potential fragility, and said those were the anxious words of a young doctor in love. He thought Michael worried too much about her and treated her like a porcelain doll.

But Michael wasn't proven wrong about Maggie being frail. She fell prey to severe flus every winter, and had pneumonia several times, so severely that Michael had hospitalized her and was afraid for her life. When she recovered, he urged her not to leave the house for several months. He didn't want her exposed to random germs

that put her at high risk. They had been living in an apartment in Boston then, while
he finished medical school, and he had
personally put her on bed rest when she
was pregnant with their first child. She didn't
see an obstetrician, or need any other doctor, Michael took better care of her than
anyone else. But the long months in bed
made her legs weaker, more unsteady, and
she could hardly walk after she gave birth,
and to keep her from falling and injuring
herself, she was in a wheelchair for several
months. It was a small price to pay for the
handsome baby boy they named William.
She was only sorry that Michael felt she
was too weak to nurse, and they took turns
giving him bottles whenever Michael was
home. He was a strapping, handsome little boy.

While Michael did his residency in anesthesiology, Maggie managed fairly well.
She was walking better again, although it
was hard for her to care for the toddler, and
she was always relieved when Michael
came home to keep him from getting hurt.
He worried a lot about Maggie's nerves. He
reluctantly admitted to her that after a head
injury like the one she had sustained, she

was far more at risk for a stroke or cere-
bral hemorrhage at any age. The thought
of that happening while she was caring for
their baby terrified Maggie, and they hired
a babysitter to keep him safe and so she
could rest more. She missed going to the
park with Billy, but she was always waiting
with open arms when he came home. He
was the joy of her life, as was his father.

Everything became simpler for them
when Michael's father invited him to join his
practice, and they moved back to Ware.
She easily found young girls to help her
there. When Maggie got pregnant with Lisa,
Michael put her on bed rest again, this time
for eight months. It weakened her considerably, but once again the delivery was
easy, and the baby a healthy little girl. And
after eight months on bed rest, Maggie was
weak and fell in their bedroom after the
birth. Michael insisted that she use a walker
after that, which embarrassed her, but he
was adamant that he didn't want her seriously injured, or to hit her head again. He
was convinced that she wouldn't survive it
a second time. And a year after Lisa was
born, his parents died, and they moved into
their house. The only problem was that

there were several flights of stairs, which made it hard for Maggie to get around. She was absolutely forbidden to negotiate the stairs on her own. Michael brought her downstairs in the evening when he got home, and gently laid her on the couch where he could keep an eye on her, but he didn't want her wandering the house, on any floor, while he was gone. It limited her activities considerably, and it drove her crazy listening to her children playing down-stairs with the babysitter, and she couldn't go down to join in the fun. She had to wait for them to visit her, or until Michael came home and carried her downstairs to the liv-ing room.

Several times she suggested that they buy a house all on one level, so she could get around with the walker, but Michael looked heartbroken at the thought of sell-ing his parents' house. She didn't have the heart to do that to him, after all that he had done for her. He had given up his life, ex-cept for working as a doctor, to care for her in every possible way. It was why she had listened to him yet again when he insisted that she abort their third child. She trusted him implicitly. Michael was always right when it came to her health. And he was right too that she would grow weaker over the years. Michael had said it early on, and it appeared to be inevitable.

In recent years, her father's death had come as a great shock and source of grief to her, as had their son Bill moving to London to go to school several years before. He was twenty-two now and she missed him terribly. He almost never came home, although they called each other often and communicated by e-mail. Michael worried that the shocks she had sustained had once again impacted her health, which had deteriorated noticeably in the last two years.

Their daughter Lisa was their pride and joy. She wanted to be a doctor like her father, and she was a very efficient nurse whenever Maggie felt weaker than usual, or particularly ill. Her health had been on a slow downhill slide for years, and it was beginning to seem miraculous to all of them that she was still alive at forty-four. She had survived the accident that happened twenty-four years earlier, but just as Michael had said it would, her health had grown markedly worse over time. She had recently been diagnosed with Parkinson's, which was a source of great concern to Michael. He tried not to worry her, or alarm her, but she could always see in his eyes how concerned he was about her.

He was a devoted, adoring husband, and she was immeasurably grateful for his lavish kindness, their children, and the life they shared. She felt guilty frequently for how little she could do for them. She was trapped in her bedroom most of the time, a prisoner of her own body. As the Parkinson's progressed, she could hardly walk anymore, and never without a walker. Michael preferred her moving around in a wheelchair so she wouldn't fall and hit her head again. He did everything possible to protect her. And Maggie felt useless a great deal of the time.

Without question, Maggie's children were the greatest source of joy to her, and Lisa was tireless in the help she provided her mother. And in spite of her infirmities, Maggie had managed to derive joy from other things as well. She was by nature a cheerful, optimistic person, although with Michael's constant warnings, she had grown more fearful about her health over the years. And she hated the idea that one day she would leave Michael and her children, long before she was ready to do so. She tried not to think of it too much, but the specter of her failing health and what it could mean to all of them was ever present.

Instead of dwelling on it, thanks to a Christmas gift from her son Bill, she distracted herself with the Internet and had become addicted to it. It was Maggie's magic carpet to the outside world. Michael complained that it exhausted her, and confused her with unreliable facts from medical websites, but with Bill's wonderful gift of a laptop computer, she could shop for Lisa on eBay, write e-mails to Bill in London whenever she chose, and learn fascinating facts about history, art, and the travel she would never be able to do. The Internet had given her access to a whole new world. She stayed abreast of all the news happening around the globe, and was well informed on many subjects. Sometimes Michael burst out laughing when he got home and she announced some obscure world event, or fact about something he had never thought about and had no need to know. She was insatiable in her passion for information and knowledge. Maggie entered chat rooms occasionally, corresponded with people she had never met and wouldn't have otherwise, and looked up old friends on Facebook, although she herself wasn't listed there.

And once in a while, although she rarely admitted it to him, she Googled articles and medical data about her health in order to learn more about her ailments, since Michael sometimes kept harsh facts from her to protect her, although she could always see his deep worry for her in his eyes. And most recently she'd been reading about Parkinson's, since Michael had diagnosed her with it two years before. She knew that Michael was always the best judge of what was good for her, but she liked to be informed about her health, and she constantly learned new things on the Internet. But she never wanted Michael to feel that she questioned his medical opinions, so she almost never mentioned the medical research she did. He was so devoted to her that she didn't want to upset him. And he said that a lot of medical data on the Internet was inaccurate. But she found it interesting anyway. She had a voracious appetite for information.

Recently, she had corresponded with a woman she'd "met" in a chat room for shut-ins. They were exactly the same age, although Maggie had been housebound for longer. Her new friend had been in a wheelchair for ten years after a car accident. And they had exchanged information about Parkinson's when they discovered they both had it. And Maggie had been somewhat relieved to discover that her symptoms seemed less acute than her correspondent's, although she didn't say that to her. She seemed like a nice woman, and they corresponded several times a week. Michael frequently expressed concern that she could be victimized by dangerous people preying on her through the Internet, but Maggie didn't worry about it. She had fun talking to people in chat rooms.

Most of all, Maggie enjoyed the freedom that the Internet gave her, and sometimes she stayed glued to it all day, learning new things, and reading about subjects that fascinated her. Michael had been annoyed about it at first, and had scolded Bill for giving his mother a gift that would exhaust her. Bill had ferociously defended his mother's right to explore the Internet, and Michael knew he had lost the battle. Maggie loved everything about it, and the doors it opened to her. She had became a master at home shopping, and had redecorated their dining room at IKEA two years before, without ever leaving her bed.

Most of all, it was fun for her, and had been a precious gift from her son that she cherished. She sent him several e-mails a day, which he responded to from his Black-Berry. He had promised that that would be his next gift to her, whenever he came home, although he had no plans to do so at the moment. She missed him terribly, but she tried to sound cheerful whenever she reported on things at home. And she never complained about her health. She didn't want to upset her son, and kept her reports from home upbeat.

Recently, she had even started watching movies on her computer. Sometimes she got Lisa to sit in bed and watch them with her, when she didn't have homework to do. Her computer had become the most important possession in Maggie's life. It provided information, escape, entertainment, and knowledge. It was perfect for someone who spent most of her life in bed. The Internet had added a whole new dimension to her life.

And the other great blessing in her life was Prudence Walker, who came three times a week to clean their house, and make lunch for Maggie when Lisa couldn't get back from school, and Michael was too busy with patients. Pru was nearly seventy, had raised six children, and had boundless energy, although she thought that Maggie's fascination with the Internet was a little strange and possibly even dangerous. She didn't even have a microwave in her house, and felt sure that spending so much time on the computer would end up giving Maggie some terrible disease that would be the end of her. She had warned her of it often. But other than that, the two women saw eye to eye on most things, and Prudence was very fond of Michael, whose father had delivered all six of her children.

Pru was a widow now, and she loved helping Maggie, and for Maggie it was a joy having someone to talk to, other than her husband and daughter, who were both busy. Pru brought Maggie the books and magazines she asked for, and took books out from the library for her. And the two women laughed and talked as Pru diligently cleaned the house and muttered about how much dust had accumulated from one time to the next. She had none of Maggie's interest in world affairs, but she was always well versed on all the local gossip, which Maggie loved to hear, although she hardly saw anyone anymore. Michael was so discreet that he never told her anything, and Lisa was too young to care what the adults in Ware were doing. She was only interested in what was happening at school. Pru Walker livened up Maggie's life considerably, and was a godsend for her. She had been cleaning house for them for fifteen years, since they had moved into Michael's parents' house. It was a big rambling old home, and needed more than just Michael and Lisa to clean it. And Maggie loved every bit of the local news she heard from Pru. Between Pru and the Internet, Maggie was thoroughly informed.

*   *   *

When Michael bounded up the stairs at the end of his day, and let himself in through the front door, he hung his hat and coat up in the front hall. There were delicious cooking smells coming from the kitchen. Lisa had called him an hour before to see what time he'd be home. Because of her mother's infirmity, she often acted more like a wife than a daughter. At sixteen she ran an excellent home. Michael often came home at lunchtime to give Maggie lunch, if Pru wasn't there, but Lisa did all the rest. She cooked dinner and bought their groceries, and in spite of her domestic duties, Lisa got excellent grades. Michael's face exploded into a smile the moment he saw her, with an apron over her short denim skirt, as she wandered out of the kitchen to greet him. His wide smile was matched by her own.

"Hi, Daddy, how was your day?" She looked ecstatic to see her father. The house was always much too quiet until he got home. And while cooking dinner, she had done her homework in the kitchen. She had made leg of lamb from a recipe she'd taken out of a magazine. She always had a hot meal waiting for him, and they ran a tray up to her mother if she wasn't well enough to be carried down, which was often the case these days. The Parkinson's was worsening at a rapid rate, much to Michael's dismay. He never mentioned it to Maggie and Lisa, but Maggie could see it in his eyes when he observed her.

"My day was pretty good. Better now that I came home to you. How's Mom?" he asked her quickly as he gave her a big hug and pulled her into his arms. He looked a great deal like Peter, but was shorter and stockier. Peter had always been tall and thin and better looking, and Michael had a more powerful build. He looked like a blond teddy bear as he held her.

"Mom seems pretty good," Lisa said with a broad smile. Her eyes danced as she looked at her father. He had been her hero all her life, and everyone else's in Ware. And Maggie's too.

"I'll run up and see her before we eat. What's for dinner? I'm starving." He had had lunch at noon on the fly, and hadn't had time to eat anything since then. He usually started work at seven with house calls. It was a long day for him. And all Lisa wanted was to join him in his practice eventually and follow in his footsteps. Just as Michael had done with his father, Lisa's ultimate goal was to work with him.

"Leg of lamb. New recipe," she said proudly. She had her mother's dark hair and her father's blue eyes, but she was petite like her mother, without looking frail like Maggie. And Maggie was very thin after many years in bed, and with a poor appetite. It was always a struggle getting her to eat, especially lately. Lisa had a fuller, more womanly figure. She looked like a ballerina with her long dark hair that she had pulled back in a knot. Michael ran up the stairs then to see his wife. She was lying on her bed with her computer on her lap, and beamed at him as he walked into their room. He was so vital and alive, like a breath of fresh air in her room.

"Hi, sweetheart," she said happily. "Long day. You must be exhausted." She hadn't seen him since breakfast. She always worried about him, as he did about her. He smiled when he saw that she was watching a documentary about Japan on her computer. It was a tour of the temples in Kyoto. He leaned over her bed and kissed her, and as soon as he did, he frowned, and then smoothed his brow so as not to worry Maggie, but she had seen it. She knew all his expressions and what they meant, always about her health.

"Something wrong?" She looked suddenly anxious. He was her barometer for how she was doing, and she could always read it in his eyes, regardless of what he said. She knew all the unspoken signals, no matter how well he tried to hide them. She could see right through him when he was concealing his concern.

"Are you having chills?" he asked casually, as he pulled a blood pressure cuff out of a drawer next to her bed, and she turned off her computer.

"No, I'm feeling fine. Actually, really good. I wanted to come downstairs tonight for dinner. It smells delicious." There was a hint of garlic in the air, which made it even more appealing.

"Let's see what the magic puffer tells us," he said, as he leaned over and kissed her again, and pumped the cuff until it squeezed her arm and then he released it and frowned again. She could tell instantly that he didn't like what he read, but he slipped it off her arm before she could see what it said. He never liked to worry her. But she was well aware of her bad health and slow but steady deterioration.

"Bad?" she asked, looking worried. And he paused a beat before he answered. She knew what that meant too. It meant that something was wrong again. She had low blood pressure often, which made her dizzy, but she had been feeling strong that night, until then.

"Of course not," he reassured her. "But I don't think you should come downstairs tonight. I want you to stay up here and take it easy." She looked instantly disappointed, like a child who had been told her birthday party had been canceled. She had waited all afternoon and evening to see him, and was looking forward to having dinner with him and Lisa. Michael hadn't let her come downstairs to dinner all week. She was used to it, but she lived for these moments with them. No one visited her anymore except Pru, to clean their house. She had been shut in for too long. The only people in her world were her husband and daughter, now that their son was in London. And Michael discouraged people from visiting her because he didn't want her getting sick. Ever since her accident, her lungs weren't

strong. And she had no resistance to diseases they might bring in. For Maggie, it
could mean death. Sometimes he even told
Pru not to come if Maggie was sick, or Pru
had a cold, which could be dangerous for
Maggie.

"I was hoping to come down to dinner."
She looked at him with pleading eyes. "I felt
really good today." But now, after seeing
the look in his eyes, she realized that she
was a little dizzy. Maybe he was right.

"We don't want you falling out of your
wheelchair," he said gently. She had been
hoping to use her walker, but she didn't
want to insist. If she fell and hurt herself, it
would upset him and Lisa, and she didn't
want that. She was such a burden to them,
and she knew it. "I'll bring you dinner up
here. You can put on a movie." She had
already seen two that day, and all she
wanted was to have dinner with her family,
which she was able to do now less and less
often. The Parkinson's was making her
even more shaky, and unsteady. And she
knew from what she read on the Internet
that eventually it would get worse.

"All right," she said sadly, as he kissed
her again and left the room. He was back

five minutes later with a tray Lisa had prepared for her with a pretty linen placemat
and napkin. She wished that she could be
doing these things, instead of her daughter.

"Room service," Michael said with a bow
as he set the tray over her knees. She was
tired of eating in her room alone, but she
could hardly ask them to eat on trays with
her. They had a right to a normal dinner.
But looking at the tray he left with her, she
was no longer hungry. It smelled delicious,
but she couldn't eat. She just sat there looking at it, as tears slid down her cheeks.
She had missed an entire lifetime while lying in her bedroom, but she was immensely
grateful that she had Michael and her
children. She picked up her fork and began toying with the food. She had to eat
something—she didn't want to hurt Lisa's
feelings. She had the same ballerina looks
as her daughter, but after a lifetime of ill-
ness, she looked more like a doll, laid gently on her bed. And Michael treated her like
one. She was the doll that he had kept alive
since they married, and she was grateful to
him for that. She thought about sending Bill
an e-mail then, but she didn't want him
to sense that she was sad, and he knew

her well, sometimes even better than his father.

Downstairs, Michael and Lisa were laughing at the kitchen table. She was telling him what had happened at school that day, and about her friends, but her best friend was her father. She told him everything and always asked for his advice. She couldn't do that with her mother—she had always been taught to shield her and care for her almost like a child. And her father had warned her and her brother since they were young not to challenge their mother's nerves—she was too fragile. So they turned to him with all their joys and heartaches, and not their mother. Maggie had spent her entire life on the sidelines, since that fateful day skating on the pond. But Lisa and her father were full of life as they chatted. He helped her do the dishes afterward while they continued to talk. Like her, he couldn't wait for the day when she joined him in his practice. It had been his life's dream, and now it was hers too. They were soul mates. And it was after ten when Michael went upstairs to Maggie, and Lisa went to her room to watch TV and talk to her friends on the phone.

Maggie was awake when he walked into the room, and she looked bored and lonely. She had turned her computer off for the night, and was silently worrying about her health after Michael's visit to her room before dinner, when she had seen his concern. What she had glimpsed in his eyes had dampened her spirits. And sometimes she wished that he and Lisa didn't spend quite so long over dinner, but they always had a lot to say to each other, and she had so little to contribute since she did nothing all day and was sequestered from the world. All she could tell them was what she had seen on the Internet. Her husband and daughter were both involved with real people and real life.

"Tired?" he asked her, as he sat down on the bed and looked at her. She could see something in his eyes again, that fleeting hint of worry that always scared her.

"No, I'm fine," she said, smiling at him, and reached for his hand. He took her pale delicately carved hand in his own and held it.

"I'll give you a sleeping pill in a few minutes," he promised, as though she were longing for it, but she wasn't.

"I don't need one. And I'm not sleepy yet. Let's talk for a while." He laughed as she said it, as though she were a child with a totally ridiculous idea, like going to the zoo at night.

"Let's see. I got up at five this morning, and visited my first patient at seven. I did eleven home visits, had office hours, and worked a twelve-hour day." He glanced at his watch then. "And I have to get up in seven hours, and start all over again. If you're expecting intelligent conversation from me at this hour, my love, I'm afraid you're going to be seriously disappointed. Even without a sleeping pill, I'll be asleep before you are! And I don't have time to learn new facts on Google all day."

"I'm sorry!" She looked instantly guilty for wanting time with him. "You must be exhausted." He was, and all he wanted to do was shower and get into bed. And he wanted her to get a good rest too. She looked worn out to him, even if she claimed not to feel it. He was still convinced that she spent far too much time on the Internet, instead of resting.

He went to a drawer across the room then, took out the bottle of sleeping pills, and handed one to her with a glass of water.

"Honestly, I don't need it," she insisted. If she had trouble sleeping, she could always watch a movie on her computer with earphones, and would have preferred it. But Michael preferred medication, since he was a physician.

"Who's the doctor here?" he asked mock sternly, and she laughed.

"You are. But I'll sleep fine without it."

"Let's be sure. I'll feel better if you take it." They lived by hospital rules, with Michael in charge of her medications and treatment, but he always knew what was best for her, and he was always proven right. And she didn't like going against his wishes. She swallowed the pill and looked up at him with a smile. She was a gentle, loving person, and had been docile for their entire marriage. He loved being married to her, no matter how ill she was. He knew what to expect right from the beginning, and had no illusions about it. He hadn't expected her to get better, and she hadn't. "I'll be back in a few minutes," he said as he left to take a shower. And by the time he got back half an hour later, Maggie was drifting off to sleep. Her eyes fluttered open, and she smiled at him peacefully.

"I love you," she murmured, already half asleep.

"I love you too," he said, as he got into bed next to her and kissed her. She kissed him back and then fell asleep in his arms, as he looked down at her and gently smoothed her hair. He knew that one day she would no longer be with him, and he wanted to make her as comfortable as possible and do everything he could for her now. They had been lucky so far, but he knew that one day that wouldn't be the case. They had been fighting the inevitable for years.

Chapter 5

When Peter walked into the house on Lake Wickaboag, a thousand memories engulfed him immediately. He picked up the key at a local realtor in West Brookfield who had kept an eye on the house for him for years, and reported on annual repairs that needed to be done before the winter. He had put on a new roof several years before after there had been some leaks. There was a flood when some pipes froze one year and then burst. On the whole the house looked dreary but was in good repair. Nothing had changed since he'd last seen it. Its last occupant had been his mother.

She had spent her final summer there
when she was very sick, and died shortly
after she left it. And the furniture was the
same as he remembered from his childhood. The upholstery had faded, but the
memories hadn't. He still remembered
the regattas, the sailboats on the lake,
swimming to the raft, fishing with his father
and brother. Despite his frequent problems
with his twin, the lake had been a happy
place for him.

He turned the lights on in the house, and
saw how dusty everything was, but he was
too tired to go back to Boston, so he had
no choice but to spend the night. He found
some old bedding in a closet, and walked
into his boyhood room. There were two
narrow beds in it, and he made up the one
that had been his for all the years they'd
gone there. They had selected a place
close to home, so their father could still go
back and forth to Ware to work when nec-
essary to see patients. He tried to lighten
his work schedule in the summer, but rarely
took off completely.

Peter walked through every room in the
house and then opened a back door and
went to sit in an old chair on the deck and

looked up at the stars. It was strange to think how far he'd gone since he'd been there, and now he had to start all over again. He wondered if he would have done anything different if he had known how his career on Wall Street would end. Probably not.

He thought about his parents more intensely than he had in a long time, and his twin. It had been such a fierce competition between them for their parents' affection, and Peter had felt through his entire childhood that Michael always won. Michael **had** to have their attention and approval, and did whatever it took to get it. Peter wondered what had happened to Michael, what kind of life he was leading, and if Maggie was still alive. He had always liked her. They had dated for a short time in high school, when she was a sophomore and he was a senior, but nothing ever came of it, and then he left for college. He didn't see her again until after the accident, when he came home for a visit, and Michael was courting her by then. He had been devoted to her after she was injured, and fiercely protective of her. She was a beautiful girl, but she had been seriously impaired after the incident on the pond. Her mother said that the doctor was sure she would improve over the years, but when Peter had seen her at his parents' funerals, she had seemed even more frail. He hadn't seen her since, nor his twin, after their vehement arguments over the will. It seemed unlikely to Peter that she was still alive fifteen years later, given the condition she had been in, and with no contact with anyone in Ware, he had no way of knowing if she'd died. He hoped she hadn't, she had been such a sweet girl and the accident had been so devastating. She had been a champion figure skater, but after her injury there was no way she could lead a semblance of a normal life. It was impressive and touching that Michael had married her in spite of it and wanted to take care of her. No matter what Peter thought of his brother, for Maggie's sake, he hoped that she was happy and alive.

Their last child had been just a baby when he last saw them. Maggie had held her in her arms while Michael pushed her in a wheelchair. The church had been filled to the rafters for his father's funeral, and nearly as much so for his mother. He closed his eyes and thought of all of them as he sat on the deck in the cold February air. There was a chill wind off the lake, and finally he went back in the house, but could find no food in the cupboards or refrigerator, and he wasn't hungry anyway. A little while later, he turned off the lights and went to bed. He woke up stiff and tired in the narrow bed as the sun streamed into the room. It was still early, and he had to get back to New York. Nothing had come of the meeting in Boston, and he wanted to go to L.A. as soon as possible to see Alana and the boys.

Peter folded the bedding neatly and put it back in the closet. Seeing the house again made him realize that there was no point keeping it. He was never coming back here. It was time to sell it. He should have done it years before.

He drove back to West Brookfield, and dropped the envelope with the key back into the realtor's mail slot. It had been a trip back in history for him, but it was one he knew he didn't need to make again. He put a note in the envelope telling the realtor he was putting the house on the market and to call him and suggest a price. He doubted that the house was worth much, although it had a small beach and was well located. He remembered that his parents had loved it, and had bought it for their boys. And now Peter was selling and severing his last tie with his early life. It was time. He had no idea why he hadn't done it before this.

It took him four hours to drive back to New York, and he arrived at the hotel where he was staying, tired and happy to be in the city. He called Ben and Ryan as soon as he got to his room, and told them he would be out in a few days. Ben was vague about it, and Ryan sounded relieved. It had been five weeks since Peter had seen Alana and the kids. He called her regularly too, but she sounded distant on the phone. He was still hoping that the tension between them would calm down again. The essential thing to Peter now was saving his relationship with Alana, if it was still possible, and being with her and their boys. Peter was willing to sacrifice almost anything for that, within reason, and without selling his soul to her father.

He thought about it again on the plane to L.A. two days later. And he had no idea what he would do with himself in L.A. He had no desire to be idle, or a lackey to her father, or to collect a check for sitting in an office, doing nothing, between massages and tennis games. All Peter wanted was to go back to work, but there were scores of others like him who were out of work at the moment, and no one was ready to hire until the economy stabilized again, and it hadn't, and maybe wouldn't for several years. It was grim to think about, and he had no idea what to do in the meantime. He had some money in the bank after selling the apartment, but it wouldn't last forever, not the way Alana liked to live. And they had the monthly rental money from the house in the Hamptons. But it was slim pickings compared to what they'd been used to. She had made an easy lateral move when she moved to her father's in L.A., and Gary was delighted to pick up all their bills, which Peter hated. He wanted to support his own wife and kids.

He had let Alana know when he was coming, and her father's car and driver picked him up at the airport. He was pleasant to Peter and put his suitcase in the trunk of the Rolls, and they headed toward Bel Air. The weather was warm and balmy, and it was a far cry from the freezing cold in New York when he left. It felt like spring in L.A. They wouldn't have weather like that in New York until May or June.

Alana was out when he got to the house—the maid told him she was at a luncheon at the Beverly Hills Hotel—and the boys were still in school. They got home before she did, and both boys threw their arms around his neck as he hugged them, and they shouted in excitement and delight. Ben looked as though he had grown a foot since his father had seen him, and Ryan looked suddenly more mature. Not seeing them for five weeks made him more aware of changes than usual. And he thought Ryan looked very serious once the excitement over his arrival abated.

"Everything okay?" Peter asked him as they headed to the kitchen for a snack. Ryan nodded with a smile.

"Yeah, it's fine."

"I thought maybe we could get some skiing in during your break," Peter suggested as they both made sandwiches. Ben had gone to his room to watch TV.

"Grampa is taking us to Aspen," Ryan said noncommittally, and Peter noticed that he didn't look thrilled about it. And Peter would feel like a freeloader going along with them on his father-in-law's tab.

"That sounds like fun," Peter said as they sat down at the table.

"Yeah, I guess," Ryan said, taking a bite out of his sandwich, as his mother walked into the kitchen and saw her husband for the first time in five weeks. She looked considerably less excited about it than the boys. She kissed Peter on the cheek, and she looked nervous when he put his arms around her and kissed her on the mouth. She was quick to move away, and asked Ryan how school had been that day.

"It was fine. My chemistry teacher is a jerk," he said grumpily as he finished his sandwich and put the plate in the sink. Peter was watching him and thought he looked unhappy, and a minute later Ryan walked out of the kitchen, saying he had some homework to do.

"I missed you," Peter said, smiling at Alana. He put his own plate in the sink and followed Alana out of the kitchen, as she chatted about lunch. Her circle of friends seemed to have widened since he left. She was hanging out with an assortment of celebrities and Hollywood wives. She looked as beautiful as ever in a tight white silk dress and high heels. She was looking very L.A. these days, without a trace of New York. "Did your clothes get here?" he asked her, and she nodded.

"I put it all away. I can't wear that stuff here. I put your things in the closet too."

They were in their bedroom by then, and Peter looked at her as though seeing her for the first time. He had a sudden, overwhelming desire to make love to her. She looked so beautiful, he had missed her, and it would be so comforting to be in bed with her again. And then he saw how strangely she was looking at him from across the room, and he remembered how distant they had felt from each other when he last saw her. And she'd been cool on the phone, or out.

"Something wrong?" he asked, picking up on an odd new vibe, as though she had turned into someone else while he was gone.

She looked at him endlessly from across the room and nodded, and then she said the words he never thought he'd hear from her and nearly stopped his heart. "I want a divorce," she said in barely more than a whisper. Her eyes apologized to him, but her mouth was set in a firm line.

"Are you serious?" was the only thing he could think of to say to her. "Why?"

"I don't know," she said, as tears filled her eyes. She was still standing and looking at him from across the room. "This just doesn't feel right anymore. It's all over, your job, our life in New York, us. We can't go back. I don't want to live there anymore, you don't want to live here. I think too much has happened. We've grown apart." Peter was silent for a moment as he sat down in a chair. His head was reeling, and he felt sick. He had just been trying to adjust to the idea of living in Los Angeles with her, and now she wanted out. His next question crossed his lips before it even went through his mind.

"Is there someone else?" He didn't even want to know, but he had asked. It was the only explanation he could think of for her asking him for a divorce. And he still wanted her, and the life they had shared for fifteen years.

"No," she said cautiously, but she hesitated, and he heard it in her voice. "But I'd like to be free to lead my own life here. I think we both need to move on."

"Just like that? Why? Because I lost all our money? When the market settles down again, I can make it all back. I made it before."

"It's not about the money," she said unconvincingly. "We don't want the same things. You hate my life out here. You said it yourself."

"I don't want to live here forever, but I could do it for a year or two. And maybe I could get a job out here, a real one, not working for your father. There are investment firms out here too. Shit, we have two kids. We love each other. You don't just dump that in five minutes, Alana." But she had, and he could see it. She was already a million miles away. He had heard it in her voice when he had called her, but he thought things might be better when they were together again. He could see that he'd been wrong. And then he thought of something that made a chill run down his spine. "Do the boys know?" Alana looked embarrassed and shook her head. "Ryan looks unhappy. I thought maybe it was about school."

"I talked to my dad about it, maybe he overheard something, but I don't think so."

"I think he knows, or he suspects it," Peter said, looking upset.

"Well, they'll have to know eventually, so it might as well be now. I went to see a lawyer last week. It's pretty simple if we do it on friendly terms." She was expecting a lot of him, and for an instant he felt one of his old rages boiling up in him, but he resisted it immediately, and never lost control. Those days were gone. He wasn't a frightened, angry kid anymore. He was a man. Whose wife wanted a divorce. It had happened to a million others before him, many millions, but he had never thought it would happen to him. Their life had been so perfect and so sure, but nothing was anymore. Their marriage was over, and he felt as though his life was too.

"At least the financial side will be simple," he said cynically. "There's almost nothing left. Are you planning to live with your father, or do you want your own place?" He hoped she didn't, it would leave very little for him.

"I want to stay here," she reassured him, "but I still need something, and money for the boys." She had thought it all out and discussed it with her lawyer. Peter could tell it was a fait accompli. He'd been fired. Again. The same sense of failure he'd had before nearly drowned him as he listened to her and tried not to react.

"Of course," Peter said coldly, and stared at her from across the room. "Are you willing to discuss this, or try counseling? We could give it another shot." Other than losing most of their money in the financial crisis, he had done nothing wrong. He had been a model husband until then, but winding up penniless was not in Alana's plans. She shook her head in answer to his question. She had made up her mind. It was written all over her, and he seriously wondered now if she was involved with someone else. He didn't have the guts to ask again, and he wasn't sure he wanted to know. "When do you want to tell the boys?"

"I don't know, before you go back to New York. You can enjoy them for a few days first. We're going to Aspen in a week anyway. I guess you'll want to go back to New York then." And then she looked panicked for an instant. "Or do you think you'll stay out here?" Having made the decision, she wanted a clean break.

"I don't know," Peter said, thinking about it. "I'd been thinking about staying out here with you. But there's no point in that now. At least here I'd be close to the boys, but I have nothing to do here, and even less if I'm not with you. I don't want to sit around in an apartment, waiting to see them. They have their own lives too. I'd rather fly out to see them, or have them come to New York for a chunk of time. If I'm not with you, Alana, I really have no life out here." She nodded and agreed. She didn't want him to stay.

She walked out of the room then and disappeared for a while. The four of them had dinner together that night, and Peter did his best to keep the conversation lively and entertain the boys. His heart was breaking while he did it, and it was the hardest thing he'd ever done. He didn't speak to Alana again until they went to bed that night. He had thought about staying in a guest room, but that would have said everything to the boys, and Alana agreed. So they were sharing a bedroom and a bed, and he was stunned by how lonely he could feel lying right next to her. Neither of them said a word once the lights were out, and it took him hours to fall asleep.

He got up at six o'clock the next morning and went to use the gym in the main house. He ran into his father-in-law as he walked in too, and Gary greeted him with a friendly expression.

"Sorry, Peter." He went right to the point, as he stood on the treadmill and looked at his about-to-be ex-son-in-law. "I think it's for the best."

"For who? I don't," Peter said honestly. "This is going to be hard for the boys, and for me, even if it's what she wants."

"You'll get back on your feet again. You're a very smart guy. I'm not worried about you. But it would be hard on Alana sticking by while you go through all the crap you'll have to, to get to the top again."

"I thought that was what 'for better or worse' was all about," Peter said grimly.

"Not in real life," Gary said firmly. "She went through enough when she lost her mother at fifteen. I don't want her ever going through hard times again. She's not made for that. She deserves an easy life."

"Life isn't always easy," Peter said doggedly. "That's what love is all about."

"You'll want things easy for your kids one day too. I don't want Alana to suffer while you put your life back together again. It could take years. It would be different if you were along for a free ride, but you're not that kind of guy. You'd go crazy hanging around an office doing nothing. I respect that about you."

"But not enough to encourage your daughter to stay married to me."

"She'll be happier out here, and so will your boys. You can come out and see them anytime you like. You're welcome to stay here," Gary said magnanimously as he upped the speed on the treadmill and adjusted it for a hill. He was in great shape for a man his age.

"That's not the same thing," Peter said unhappily. "I want to live with my kids." Not a continent away. And staying in L.A. was not the answer for him either, if he and Alana weren't together anymore. It would have been a painful life for him, and an empty one.

"Things don't always work out the way we want. I lost my wife, and we had a great marriage. She was thirty-nine when she died. Only a year older than Alana is now. That isn't fair either." There was nothing Peter could say to that. Peter realized he had been crazy to think that he could ever interfere with the sacred pair. They were a team, and he and Alana no longer were. He had lost his membership to their secret club, or maybe he had never had it after all. But he was an outsider for sure now. He left the gym a few minutes later and went back to their room. Alana had already left, and the boys had just gone to school. He had nothing to do that day until he picked the boys up at school.

It was a painful week, and they finally told the boys two days before he left. All four of them cried and Alana made it sound like it was a joint decision, which it wasn't, but he didn't want to make her look bad to their kids. He said he had to be in New York to find a job, and they could come to visit him anytime they wanted, and he promised to come out and see them once a month if he could, or every six weeks at most. It was the best he could do. Ryan just clung to him and cried.

It was wrenching leaving them this time.

Ryan took it harder than his younger brother, and Peter felt as though his heart had been torn out of his chest when they left, and he gulped down sobs. His plane was leaving two hours after the boys left for Aspen with Alana and her father, and Peter had tears streaming down his face in a cab on the way to the airport. And on the flight back to New York, he felt as though someone had died. He checked into the residential hotel again and tried to figure out what he was going to do. There were no jobs to be had at the moment, and there was no point being in New York, but he had nowhere else to go.

He was sitting in his hotel room the next morning, when the realtor from West Brookfield called him about the house on the lake. He wanted to discuss the price with Peter, and come up with something realistic since the house had been uninhabited for years, needed work, and hadn't been remodeled in fifty years. And as Peter listened to him, he realized what he was going to do. It was the only piece of property he owned right now that was available, since the house in the Hamptons was rented, which meant that living there would be free. It was about the only thing it had going for it. He could do some of the work on it himself, he had nothing else to do. And he could put it on the market when he was ready to move back to New York.

"Never mind," Peter said curtly, and the man on the other end was confused.

"Does that sound too low to you?" Peter hadn't even heard what he'd said.

"I'm not ready to sell it yet. I think I'm going to stay there for a while." The idea suddenly made perfect sense to him.

"Now? It's colder than hell out there this time of year. There's a bad wind that always comes off the lake. It's freezing cold."

"It's almost spring," Peter said calmly. March was just around the corner, and he and his brother had been out there with their father plenty of times in the spring. It might even be good for Ben and Ryan to come and see him there. They could have as much fun as he and Michael had had, fishing and sailing in summer, and water-skiing on the lake. It would be something different and new for them, and a simple, wholesome country life they'd never had. He liked the idea. "Maybe I'll put it on the market in the fall," Peter said to placate the realtor. "I can start cleaning the place up."

"Well, let me know when you're ready," the realtor said, sounding disappointed. It was rare for him to get a lakefront property to sell, even if the house was old-fashioned and needed work.

"I will," Peter promised, and hung up. He called a few contacts that morning, and came up dry again. And by that afternoon, he was driving north toward Ware. It was a far cry from the life he had considered living with Alana in L.A., or the one they had until recently in New York. It had been almost five months since their life had fallen apart, and now everything had changed again. He missed his boys as he drove to Massachusetts, but he felt better than he had in a while. And he wondered if by going back there he would find a piece of himself that had been missing for a long time, and make peace with his past finally. It was worth a shot, and the only one he had right now.

Chapter 6

Peter spent the first week at the lake house throwing things away—old pillows, stained bedding, tattered towels, pots with broken handles, ancient utensils that could no longer be repaired. He had a small mountain in the backyard of objects that needed to be hauled away, and realized that he needed a truck to do it. And after that, he spent another week scrubbing everything down, until the windows and woodwork gleamed. The kitchen looked ancient, but it was sparkling clean. He bought cleaning supplies at the local market, and he had a long list of items he wanted to replace, most of what he'd thrown away. And doing the work felt good. He ate easy dinners he cooked on his mother's old stove. He built a fire in the fireplace every night, which kept him warm. The wind off the lake was as icy as the realtor had said. But he slept well under some old blankets, and he called the boys in Aspen every night. He told them what he was doing and that he wanted them to come and stay with him.

The boys were shocked that he wasn't in New York, but they could hear that he was excited about being at the lake, and they were slowly adjusting to the idea that their parents were getting a divorce, although it still felt unreal to Peter too, and his heart ached when he thought of no longer living with his boys. Strangely, losing Alana wasn't as hard. Maybe she was right, and they had grown apart. He was feeling bitter that she wasn't willing to stick by him, and now that the golden days were over, she had bailed. It told him who she really was. And made it less agonizing to lose her.

For the moment, his life consisted of simple pleasures, and he was beginning to enjoy them. By mid-March, he realized that he needed to start stocking the house, from the long list he had made. There were tools he wanted to buy to make some repairs, a few pieces of furniture he could use, and he was going to buy a decent bed. The narrow beds he and his brother had slept on were wreaking havoc with his back, and his parents' bed was even older and in worse shape. He needed to get a line put in for his computer. He was getting all his e-mails on his BlackBerry, which wasn't enough. And he couldn't get everything on his list in West Brookfield, so he decided to drive the seven miles to Ware, where he'd grown up. It was going to be the first time he had seen it in fifteen years. He had been hesitant about going there, because he didn't want to run into his brother, and with any luck he wouldn't. His first stop was the hardware store, and he had decided to go to the used-car lot and buy a truck afterward. He still had a mountain of things he needed to haul away. The realtor had come out to check on him, and he was impressed by all that Peter had accomplished. The place was already looking better, and Peter was getting it in great shape. He was doing it now not so much to sell it as to show his boys. He wanted them to love it when they saw it, and enjoy it as much as he had when he was young. It was a piece of his history he wanted to share with them and never had before, because he hadn't come back here himself.

Peter felt strange when he drove into Ware. He went to the hardware store and went down his list with a young boy working there. They had everything he needed, and the boy helped Peter carry it to the car. There were tools, and several pieces of lumber, hardware for the kitchen cabinets, and utensils he needed for the kitchen. He was just coming back in for the last load, when an old man walked toward him from the back of the store. He looked ancient to Peter, but Peter recognized him immediately. It was old Mr. Peterson, the owner, who had already looked ancient fifteen years before, and he was still sharp as a tack. He narrowed his eyes as he looked at Peter, and he saw a flicker of recognition there. But Peter had changed a lot more than he had in the past fifteen years. Walter Peterson had to be close to ninety years old.

"I know you, don't I, son?" There was

something totally familiar to him about Peter's face.

"I haven't seen you in a long time, Mr. Peterson," Peter said politely, as he extended a hand. It was too late to avoid the meeting now. "Peter McDowell." The old man broke into a smile.

"Well, I'll be damned." He didn't tell him how much he still looked like Michael. He knew there had been bad blood over their parents' will. "What brings you to town? Do you live in Boston or New York?"

"I'm doing some work on the house at the lake," Peter said, avoiding his second question. He wasn't sure where he lived right now. Lake Wickaboag was the only address he had.

"It'll need a lot of work," the old man ventured.

"Yes, it does," Peter concurred. "How've you been?"

"I'm holding up. I'm turning ninety in June. I still manage to run this place."

"You're looking great," Peter said with a smile, scooping the rest of his purchases into his arms. "See you again sometime," he called out as he left, and Walt Peterson stared after him, thinking it was too bad that he hadn't come back to town in all these years, and even more so that the two brothers were estranged. Peter looked like he had calmed down a lot with age. He'd been a wild one in his youth, rowdy a lot of the time, not like his brother Mike, who'd been easygoing all his life. It was funny how different they were, Walt Peterson mused, since they were twins.

After the hardware store, Peter went to the used-car lot, and checked out the trucks. There was an old blue one with a big bed in the back that was just what he needed. He paid for it, and the dealer offered to drive it out to the lake for him when his son came in that night to do deliveries for him. He offered Peter a very good deal, and he didn't recognize Peter since he'd only owned the dealership for three years. The previous owner had died. It was rare for businesses in Ware to change hands, in the old days anyway.

By twelve-thirty, Peter was back at the lake, and he spent an hour putting his tools and supplies in the garage, and then he went inside and made lunch. He heard his cell phone ring and was startled when it was Alana. She wanted to know if he'd called a lawyer yet. It was a wake-up call back to real life. He'd had a nice day until then.

"I haven't had time. I've been busy here," he lied. He had been busy, but not too busy to make a call. He hadn't felt ready to face calling a divorce lawyer yet. As far as he was concerned, there was no rush. This was her idea, not his. And he still hoped she might change her mind, although he was angry at her for what she'd done and deeply hurt by it. But he would have preferred to stay married to her, if she was willing. It was obvious from what she said that she wasn't.

"What are you doing at some lake?"

"It's where I grew up. I used to spend the summers here. I'm living at the house for now. It's free. And the boys will have fun here this summer. I'm cleaning the place up so I can sell it in the fall." Alana remembered hearing about it—he had just inherited the house from his parents when they got married—but he had never gone there during all the years they were together, and never wanted to, from what she could tell.

"Where is it?"

"About two hours out of Boston. It's a

nice place." He wouldn't have said that six months before. "There's nothing happening in New York, so I figured I might as well be here."

"Well, call a lawyer," she said, sounding impatient.

"I'll do it next week," he said, and she was annoyed when they hung up. He was dragging his feet, and she was ready to move on. She wanted to file. Once she made up her mind, it was done.

He called his tax lawyer the next day, and got the name of a divorce lawyer from him. He told Peter he was sorry to hear he needed one.

"So am I," Peter said with a sigh. "It wasn't my idea."

"I think a lot of marriages bit the dust with the crash," his attorney said philosophically.

"It kind of lets you know what those marriages were based on," Peter said, sounding bitter for an instant. "Alana went back to L.A. as soon as she could."

He left a message for the divorce lawyer that afternoon, and he called Peter back the next day. He took down Alana's name, and Peter's information, and said he'd let him know if he heard anything from her lawyer. Peter didn't know her lawyer's name, and he texted her with the name of his. And then he went back to work on the house.

While Peter was working hard at the lake, Walt Peterson sprained his ankle at the store. He missed a step when he came down from his apartment upstairs, and the boy he had working for him thought it might be broken and talked him into going to the doctor. He drove him to Michael's office to get it looked at. But when Michael examined him, he said it was just a sprain.

"You were lucky with that," Michael said, smiling at him. He hadn't seen Walt Peterson in a while. He was in good health. "How did it happen?" he asked as he bandaged it for him. He told him he'd have to stay off it for a while, although he knew he wouldn't. He'd be back at the store that afternoon. And at the local bar that night, where he hung out since his wife died.

"Progress is a dangerous thing. I've been wearing two pairs of spectacles for fifty years. One for distance, and one to read. I wear both of them around my neck. My eye doctor talked me into a pair of those bifocal progressives, and I can't see a damn thing with them. They make me dizzy, and the ground goes all fuzzy under my feet. I missed the step when I was wearing them. I'm going to throw them away." He looked outraged as he said it, and Michael grinned.

"They take a while to get used to," he confirmed. And then he saw that Walt was staring at him, measuring his next words, and he had no idea what he was going to say. "Something else?" Sometimes his patients were shy about their problems, even at Walt's age.

"Someone came into my store the other day whom you used to know," Walt said cautiously. He hadn't heard Michael mention his brother in years. It was as though his twin had died.

"And who was that?" Michael asked pleasantly, as he finished wrapping Walt's ankle, and set his leg gently down.

"Peter," he said simply, which meant nothing to Michael. There were a lot of Peters in town.

"Peter who?"

"Peter, your brother. He came in and bought a load of stuff from me. He says he's working on the lake house. Maybe he's getting ready to sell it. He hasn't been here in all these years." Michael knew that as well.

"That's interesting," Michael said coolly, showing none of the emotion he felt. It bothered him to know that his twin was in town, but he didn't want Walt to know that. He wasn't about to feed the gossip mills, it was a small town, and people liked to talk. There had been enough of that when his parents died, about the inequities in the will. "The prodigal son returns" was Michael's only comment, but Walt could see that he wasn't pleased by the news, and wondered if he should have stayed quiet. He didn't like upsetting Dr. Mike, he was a good doctor and a nice guy.

"I'm sure he won't stay long," Walt said to reassure him, although he had no idea if that was true. Peter hadn't told him his plans.

"Let's hope not. This town's not big enough for both of us. It never was," Michael said, and helped the old man up and onto his feet. He gave him a pair of crutches to take with him. "Now you stay off that foot. And watch out for your new glasses until you're used to them," he reminded him, and said not another word about his brother. And Walt Peterson took his cue from him.

"Thanks, doc," he said, and hobbled out with his employee's help. And as Michael moved on to his next patient, he decided to put the unpleasant news out of his mind. As far as he was concerned, his twin brother was dead, and had been for fifteen years. And after all the trouble he'd given Michael when they were growing up, he had no desire to see him again.

Chapter 7

Alana's lawyer called Peter's the following week, and his lawyer then called him. He told Peter that Alana wanted to file the divorce, but they had to work out their financial settlement first. She was willing to hold off on alimony until he was employed again, although she expected him to support their boys, and Peter had no problem with that. He wanted to support them too. He suggested an amount to the attorney, which sounded reasonable to him as well. And she wanted back alimony with interest once he had a job. Peter didn't like that as much, and it sounded greedy to him, since her father was supporting her lavishly, but they had been married for fifteen years, and she deserved something for that. Peter thought the conversation was over after he made that point, but the lawyer said she had one more request. Peter couldn't imagine what it was, as he waited to hear.

"She wants the Southampton house as a settlement," he said simply. It was the only thing Peter had left of any value, other than the lake house, which was worth next to nothing compared to it. He whistled through his teeth.

"That's pretty much all I've got right now." There was very little remaining from the sale of the New York apartment, and she still wanted half of that. Peter was sure that her father was advising her. The South-ampton house was a valuable piece of real estate, particularly if she kept it until prices went up again. Asking for it was a smart move. Peter was living off the monthly rental they were getting. It would hurt to lose that, particularly while he was unem-ployed.

"What if we split it when we sell it?"

"She says she wants to use it with the boys."

"We can still split the proceeds when we sell."

"I'll try," the lawyer promised. Other than that, it didn't sound like there was much left to divide. He was handling several divorces like theirs, particularly of Bernie Madoff's past clients who had nothing left at all. In March, Madoff had pleaded guilty to the charges of investor fraud against him and was waiting for sentencing in June.

The lawyer called Peter back the next day, after talking to Alana's lawyer again. "No deal," he told him bluntly. "She wants the house, no split. She wants it all free and clear. They sounded pretty tough about it, but we can put up a fight for it in court. Since it's the only asset left, a judge is liable to give half of it to you." Peter thought about it for a long moment, and about his boys and the years he had spent with her. He was angry at her for bailing on him, but he still loved her. And he felt bad to have put her through hard times when he went broke in the crash, but it certainly wasn't his fault, and if that hadn't happened, they'd probably still be married, although that was a damning statement about her. But he didn't want to fight. She was a woman who was willing to be there for the good times, but not the bad. She was spoiled. And he also knew that her father would help her fight like a demon to get what she wanted.

"Give it to her," he said quietly. It was like emptying his pockets to make amends. After that, he had nothing left except the house at Lake Wickaboag, which was worth too little to fight about.

"Are you sure?" his lawyer asked him. "Why don't you think about it for a few days? There's no rush here. The final decree will only take six months once we get this worked out."

"I'm sure." He wanted it over now. If all she wanted was the house and back alimony with interest, it was a business deal now, not a marriage. It was over for him now too. Fifteen years down the tubes, just like everything else. He felt like a failure across the board. At least he could make one last grand, elegant gesture with the Southampton house. "She can have it."

"Do you want some kind of restriction put on it that she has to keep it for the boys?"

"No, it's hers." Peter knew that his father-in-law would provide handsomely for Ben and Ryan in his will—he didn't need to worry about them. And one day, he would be solvent again too. Maybe not as rich as he had been, but you never knew what could happen. He had a lot of years left to earn big money, if that was what he wanted to do.

"That's it then. I'll send you the papers to sign," the lawyer said simply.

"Thank you," Peter said quietly, and hung up. It was a strange feeling suddenly. Un-encumbered. Unfettered. He had nothing left, except the house he was working on. He went back outside and repaired the loose boards in the front steps. His life had suddenly become very simple, and for now, he liked it that way. There was something very symbolic about it, and very Zen. It was 180 degrees from his old life, and the passion he had had for making money for twenty-one years. Now he was giving it all away.

Two hours later he got a text from her. All it said was "thank you," just those two words. He knew what it meant. The house meant more to her now than their marriage, or him. The only thing they had left in common was their boys. The rest was gone. And in the end, it came down to money for

Alana. It was a sad thing to learn about her. Success meant everything to her and her father, and Peter had failed. He had lost his grip on the brass ring and fallen off the merry-go-round. Alana was still on it, but Peter wasn't. For now, he was living in a whole other world, one that Alana wanted no part of. She would have died if she could see the house at the lake. There was nothing grand or elegant about it. But Peter was proud of the work he had done on it with his own hands. The place was starting to look good again. It was flourishing with his attention and hard work, and there was satisfaction for him in that. His life was really down to the basics.

Peter went into Ware again the next day, to buy groceries and get more cleaning supplies. He drove to the supermarket in his new truck, and as he parked it, he saw a woman sitting in a car in the space next to him. She looked familiar, sitting in the passenger seat, and he realized instantly who she was. She looked older and more fragile, but the minute she smiled up at him, she looked the same. It was Maggie. Lisa had taken her for a ride, when she went to buy groceries for them. Maggie loved getting out on the rare occasions she could, and she looked at Peter now with disbelief.

"Is that you?" she asked, smiling in delight. She had been no part of the battle between the two brothers, and she'd always been sorry it ended so badly for both of them. Peter had been a good friend and date for a while when they were kids, and she often wondered how he was.

"No, it's just a ghost," he said, laughing, getting out of the truck. He bent down into the window and kissed her cheek. She looked frighteningly frail, and he could see how thin she was. Her hand resting on the open window looked transparent, it was so thin. "How've you been? Any better?"

"I'm fine," she said with a shrug and a rueful smile. "Michael manages to keep me together." She didn't tell Peter about the Parkinson's, but he could see that her hand on the window was shaking.

"Are you going in?" Peter asked her, gesturing toward the supermarket. He would have helped her if she needed it. He didn't ask about his brother, but he had always liked Maggie. Even when they were younger, she'd been a lovely person.

"No, I'm waiting for my daughter. She does the shopping for us." And everything else, Maggie thought but didn't say. Lisa was more of a wife to Michael than she was, with all the help she gave them both. She felt guilty about it often, but there wasn't much she could do, lying on her bed, other than surf the Internet, and Michael didn't like her to go out. There was too much risk for her, especially with the Parkinson's in the last two years. He was terrified she'd get pneumonia, and knew she might not survive if she did. Even a cold was a danger to her. "What about you? Married? Kids?" She was smiling at him, obviously happy to see him.

"Yes to both. Well, sort of." He hesitated. "I have two great boys, Ben and Ryan, they're nine and fourteen. They just moved to L.A. with their mother. She's filing for divorce. So, married, but not for long." He shrugged, looking embarrassed and feeling like a loser as he said it. "How is your dad?"

"He died two years ago."

"I'm sorry. He was a nice man."

Maggie nodded, looking sad for a moment. "Yes, he was. I really miss him.

It's weird to see the lumber mill in someone else's hands now, after three generations. Michael and I had to sell it after he died. None of us knew how to run it. Times change." Peter nodded in silent agreement. They certainly had for him as well, in a major way.

And with that, Lisa got back to the car, pushing a cart piled high with their groceries in bags. She looked startled to see a tall, handsome man talking to her mother, and she was struck immediately by his resemblance to her father. Her mother looked happy to be talking to him. The two adults exchanged a look, and Maggie decided to tell her the truth. They had nothing to hide. Even if Michael didn't acknowledge his existence, Peter was still her uncle, after all, and she had a right to know it. Maggie never liked secrets.

"This is your uncle Peter," Maggie said simply with a gentle smile, as Peter smiled at the niece he hadn't seen since she was an infant in his arms. She was a beautiful girl and looked a lot like Maggie, except that she had her father's eyes. Lisa stared at him in amazement and then broke into a smile.

"I've always wanted to meet you," she said shyly. "You look a lot like my dad." Except that he was taller and better looking, but Lisa didn't say that. She adored her father and would never have been disloyal to him. And she thought her father was the handsomest, smartest, nicest man in the world. But Peter looked pretty cute to her too.

"Are you visiting?" Maggie asked him then.

"I'm cleaning up the lake house. It needs a lot of work." They had had some good times there as kids. Maggie had been the water-skiing champion at the lake every year. It was there that their high school romance began, over a hot summer. He had kissed her after they swam to the raft. But the infatuation had only lasted the summer, and then he left for college, and two years later so did she. And after that she had the accident, and everything changed radically. No one had been more surprised than Peter when Michael started dating and then married her. But he was happy for them both. Peter wouldn't have been able to take on a responsibility like that at the time, or maybe even later. As a doctor, Michael was perfect for her and just the husband she needed.

"Are you moving back here?" Maggie looked surprised at that. He had outgrown Ware years ago, and he'd been in New York for a long time.

"I got caught in the market crash. The investment banking firm I worked for closed. The rest is history, and so is my money and my marriage. I'm taking a breather, and when things calm down, I'll go back. Right now, I'm happy here, except I miss my boys."

"I miss mine too," Maggie admitted sadly. "Bill did his junior year in London two years ago, and never came back. He swears he never will. He's a lot like you," she said, without expanding further on the subject. "He's only been back twice since he left." She looked sad when she said it, and Peter helped Lisa load the car. He wondered who was going to help her when they got home. She seemed like a very capable girl, mature far beyond her years. Having an invalid mother had probably made her grow up faster. She seemed to have everything in control as she thanked Peter. He was upset to see how fragile Maggie looked and how pale. She looked as though she never got out and she probably didn't. She had been a shut-in for years, and Peter had always thought that Michael was overprotective of her. Peter would have gotten her out more, and tried to give her a normal life, but maybe then she wouldn't have lived as long. It was hard to know. Maybe Michael was right if she had survived this long. But Maggie looked like a ghost from another world. Only her smile was the familiar one he knew so well.

"I hope we see you again sometime," Lisa said shyly. He would have invited them to come out to the lake, but he knew Michael would have had a fit over their visiting him, and he didn't want to cause trouble for Maggie or her daughter.

"I'm sure we will," Peter said warmly and kissed Maggie on the cheek again. "It was nice to meet you, Lisa. You make your uncle very proud." She giggled and got in the car. Maggie waved as they drove away a moment later. It had made Peter happy to see Maggie, and sad at the same time. She looked as though she were clinging to life by a thread.

Before Peter went back to the lake, he

stopped and had a hamburger at the diner. He'd been hungry for one for several days, just the way they made them. The diner had been, and still was, the main teenage hangout in Ware. And everyone else in town went there too. Workers, truckers passing through, people stopping in for their lunch break, or having breakfast before they went to work. Most of the police department usually ate there, single men who had no one to cook for them, families that wanted an easy night out, or women who didn't feel like cooking. Just about everyone in town was a patron of the diner at some time or other. And they mainly featured good home-cooked meals—meat loaf, pot roast, roast turkey, and Irish stew were main features, with great fries and mashed potatoes, and their hamburgers were famous in the region. And their fish dishes were always good on Friday. Peter had been longing for a meal there or a hamburger since he'd been back. He finally wandered in right after he saw Maggie. And when he looked around at the packed diner, he felt like it was a time warp and he had never left. It was the middle of the afternoon, and in spite of that, half the town was there. Peter slid into a small back booth, and a waitress in a pink nylon uniform with a frilly apron took his order for a burger and fries.

He was halfway through his hamburger when a woman at the cash register looked at him, stopped what she was doing, and ran right over. She gave him an enormous hug and kissed him on the cheek. Violet Johnson owned the diner. It was a gold mine for her, and in spite of his checkered reputation as a kid, Vi had always been crazy about Peter, and stuck up for him whenever his name had come up when he was in high school. He had been one of her best customers. With her he had never been a troublemaker, just a handsome young kid. She hadn't seen Peter in fifteen years, and she thought of him whenever she saw Michael when he had lunch there occasionally, usually with the chief of police. But she knew not to ask Michael about his brother. Everyone in town knew they hadn't spoken for years and that Michael had gotten almost everything in his parents' will. In a small town, people knew.

"Well, look what the cat dragged in. Where've you been, sonny?" she said, beaming at him. She was a big woman, well into her sixties now, with a red beehive she always combed herself. She wore a pink uniform like all the other waitresses, and she watched them like a hawk. Dawdling, being rude to customers, eating or smoking on the job, and God forbid stealing were all major crimes at the diner.

"I was in New York," Peter said to Vi with a big smile, as though he'd gone there for the weekend for a basketball game or a prom, not for twenty-one years.

"I heard something like that." Vi nodded. She knew everything that happened in town. "You gonna stick around for a while?" She didn't ask why he'd come back. She'd already heard about his being in town from Walt Peterson, who ate dinner there every night.

"Maybe." Peter was vague, and so was his life at the moment.

And after another enthusiastic hug, she went back to the cash register where people were piling up. "Welcome back!" she said over her shoulder as she got back to work. It made Peter feel like a kid again when he saw her, and brought back a thousand memories of high school and even college. Even Vi's hairdo and the color of it hadn't changed in thirty years.

He gave her a big bear hug again when he paid for his hamburger, and drove back to the lake. It really felt like old times running into Maggie, and then seeing Vi at the diner. She had always been one of his staunchest fans and insisted he was a very polite boy, which not everyone would have said at the time, given his temper in his teens.

When Peter got home with his own groceries, after stopping at the diner, he was thinking about his chance meeting with Maggie and then decided to play hooky and go fishing in the lake for a few hours. He had found some old fishing poles in the garage, and he had already used them several times. He didn't catch anything in the late afternoon, but he had fun anyway. And he called to tell Ben and Ryan about it that night.

He invited them to come and stay with him over Easter, but his grandfather had invited them to Hawaii, and they were both looking forward to it. Peter was beginning to feel that there was no room in their life for him. And it was hard competing with a grandfather for whom money was no object, and who kept devising exciting vacations for them that their father could no longer afford. Peter felt like a loser all over again, and he was depressed when he hung up the phone. He had promised to visit them when they got back from Hawaii, and he wanted them to come to the lake that summer. Both boys said they thought it would be fun, and Peter hoped it would. There was so little he could offer them now. Alana and her father had cornered the market on fancy vacations and all the things that had been commonplace to them before. At least a trip to Lake Wickaboag would be something different, and they might enjoy it as much as he and his brother had as boys.

Peter cooked dinner and went to bed early that night. Before he fell asleep, he lay thinking about his sons and how much he missed them. He thought about Alana too, but he tried not to do that anymore. He had already mourned their marriage in the past weeks, and after everything Alana had done, there was nothing left for which to grieve. His thoughts drifted to Maggie then, and her luminous face looking up at him from the car window that afternoon. There was something haunting about her, as though she had already drifted into another world. She looked almost like a ghost, but when she smiled at him, he could still see the girl she had been years before. And he enjoyed meeting Lisa—she was so young and full of life. It was a crazy thought, given the situation with Michael, but he would have loved to introduce Maggie and Lisa to his boys when they came out. Maybe they would run into each other again sometime. Peter hoped they would. She was his only friend from his boyhood days, and they were family after all. And it had been so nice seeing her. He felt so isolated and lonely now without Alana and his boys. Life as he had known it for twenty-one years had virtually disappeared. He was still thinking about Maggie as he drifted off to sleep.

Maggie didn't tell Michael about running into Peter when he came home that night, although she had looked up Peter on the Internet and read all about the fiasco when Whitman Broadbank closed, and felt sorry for him. She had been so excited to see him. He was a happy piece of her own youth. She didn't want to keep it a secret from Michael, but it was awkward telling him because he and Peter had been on such bad terms and she didn't want Michael to think her disloyal. Lisa hadn't said anything about the chance meeting either.

Maggie mentioned it casually as he took her blood pressure the next morning, as he always did, before he left for work. He told her that it was low again, and he didn't want her getting out of bed all day. She was glad he hadn't said that the day before or she might never have seen Peter again, and she was glad she had.

"We ran into someone yesterday," she said casually, as he put the cuff away.

"Where was that?" He looked startled. Maggie never went anywhere.

"Lisa took me with her when she went to buy groceries. It was nice getting out and sitting in the car. We saw Peter there," she said simply, and immediately saw a look of pain in Michael's eyes. He sensed instantly what Peter she meant, his twin, and he stiffened visibly.

"Did he talk to you?" Michael asked, looking unhappy.

"Just for a few minutes. He says he's cleaning out the lake house." She tried to sound low-key about it, not to upset Michael more than she had.

"Did Lisa see him?"

"For a minute when she came out of the store." Maggie tried to make light of it, but Michael looked as though a bomb had hit him as he sat on the bed.

"I hate to say it, but, Maggie, there are some dark people in the world, people who do nothing but hurt others, and cause pain and havoc wherever they go. Peter is one of them. He disappointed my parents. He lied and cheated and bullied his way through our childhood. He's just not a nice guy. I know you two were friends when you were kids, but I hate to think of him getting anywhere near you or Lisa. Don't talk to him if you see him again. I don't trust him, and he might do something to get back at me. He hates me for what our parents left me. But he abandoned them. And he forgot all about us the minute he got to New York and started making money. Now all I want to do is forget him." Maggie knew it was somewhat true and that Peter hadn't come home often, but their estrangement pained her for both of them. She knew a side of Peter that Michael didn't. He had always been wonderful to her, and was a truly lovely person.

"I wish you two would find a way to make peace. It's not right for two brothers to spend the rest of their lives hating each other."

"I can't make peace with a man like him. He wouldn't let me. All Peter knows how to do is fight and hurt the people who love him. He nearly broke our mother's heart. He hardly came to see her before she died. I can never forgive him for that," Michael said clearly with a look of sorrow.

"You'd be the bigger man if you ended this war between you," she said gently. "You're both forty-six years old. Maybe it's time for you two to forgive each other. He says he's getting divorced, his boys are living in California, and things can't be going well for him if he's living at the lake."

"He probably got hit hard in the market crash. He wouldn't come back here if he didn't have to. He hates it here." She suspected that was true after what she'd read on the Internet the day before.

"I just don't want you carrying all that anger and pain around forever. It's too heavy to carry, for both of you," she said wisely.

Michael nodded and stood up. He had to go to work. He had house calls to make. And then he looked down at her with a worried expression, which reminded her of when they were young.

"You're not still in love with him, are you?" He was frowning when he asked her, and Maggie laughed with the broad smile of her girlhood.

"I was never in love with him. I was fifteen and I had a crush on him. You wouldn't give me the time of day then. You were going off to do pre-med. Peter and I were just friends by the time I was sixteen."

"And now?"

"I'm in love with you. I just think you should make peace with each other, before it's too late, or something happens to one of you. You've suffered enough for the last fifteen years. I hope one of you figures out a way to put this to rest. It would be a good time, now that he's here."

"I'll think about it," Michael said quietly, and then he leaned over and kissed his wife and left for work. Maggie lay in bed thinking about it afterward, wondering if she had made any headway convincing Michael. It was hard to tell with him. In Michael's case, still waters ran deep, and she had meant every word she said. She didn't want him carrying the burden of anger and hostility for the rest of his life. And as she thought of it, she nestled back into her bed and reached for her computer. She wanted to see if her friend was in their favorite chat room yet. Maggie's day had begun.

Chapter 8

While Peter was chopping down a small tree behind the lake house, Michael was visiting one of his elderly patients in the late afternoon a few days later. Mabel Mack, the woman he was visiting, was ninety-two years old, had never married, had no children or living relatives, and she was entirely alone. Michael was the only kind, caring soul in her life other than two neighbors who were nearly as old as she was. All three elderly women were Michael's patients, and he was trying to visit Mabel every day at the moment, and made time to listen to her complaints and problems.

She had broken a hip two months before, and was getting around on a walker, but he was afraid she might fall again at night. She had stubbornly refused to have a nurse come to live with her, and Michael worried about her. He sat patiently while she served him tea and told him about an argument she'd had with one of her neighbors about a soap opera they watched together every day. He had infinite patience, and it was a full half hour before he gently told her that he had to leave to see other patients. She smiled shyly at him—she loved the young doctor. He seemed like a boy to her, and she had known him all his life. She always inquired about Maggie and the children. She had been the town librarian until she retired thirty years before.

"You tell that pretty wife of yours that I'm saying prayers for her," she told Michael as he was leaving. "How's Lisa? Still wants to be a doctor?"

"So she says. That's still a long way off. She's in high school," Michael said, smiling. "She takes wonderful care of her mother." It was easy to see how proud he was of his daughter. And she inquired about Bill in London, and when he was coming home.

Michael said not for a while. Mabel patted his arm with her clawlike hand as she stood in the doorway. Considering her age, she was doing pretty well, and Michael waved as he got in his car. There were three messages on his cell phone about patients whom he still had to see before he went home that night, and he headed back to his office. But the most recent message was a cancellation. The patient he had been planning to see for a rash said she was feeling better and didn't have time to come in after all.

He started the car, and then bowed his head for a moment, wondering if Maggie was right. Her words had haunted him since she said them, and as he looked up, he turned the car in the direction of West Brookfield. He didn't really have time, but something told him that her point was a good one, and he should see his brother, even if he didn't want to. Once he made the decision, he stepped on the gas, and drove steadily until he got there. It took him just under half an hour. He hadn't been out to the lake house in years, and it still held the same happy memories for him as it did for Peter.

He turned into the driveway, and could see a man chopping down a small tree. He recognized him immediately, even from the back. Peter was listening to an iPod as he hacked away at the tree and didn't hear the car approach. Michael got out of the car and walked toward him with a hesitant step. He was two feet away from him, when Peter became aware of someone in his peripheral vision, and his eyes grew wide with astonishment when he saw his brother. Michael was wearing a shirt and tie, corduroy pants, and a heavy coat, in the still-chilly April afternoon. It was almost dusk, and the tree had just fallen as the two brothers stood and stared at each other, and Peter took off his iPod. He had no idea why Michael had come, possibly to ask him to leave town, or never to speak to his wife and family again. Peter frowned when he saw him, instantly on guard for what might come next.

Michael looked shorter somehow, and heavier than when Peter had last seen him. For a long moment, neither brother said a word to each other, and the weight of the years hung between them. Peter felt his hatred and disgust well up in him like a volcano, but as he looked into Michael's eyes, he saw something different there. He wondered if time had changed him, or softened him, after years of caring for a sick wife, and the gentling effects of his children. Peter almost wondered if he was human after all, and not the monster he had thought him when they were growing up. After all, he had mellowed too. Life wasn't always easy, and had a way of filing down the sharp corners and rough edges. Peter wondered if that was the case for both of them. It was Michael who spoke first.

"I thought I'd just come out and say hello," Michael said cautiously, looking embarrassed. This was even harder than he had feared, and he couldn't read the wary expression in his brother's eyes. Was it hatred or hope? Peter always appeared fierce when he knit his brows, and in his boyhood it had been what he looked like just before he unleashed a mighty punch at someone he felt threatened by, but as he wiped his brow on his shirt, after felling the tree, he slowly smiled at his brother.

"That was nice of you," he said honestly. He wouldn't have done the same himself, and he had made no effort to contact his brother since he had come back to Ware two months before. And probably never would have, if Michael hadn't come out to the lake.

"It was Maggie's idea," Michael said with a sheepish expression, not wanting to take credit he didn't deserve. That was new, Peter noted. In the past Michael had claimed anyone's good deeds as his own, mostly Peter's. He didn't do that this time, and gave his wife the full credit for the gesture he had just made. It showed a modesty and humility Peter had never seen in him before. Michael had also attributed all of his own misdeeds to his twin. But they weren't children anymore. There was a remote possibility that he had changed.

"How is she really?" Peter asked with a look of genuine concern. "I was happy to see her the other day, outside the supermarket, but it was hard to tell how she is, sitting in the car."

"She doesn't get out much," Michael admitted. "She can't afford to risk exposure to infection, and she's had a pretty rough time for the past two years. She was heartbroken over her father's death and selling the mill, but there was no way we could keep it, and then she was diagnosed with Parkinson's right afterward. It's still in the early stages, but we can't hold it in check forever. It's a progressive disease, and she was already so fragile before that." Peter could see all the love and worry on his brother's face and in his eyes, and he felt sorry for both of them.

"You've done an amazing job taking care of her for all these years," Peter reassured him. "She's still alive. Do you want to come inside for a cup of coffee or something?" He had bought a bottle of Johnnie Walker for himself, but he didn't want to sound like a drunk offering it to him right off the bat, although it might have made the meeting easier for both of them. But Michael shook his head.

"I'd love to come by another time. I haven't been here in years," not since their parents died. "I've still got patients to see right now. I just wanted to come out to see you." He had felt compelled to do so, and now Peter was glad he had. It was a bridge to the present from the past, and for the first time in so long, Peter was beginning to think it was possible to build one, maybe thanks to Maggie. He had never thought that could still happen.

"I'm happy you did," Peter said sincerely, the storm clouds lifting from his eyes.

"How did you make out in the financial crisis on Wall Street? I saw that Broadbank closed," Michael commented, which explained why he was here. He was obviously out of a job. It was a dark intermission in an otherwise stellar career, from what Michael knew of his professional life. In spite of his awkward beginnings, Peter had turned into a star. But for now Peter was living in poverty at the lake. The seesaw of life.

"I'm wiped out," Peter said honestly with a rueful smile. "Ground zero. It's all gone, so I'm here for a while." He didn't tell Michael about the collapse of his marriage, but Maggie had told him about that, and Peter had assumed that she would if she admitted to seeing him at all.

"You'll get back on top one of these days," Michael said reassuringly. There was obvious empathy in his voice, and Peter was touched. This was a man he didn't even know. "I know it must be tough."

"It is. It's hard on everyone right now. My kids just moved to L.A. to live with their mother and grandfather. I want them to come out to the lake this summer, to do the things we used to do."

"Fight, argue, and beat each other up?" Michael said, laughing, and Peter laughed too.

"Yeah, among other things. Like fish and water-ski."

"It must be hard for you with them out there." It was obvious that Peter missed them, and Michael knew it had to be lonely for him without his kids.

"Yeah, I miss them like crazy," Peter admitted. "I'm getting a divorce. End of an era. It's a fresh start, but not one I wanted. It's kind of nice being here at the lake. It's a simple life." Michael could see that from Peter's lumberjack shirt, heavy workman's boots, and stained jeans. He was doing manual work, and living nearly cost free, except for food.

"Would you like to come to dinner tomorrow night?" Michael asked on the spur of the moment. "Lisa is a pretty good cook. And on her good days, we bring Maggie downstairs. I'd like it if you'd come, and

Maggie would too. She hardly gets to see anyone anymore. People forget you when you're shut in the way she is."

"I'd love that," Peter said with a look of genuine gratitude. This was a whole new brother, and Peter longed to have family in his life again, even the twin he had hated for years. This seemed like an entirely different man to him. They were like two old friends as they caught up on each other's lives, standing outside their parents' old cottage at the lake. "Are you sure it's not too much trouble?"

"No," Michael said with a slow smile. "It would be great." Maggie had been right, and he was so glad he'd come. They both felt enormous relief, as though the pressure had been let out of an old wound. Healing had finally begun, for both of them. "Eight o'clock? I don't get home much before that," he said apologetically, and Peter laughed, with a peaceful look.

"My social calendar is pretty free up here. I'm looking forward to it. Anything you want me to bring?"

"Just you," Michael said, as he reached a hand out and touched his brother's shoulder. "It's good to see you, Peter." He sounded as though he meant it, and Peter's heart instantly went out to him. He hadn't known it, but this was the moment he had waited for, for fifteen years. It was time now for both of them to make amends, and they were ready for it. Michael's gesture of coming out to see him at the lake had been an important one for them. Peter knew their parents would have been pleased. His mother had hated the constant rift between them, and had begged Peter to make peace with his brother the last time he saw her. Both brothers had refused. But fifteen years was a long time, and many things had changed.

"It's good to see you too," Peter said in a choked voice as he walked Michael back to his car. "Thank you for coming out here," particularly knowing how busy he must be, running between patients all day long. "See you tomorrow," he said, as Michael got back in his car, and looked up at Peter with a smile.

The two brothers waved to each other as Michael drove away, and then his car was out of sight, and Peter walked into the house and poured himself a glass of Johnnie Walker, not to numb himself this time, but in celebration. For the first time in his life, he felt as though he had a brother who cared about him, and whom he in turn could love. It was a great feeling as he put the glass to his lips, took a long swig of the scotch, and smiled. Maggie had given both of them a fantastic gift, a chance to have the brother they had longed for all their lives.

Chapter 9

Dinner at Michael and Maggie's the next day was a festive event. Lisa had made her recipe for roast chicken, with cornbread stuffing, mashed potatoes, and fresh string beans. She had even bought an apple pie and ice cream on her way home from school. She wanted to impress her uncle with what a good cook she was.

Peter arrived promptly at eight o'clock, and Michael managed to come home a few minutes early and helped Maggie into a warm white cashmere sweater and a pair of comfortable jeans. She had brushed her dark hair till it shone. She didn't put on makeup, she rarely felt well enough to bother anymore, and Michael said he didn't care. But she looked pretty and young, as he set her down gently on the couch. The smells from the kitchen were delicious, and Peter commented on them immediately when he arrived, as Lisa bounded out of the kitchen with a broad smile, and her hair piled up on her head. She was wearing a pink sweater and jeans, and she looked a lot like Maggie had when she was young.

Lisa stood next to her father as they greeted Peter, and they looked almost like a couple, as Peter said hello to both of them. And then he saw Maggie lying on the couch, waiting for him to come in. She was propped up on pillows, and her walker stood nearby. There was a wheelchair in the front hall. It was easy to see that this was the home of an invalid, and she was frighteningly pale. But she looked happy as she said hello to him, and he bent to kiss her cheek. He had brought an enormous bouquet of flowers and a bottle of champagne. They had something to celebrate that night.

"The prodigal son returns," Michael said, as he had to Walt Peterson when he first heard about Peter's return, but he was happy about it now.

"Yeah, and I didn't 'spend it all on riotous living,' I lost it all in the worst stock market crash in U.S. history since the Depression," Peter said ruefully. "But at least I'm home." He sank onto the couch near Maggie's feet. She looked so fragile that he was almost afraid to injure her when he sat down. Her skin was so white, and she had dark circles under her eyes, but she was in good spirits, and she got to the dining table under her own steam with the walker. Michael offered to carry her, but she refused. She didn't want to look like a tragic figure to Peter, however ill she was. He saw that one leg still dragged from the accident, and she seemed weak to him. It took her a little while to get to the table, with Michael walking beside her looking concerned. Peter noticed all of it, and especially how ghostly pale she was. Her delicately veined hands were almost blue. But she didn't move around much either, and Peter guessed that her circulation couldn't be good. She choked once on a sip of water at dinner, and Michael watched her closely. Her respiratory system was compromised by the

Parkinson's, and her ability to swallow was lessening and would disappear entirely one of these days.

Lisa regaled them all with stories about school, and Peter asked about Michael's son Bill halfway through the meal.

"We lost him to the big city, just like you," Michael said sadly, as Maggie lowered her eyes and looked at her plate while she continued eating dinner. He could see that she was sad about it too. It wasn't easy living far away from your kids, as Peter had learned himself recently. He missed Ryan and Ben every moment of every day. "He went to London for junior year and never wanted to come back home. He graduated last year, and he's at the London School of Economics getting a master's now. He says he wants to stay there when he finishes. He's just not a small-town guy. It suits me, and Maggie and Lisa, but it's not for him. He loves London. We can't even get him home for holidays anymore. He hasn't been home since last year." Michael looked at his wife sympathetically. "It's really hard on his mom." And Peter knew it had been hard on his own mother too, when he had left home and never wanted to return. It had been agony for Peter to come back here, because of his war with Michael, and he had always delayed it as long as he could. He was sorry about it now, especially seeing the good time they were having. Maggie looked happy as she watched the two brothers talk, and exchange stories about their childhood, some of which actually sounded like fun. Both of them had forgotten those good times until now. They were mostly fishing stories, and camping out with friends.

It was a perfect evening, and as soon as they finished dessert, Michael carried Maggie back upstairs. He looked worried about her, although she had been animated at the table, and was obviously having fun. He didn't want her getting overtired. She kissed Peter on the cheek, and he hugged her, before Michael took her up. And as he lay her on their bed, he took out the blood pressure cuff and looked instantly concerned when he saw what it said. He didn't show her how bad it was, so as not to frighten her, but he told her that her blood pressure had dropped while she was downstairs. It was never a good sign, and Maggie looked scared. There was always a price to pay for whatever she did, and sometimes an evening downstairs could cost her days in bed, until Michael felt she had regained her strength.

"It was a long evening for you," he said guiltily, sorry for a minute that he had invited Peter to come. He didn't want Maggie getting so exhausted that she got sick.

"I enjoyed it," she said with a happy smile.

"Thank you for giving me back my brother," he said with a deeply moved look. "I never knew we could have so much fun together. He turned out to be a really nice guy. I wish I'd known that before this."

"I've always known it about both of you. I'm glad you're back together too." She knew that they would need each other and the bond they shared one day when she was no longer there. She was always preparing for that, and she wanted to leave them all in a good place. This had been an important step for the twins tonight, and it was her gift to them.

"I want you to get some sleep now," he said, handing her a sleeping pill and a glass of water from her night table. "You're overtired." And they both knew that could have dire consequences for her. She didn't want that either, and she took the pill from him without complaint. She was exhausted, but she had had a great time. It warmed her heart to see Michael and Peter together. In some ways they complemented each other. Michael was more serious, and Peter was full of fun, now that he wasn't angry all the time. He had had a hard time growing up, and always felt like he was in Michael's shadow. Peter had accomplished a lot since then, on his own, despite his recent misfortunes, which he seemed surprisingly philosophical about. He seemed saddest about his divorce, and living so far from his sons. He had promised to introduce them to Michael and his family when they came to visit him.

Michael went back downstairs as soon as Maggie was settled, and there was obvious worry in his eyes when he joined Peter and Lisa. She was washing the dishes, and Peter was helping, as he told her about Ben and Ryan. He was very proud of them, and he was enjoying his niece too. Peter could see how close Michael was to his daughter, and how much he relied on her to help with her mother. She was totally reliable and responsible and an adult at sixteen. She had a lot on her shoulders and so did Michael, at work and at home. Peter was sorry for him that his son had moved away. But it was understandable, Ware was a small town, and Bill was young and wanted a more exciting career and life. There wasn't much to do here.

"How is she?" Peter asked about Maggie. He could see the worry in Michael's eyes when he came down.

"Pretty much the way I'd expect after a long evening. It's a lot for her," Michael said sadly. There was a lifetime of regret in his eyes, and Peter's heart went out to him.

"I hope I didn't wear her out," Peter said, feeling guilty. She seemed so normal despite her deathly pallor, and her will to live was strong. It had kept her alive for years, in defiance of her medical problems and now advancing Parkinson's disease. "Have you taken her to specialists in Boston to see what they can do?"

"I know her better than they do, and I love her. I don't want them destroying her quality of life any more than it is now. They would run batteries of tests on her, do unneeded surgery for some of her problems, and turn her into a guinea pig. People with head traumas like hers develop all kinds of complications over the years. She just has to live with it, and so do we," Michael said staunchly, and Peter nodded. Maybe he was right, although Peter would have been more inclined to avail himself of the latest research to help her, but there was always a risk in that too. Peter had always been more of a risk taker than Michael, and Michael made a good point about the quality of Maggie's life and not making her a guinea pig. She didn't want that either, and had said it often to him. She wanted to stay here, and be cared for by him. He would follow her wishes till the end, he just hoped it wouldn't be soon. But that could change at any moment, and he was constantly aware of it.

The two brothers sat at the kitchen table talking after Lisa went up to bed. Peter commented on what a lovely girl she was, and Michael looked fiercely proud of her. She was a very good girl. They talked about Peter's future then, and he said he hoped to be back in New York in the next few months, maybe after the summer. It would be a year after the crash, and hopefully things would have leveled out by then, and there would be jobs available for him and countless others who had gotten dumped. Michael was conscious that it was an unsettling time for him, especially now with the divorce. But it was comforting for Peter to feel he had a brother again. That lightened his load immeasurably. The brothers had found new respect for each other by the time Michael walked him to the door that night.

"Don't be a stranger," Michael said to him. "Come and see me at the office anytime." He didn't tell him to drop by the house, because Maggie needed to rest most of the time. But he seemed eager to spend time with his brother.

"Why don't you come fishing some weekend? I've been doing pretty well at the lake."

"I'd love it," Michael said as the two men hugged each other and Peter left. He got in his truck, and smiled all the way back to the lake.

Chapter 10

Peter kept busy with a variety of projects at the lake house for the next several weeks. He built bookcases, waxed woodwork, and chopped down some trees. He stopped in at Michael's office one afternoon, but he was out making house calls so Peter left him a note. Both men were still coasting on the good feelings of the night Peter had dinner with Michael and his family. Michael had called him a couple of times, and was promising to come fishing up at the lake as soon as he could. He said Maggie wasn't doing well and had caught a bad cold, so he didn't want to leave her right now, except when he went to work. Peter understood, and said he hoped she'd feel better soon. It seemed so unfair that everything was life-threatening for her, even going to the supermarket or seeing friends. Michael said she hadn't been downstairs since she had dinner with them. She was confined to her bed, with a bad cough.

Peter was thinking about her when he drove into Ware one afternoon to get some supplies again. Walt Peterson's ankle had recovered, and he had gone back to his old glasses and was much happier. The "newfangled" progressives were not for him, he had told Peter the last time he waited on him, and Peter grinned when Walt told him how dangerous they were.

Peter bought flowers for Maggie after that, and went to drop them off at the house, since she was so ill. And he was going to leave them with Lisa. He walked onto the porch and rang the bell, and was startled when Maggie answered the door, perched on her walker.

"Wow! Are you okay?" Peter said, looking surprised. "Mike said you were really sick. You must be feeling better." He stood holding the flowers, and she looked happy to see him and invited him to come in.

"I'm feeling pretty good. I have been ever since our dinner. That was really fun." Peter didn't insist, but his brother had told him she'd been very sick ever since.

"I enjoyed it too," he said benignly, and offered to put the flowers in a vase for her. She told him there was a big one under the kitchen sink, and he found it easily and set the flowers on a table in the living room. "I was worried when Mike said you'd been sick."

"He says that sometimes so people don't drop by and expose me to their diseases. But you look healthy to me." She grinned. "He'd put me in a bubble if he could. Poor thing, he always worries about me. I'm a burden on him and Lisa," she said sadly. "That isn't how I wanted it to be."

"That's not true," Peter insisted. "They love you. We all do." It was nice seeing her look better than she had the night he had come to dinner. She looked brighter and had more color in her face, and she was in good spirits. She had been lying on the couch, with her laptop, when he arrived. She turned it off to talk to Peter.

"I wish Michael didn't worry so much about me. Having you around will be a good distraction for him. When are you two going fishing?"

"As soon as he has time," Peter said easily. He didn't want to tell her that Michael had said she was too sick for him to leave her at the moment. That didn't seem like the right thing to say, since she already felt like a burden to him.

"I'll push him to do it," Maggie said. "It would do you both good."

They sat and chatted in the living room for a while, and then Peter stood up to leave. He had always loved talking to her, she was bright and funny, and had a good sense of humor, even now in her frail condition, after years of infirmity. She had an indomitable spirit that nothing seemed to break. Peter admired her a great deal for it. And he was just leaving when Michael pulled into the driveway, and looked at both of them. He had come home to check on her between two patients, since Lisa had gone to study at a friend's for the afternoon. They were doing a joint project for school, and he knew Maggie would be alone. Lisa had helped her mother downstairs before she left. Michael looked stunned to see her on the porch with Peter.

"What are you two up to?" he said as he bounded up the steps.

"I brought Maggie some flowers to cheer her up," Peter said easily, and Michael smiled at him, and then there was the merest twitch at the corner of his mouth. Peter noticed it immediately, and remembered it from when they were kids. Just a tic of some kind. And Michael was quick to say how happy he was to run into his brother.

"Do you want to come in for a few minutes?" Michael offered.

"I'm just leaving. I don't want to wear Maggie out," Peter said, hugged his brother, kissed Maggie again, and went to his truck with a wave. And Michael and Maggie went back into the house. Michael was scolding her for standing in the chill air without a coat. She reminded him that it was April and it felt good to her. She hadn't been out of the house in days, but he insisted it was too cold and she'd get sick.

Peter was backing out of the driveway after they'd gone inside, and was turning onto the street when he suddenly remembered what the twitch at the corner of

Michael's mouth meant. It struck him like
lightning, and then he shook his head.
When they were kids, Michael's mouth had
twitched like that when he was caught in a
lie or had done something really bad that
no one knew about. It gave him away to
Peter every time. But Michael had done
nothing bad this time, and if he had lied
about Maggie being sick, it was only to protect her. She had explained it perfectly
when she said Michael wanted to keep her
in a bubble. And he couldn't blame him.
She was a frail woman, with dangerously
compromised health, constantly at risk.
Who wouldn't want to put her in a bubble?
But he got an eerie feeling as he remembered the twitch. It was an unpleasant déjà
vu, a past they both wanted to forget now,
and had outgrown. The twitch meant nothing now, Peter was sure of it as he drove
home to the lake. He turned the radio on
and forgot all about the ridiculous tic.

At Maggie's insistence, Michael came up to
the lake to go fishing with Peter the following weekend. And the twins had a ball together. They caught a bucket of fish, and
Peter insisted that Michael take them home

to Maggie and Lisa. They shared several beers afterward, but Michael was sober when he drove home. He said it was the first Saturday he had taken off in ages, and it had done them both good. They were building a relationship now for the years to come.

Peter had declined an invitation to have dinner with them in Ware that evening. He said he was tired and had paperwork to do, and he didn't want to wear Maggie out. He said he'd come another time. Michael looked disappointed but understood, and said he'd had a great day fishing with him.

Peter cooked dinner that night, and sat down to eat it in front of the TV. He did his paperwork afterward, and ran out of paper on his pad. He started rummaging in drawers, hoping to find something to write on, and he found several leatherbound books instead. He had never seen them before. And as he opened them, he discovered that they were journals his mother had kept in her neat, lacy hand. He remembered that she had spent her last summer here, shortly before she died, and they had been overlooked by whoever cleaned out the house and put away her things. Probably Michael,

since there was no one else to do it. Their
father had died less than a year before, and
Peter hadn't come back to help pack up her
belongings. He didn't want to see Michael
by then, they were already at war over their
father's will. Peter sat down on the couch
and opened one of the journals. And tears
came to his eyes as he read. His mother
had written how much she missed her husband and what a wonderful life they had
shared. And then she wrote about how sad
she was not to see Peter, and how unhappy
that he and Michael were so hard on each
other. She said it broke her heart, and Peter cringed at the thought of having caused
her pain.

As he read on, he could tell that she was
already sick. She'd had cancer, and these
were the journals of her final days. As he
read entry after entry, he could see that Michael had come to visit her every day. He
had kept her company, spent the night
when he could, taken on her medical care,
comforted her, and held her when she was
in pain. He was the son that Peter had
never been to her, and suddenly everything
his parents had given him finally made
sense. It wasn't about a good son or a bad

son, or the measure of each one's need—
Peter had been at the top of the world then.
It was about one son who had been there
for them incessantly, and another who had
all but abandoned them and fled. He remembered with sorrow and regret that he
had rarely even called her then. He had
been so angry at them for always siding
with Michael and never with him, and for
believing all the lies Michael told about him.
But more important, Michael had been a
totally devoted son and Peter hadn't been.
He had been too angry over his youth to
be there for them. He had been thirty-one
years old when they died, old enough to
know better, but still young. And it made
Peter feel deep compassion for his mother
when he read how much she had suffered
physically in her last days.

The diaries were painful to read, and he
finally put them back in the drawer, without
reading all of them, and he lay awake for
hours that night when he went to bed. He
hated knowing how much his mother had
suffered and that he hadn't been there for
her. He had only visited her once that summer. It was the last time he saw her before
she died, and all through the journals he

had just read, she said she loved them
equally, whether they loved each other or
not. She had been far more forgiving than
he was at the time. But she was older and
she was dying. And in defense of himself,
if there was one, he suspected that it was
easier to forgive a son than a brother. There
was nothing he wouldn't have forgiven his
own sons, and he had hated his brother for
years. But he could see the grief it had
caused his mother, and he was sorry for
that, especially since they had made peace
now and were friends for the first time in
their lives. So what was the point of all those
years of anger and resentment? It seemed
so futile now.

Peter was haunted by his mother's diaries for the rest of the weekend and for several days after. Reading them was troubling
but deeply touching. And he finally drove
to Ware to see his brother. He arrived just
as Michael was leaving his office to see patients, and Michael had his doctor's bag in
his hand. Peter smiled when he saw it. Michael looked like the perfect country doctor, even more than their father.

"What's up?" Michael asked when he
saw him and stopped to chat for a minute.

"I owe you an apology," Peter said with a serious expression.

"What for?" Michael looked startled, and wondered what he'd done.

"I found Mom's journals last weekend, from her last summer at the lake, before she died. Reading them, I realize how much you did for her, how often you were there, how much you comforted her when Dad died, and took care of her when she was sick, right to the end. I didn't do shit for her, Mike. I came up to see her once that summer. I was still pissed at her and Dad for how they had handled my childhood. No one really understood about dyslexia then, and I was angry all the time and blamed them. And I was pissed at you for being so perfect when I wasn't. I was the hotshot of Wall Street, and the last thing I wanted to do was come here. I really let her down. You didn't. You deserve everything they gave you, the house, the money. I was a lousy son. You were a great one." Peter looked deeply apologetic and was sincere.

"No, you weren't," Michael reassured him, although he had five patients waiting for him and an old man with shingles who was in pain, and he had to get going. "We were both young and stupid in our own way. You were always the handsome one, and charming, even if you were hot-headed then. I think I was afraid they loved you more, so I tried to be perfect all the time. No one is. There was room for both of us. I just didn't know it then. Maybe it's not so easy being twins. You start competing in the womb." Michael had been twice Peter's size when he was born, but Peter had made up for it later, when he grew taller. "Thank you for what you said, though. I always felt guilty for what I got and you didn't." Michael looked as though he meant it.

"Don't worry. I did fine." Peter smiled at him. He felt better having said it, and Michael looked deeply touched. All their old wounds were healing, and the journals had given Peter perspective on everything he hadn't done for their mother, or even their father before he died. Most of all, he hadn't been there for their final years, Michael had, in spades. He had taken full responsibility for them, and their care when they got sick. Peter had been on Wall Street, making a fortune. And his parents were right, he hadn't needed what they had. Michael did, with his sick wife, and he had

earned it. He hadn't left their parents' sides
for a minute. And he wasn't a rich man now,
but he was comfortable, thanks to them.
His country practice had never been lucrative, but it was enough for the way he and
Maggie lived. They didn't need or want
more.

The two men hugged each other, and
Michael left to see his patients. And Peter
felt warm and happy all the way back to the
lake. He thought of finishing his mother's
journals when he got back, but he needed
to digest what he had read so far. It was
hard to read, and painful to realize how he
had let them down. But at least there was
no bitterness between the two men now.
Peter was grateful for that.

The following week Peter went out to L.A.
to see Ben and Ryan. He stopped by to see
Michael before he left, and told him he'd be
back in a week. He was taking the boys to
San Francisco for a long weekend, and he
couldn't wait to see them. As always, it had
been too long. And he wanted to plan their
summer with Alana. He had hardly spoken
to her since she'd filed the divorce. The
boys had already told him that they were

going to spend a month at the house in the Hamptons with their mom, when the renters left. It gave Peter a little jolt when he heard it. The waters had closed over him in Alana's life, and she was moving on, and already had. The boys didn't say much about what she was doing. And she never called Peter anymore. She knew he was coming out and had agreed to the trip to San Francisco. She said she would be going to Palm Springs with friends at the same time.

Peter was staying at a hotel this time, near her father's house. He picked the boys up at school. They were thrilled to see him, and he took them out to dinner that night. Alana was at the house when he dropped off the boys, and he felt awkward when he said hello to her. And she looked awkward too, and disappeared into the house as quickly as she could. Peter felt a surge of disappointment and bitterness again as soon as he saw her.

Peter and the boys left for San Francisco the next day after school. Alana had already left for Palm Springs when he picked them up, which was a relief.

The flight to San Francisco from L.A.

took an hour, and they caught a cab into the city. There were no limousines anymore, except with their grandfather and mom. With Peter, they were "roughing it," as he said, except that he had found a special weekend deal for adjoining rooms at the Fairmont Hotel, which was a grand old hotel on top of Nob Hill, right above Chinatown, across from Grace Cathedral, and the cable car stopped right outside the hotel. They rode it down to the Ferry Building that night, and wandered from stand to stand of lobsters, crabs, oysters, sourdough bread, and every delicacy imaginable, and they ate dinner in one of the restaurants, and then rode the cable car back to the hotel. They had had a great evening, and the boys had never been there before. They were planning to explore the piers the next day and the Science Museum, and they were going to have dinner in Chinatown. The boys loved Chinese food.

Ben said that he wanted a root beer float when they got back to the room and Ryan rolled his eyes. They wound up ordering three from room service, and Ben was sipping his through his straw when he made an announcement that shook Peter to the core.

"Mom has a boyfriend. He's nice." Ryan looked like he was going to kill him, and glanced at his father with a worried look.

"Don't listen to him, Dad. He doesn't know what he's talking about. They're just friends." Ryan had long since understood how unhappy his father was about the divorce, and that it was his mother's idea and not his. He had been angry about it since he had found out. And Ben had adjusted much more easily to L.A. Ryan missed New York, his father, and his friends.

"That's not true. He used to be her boyfriend," Ben said, looking insulted to have his information disputed. "And now he is again. His name is Bruce and he's an agent for actors who make movies. He took us to a screening of **Killer Ants**." Ryan was steaming, and Peter tried to look unconcerned as his heart sank. He knew she wasn't coming back to him, but it hurt to hear that he'd been replaced. He had suspected it for a while, but he didn't want the information from his son. And Peter knew who Bruce was. He remembered running into him when they first went to L.A. after the crash, and he had looked very interested in Alana, in more than a friendly way.

She had denied it to him at the time. He wondered now if Bruce was why she had asked for the divorce. "He has a plane, a Ferrari, and a Rolls," Ben said, adding insult to injury as Ryan dove across the bed, grabbed him, and shook him, hard.

"Will you stop, you little jerk? You're upsetting Dad!"

"Knock it off, Ryan," Peter said sternly. "I'm fine. You don't need to kill your brother for my sake. I'd rather you didn't. And if that's what's happening, Ben has a right to talk about it. Is he nice to you guys?" Peter asked with a sad look, and both boys nodded, Ben with more enthusiasm than Ryan.

"He's coming to the Hamptons with us this summer," Ben announced, looking delighted, while Ryan looked grim. He didn't like that plan at all. Bruce was nice, but he didn't want him moving in on them and their mother. And their mother was crazy about him. Ryan had heard her tell a friend that she was in love. He hated Bruce for it.

"Let's talk about your coming to the lake," Peter said, to change the subject. "When do you want to come? July and August are the most fun. There are sailboat regattas, and swimming races. And the weather is great then."

"Can we come in July, Dad?" Ryan asked hopefully. "Mom wants to send us to camp in Switzerland then, and I don't want to go."

"Me too," Ben echoed.

"We're going to the Hamptons in August," Ryan said quietly.

"Why don't you spend the Fourth of July with me, and stay for a few weeks?" Both boys beamed at the suggestion, and Peter promised to work it out with their mother. He didn't want them going to camp in Switzerland instead of visiting him. When did she think they were going to see him? Peter felt like the forgotten man. And he went to bed that night with the knowledge that Alana had a boyfriend, a Hollywood agent, it was perfect for her, and he was sure her father approved. Peter had never really fit into their plans. All he had had was money, and now he no longer did. This had nothing to do with their "drifting apart," as she had said. He had no illusions left about that.

The rest of the weekend went too quickly. They went to the piers and the museum, and walked in Golden Gate Park. They had dinner in Chinatown, and explored the Fairmont, and on Sunday afternoon, they went back to L.A. Peter stayed in L.A. for two days after that to see them, and Alana agreed to let the boys come to him for three weeks in July. He agreed to deliver them to her in the Hamptons, after he spent a week in New York with them, so they could see their friends, if they were in town during the summer. It sounded like a good plan to all of them.

He never mentioned to Alana that he knew she had a new man in her life, or an old one. He had too much pride to say anything, but he caught a glimpse of him when he dropped the boys off, just as Bruce drove Alana up to the house in his Ferrari and she got out. He looked at Peter, and the two men nodded. Bruce was the winner and Peter the loser, and it hurt more than he expected it to, or would have admitted. Peter hadn't even thought of dating other women yet. He was still trying to figure out what to do with his life now, and he was living like a hermit at the lake. It was hardly conducive to dating, and he wasn't in the mood anyway. He still felt like a loser for the job and fortune he had lost. It was going to take time to get over that. And what did he have to offer any woman right now? He could barely support himself and his boys. He was in no position to impress anyone at the moment, and he didn't want to anyway. The wound Alana had left was still wide open and not yet healed. Along with everything else that had happened in the last seven months, he had been dumped. It was hard to dazzle anyone after that.

He and the boys were sad when he left, but they had July to look forward to now. It was only two months away, until they came to visit him. He could hardly wait. And as the plane circled over Los Angeles and headed east, Peter tried not to think about Alana and Bruce. He had a twin brother again, and two great sons. For now, that was enough.

Chapter 11

When Peter got back to the lake after his trip to L.A. and San Francisco, he had a lot to do. He was still sending out e-mails regularly to look for work and new projects. And now that he knew the boys were coming to visit, he wanted to repaint his old boyhood room for them. He needed to get some new furniture, and ordered it from IKEA. He wanted to do what he could to spruce up the house a little before they came. It was very basic compared to what they were used to, but he thought it would be fun for them to spend time at the lake with him. He could hardly wait.

He was planning to drop by and see Michael the day after he got back, but he got busy with e-mails to several Wall Street firms, and picked up his mother's journals again late that night. This time he was shocked by what he read. The cancer that ultimately killed her had gotten into her bones by then and it sounded like she was in incredible pain, as he read what she had written. She sounded truly desperate in some entries, and her handwriting had gotten shaky. It made him feel ill to read it, but he wanted to read everything she had to say. It was the least he could do after not being there for her. At least he could hear her now, even if it was fifteen years too late. She mentioned several times that Michael had given her pain-killers, but they weren't working, and she said that all she wanted now was for him to put her to sleep, as he had his father.

Peter stopped as he read it, squinted, and read it again, to be sure he had understood what she'd said. His mother had written in her now-shaky hand that Michael had "put his father to sleep," to put him out of his misery at the end. In other words, Michael had euthanized him, and their mother had wanted him to do the same for her. She said that Michael was refusing, and insisted that she could still live many months. Peter was shaken by what he had read. He read on for another hour, but mostly his mother complained about the pain she was in and the fact that he had not come to visit, but she said that he was busy in New York. She had made excuses for him, but the shocking entry in the journal he read that night was that Michael had killed their father, surely with noble motives, if so. But Peter wanted to know now if he really had.

He was still troubled by it when he drove into town the next morning, and went to Michael's office, but he was out. He stopped in at the diner for a cup of coffee and spent a few minutes chatting with Vi. The chief of police was there that morning too. Afterward he went to the paint store to kill time, and a small furniture store, looking for things for the boys, and then he went to the house to see Maggie. She was upstairs, but she shouted to him to come up when he opened the unlocked door. He found her in her bedroom, sitting up in bed with her computer, intently writing an e-mail to Bill.

They had been iChatting earlier that morning, and it was wonderful seeing her look
so much better and stronger. She looked
immaculate and pretty, in a pink bed jacket,
and her hair was freshly brushed, and the
circles under her eyes didn't seem quite as
dark.

"How was L.A.?" she asked him, obviously delighted to see him. Lisa was in
school, and Michael was making his rounds.

"Great. I had a terrific time with the boys.
We went to San Francisco, and they'll be
here on July Fourth."

"I can't wait to meet them," Maggie said
with a warm smile, but she could see something in his eyes. He didn't want to tell her
what he had read in his mother's diaries the
night before. That was between him and
Michael. And he just wanted to know for his
own peace of mind. If Michael had done it,
he had clearly felt it was justified and there
was no other choice. His father had died a
martyr's death from pancreatic cancer, so
Peter would have understood it, but it was
a private matter between the two brothers,
so he said nothing to Maggie about it.

"How are you feeling?" he asked. She
looked better than he had seen her before.

"Pretty good. Michael is sitting on me. I've been in bed most of the time. But I guess he's right, I feel better, although my legs get weak and stiff, but they are anyway," she said practically. "The weather has been so pretty. I'm dying to get out." She looked wistful as she glanced out the window. She was only forty-four years old, and had been a shut-in for years. She had deteriorated progressively during twenty-three years of marriage, and only Michael's care had kept it from moving at a more rapid rate. They were playing beat the clock for her health, and with Parkinson's now, things were only going to get worse. They both knew it. Maggie was not going to live to be an old woman, but she had made her peace with it years before. It was Michael who fought desperately not to lose her.

"I wish you could come up to the lake sometime," Peter said gently. "Maybe Michael could bring you."

"I'd love it," she said, smiling at him. It sounded like heaven to her. And every time she went out, her spirits soared, but her physical condition always worsened right after. Michael was concentrating on caring for her body, but Peter wished he could do something for her soul. "I heard from Bill, by the way," she said, looking cheerful. She was always happy when she talked about him. Peter could only guess how much she missed him. "He loves his school, and he wants to find a job there when he finishes. He's never going to come home." She had made her peace with that too, but Peter could see that it was hard for her.

"He's not interested in Boston or New York?" At least then he could visit.

Peter had just learned that lesson himself, when he read his mother's journals. He had been in New York, but had visited too infrequently before she died. He knew that one day his nephew would regret it. Maggie was not going to live forever, that much was clear. She was valiant about it, but Bill was missing precious years. It was hard to see that when you were young, although Bill's mother had been sick all his life. Maybe that was why he didn't see that time was running out. Even Peter understood that when he looked at her. She was barely more than a wisp of a woman, and she seemed as though she were about to blow away. And one of these days she would just disappear.

Maggie looked thoughtful before she answered Peter's question. And then she decided to be candid with him. She trusted him, and always had. "It's not about what city he's in. He and Michael don't get along. They haven't in years. At first I just thought it was adolescence, but it isn't. They're at each other's throats every time they're in the same room. Bill disagrees with everything his father stands for. Some of it has to do with me," she said, looking guilty. "They're both fiercely protective of me, and they fight about everything. Bill just couldn't take it anymore, so he left. And Michael loves him, but he gets aggressive with him. He's very hurt by the things Bill says. Bill left here at twenty, and he's never coming back, except maybe to see me. And maybe it's for the best. They'll kill each other one day. It's better for Bill not to be here, and for Michael too. It was miserable for everyone when he was here. Even Lisa got pulled into it, and she loves them both. So do I, but I want what's best for Bill. This isn't it." She was willing to deprive herself of her child for his benefit, and Peter felt sorry for all of them.

"It sounds like what Michael and I went

through when we were young," Peter said quietly.

"No, it's worse. Much worse," she said sadly.

"Sometimes there just isn't room for two adult males on the same turf. There were three at our house, and I was one too many. I was the one who was always out of step with the other two, so I left. I had to find a place of my own, and I did. Bill will too. Maybe then it will be easier for him to come back, once he establishes himself somewhere else." He wanted to give her hope that she'd see her son again, but neither of them looked convinced. "Mike can be pretty tough when he gets pissed," Peter said ruefully, and Maggie smiled.

"And Bill is even more so. He's much too hard on his father, and the fights are always about me. They both love me, but I don't want them killing each other over me. It was terrible, but it was a relief when Bill left." Peter couldn't help wondering if his mother had felt the same way about him. His had been the one dissenting voice, trying to fight for justice in his own family. And whatever he had done and said, he couldn't get it, and his mother had forgiven him in the end, just as Maggie would. He knew that now from his mother's journals.

He left Maggie a little while later, and went back to Michael's office. He was just returning from his house calls. He looked tired and depressed, and said to Peter that he had just lost a patient. She was eighty-three years old and had been sick for several months. But he hated it when that happened.

"I should have been a pediatrician," he said with a sad look at his twin. "All they get are skinned knees." When a child died, it was infinitely worse, but they rarely did. "I get so attached to my geriatric patients. And sooner or later, they go. But it always depresses me." It was the perfect lead-in to the subject Peter wanted to discuss with him. He mentioned their mother's journals again, and Michael nodded, as he walked into his office and Peter took the seat across from his desk. It was lunchtime, and he didn't have any patients to see yet. He had already dropped off lunch for Maggie on the way back, as a treat for her. Pru had been at the house too, vacuuming the stairs. And Maggie had been happy to see him. She always was.

"This will sound awful," Peter began cautiously, "and I don't mean it that way," he said, feeling nervous. He didn't want to insult his brother or start a fight with him again. But he wanted to know. "In Mom's journals, she was obviously suffering when she wrote them, especially toward the end, but she mentions several times that you euthanized Dad, and she wanted you to do the same to her. She was pissed that you wouldn't." Peter looked serious as he said it, and his twin brother smiled. It was the tired, gentle smile of a man who had seen too much sickness and sadness, at home and in the office.

"Of course I wouldn't do it for her," Michael said with a wistful look. "Because I didn't do it for Dad either. He begged me to, and I wouldn't. I can't. I took an oath to do no harm, and I believe in it profoundly. Even Mom thought I should put him out of his misery, and he finally died on his own. I told Mom I had given him a shot that night, so she could feel that we had eased his pain and released him. It consoled her somehow, but I would never do it, which is why I wouldn't do it for her. I told her it was too soon."

"She wrote that in the journals too." Peter was relieved by his brother's answer. He would have understood it and forgiven it, but he didn't like the idea that Michael had euthanized their father. And Peter was happy to know that he hadn't. It would have been a heavy burden for Michael to bear, and even for Peter, knowing that he had.

"People say crazy things in the end. A lot of my patients want me to put them out of their misery. But I can't do that. God takes them at the right time." And they both knew that He would do that with Maggie one day too. Peter just hoped it wouldn't be anytime soon. Michael was doing all he could to make sure that didn't happen. He was playing roulette with God, but one of these days, he knew he would lose.

"I'm sorry I even asked you," Peter said apologetically.

"I'm glad you did," Michael said, looking at him warmly. "I don't want anything to ever come between us again, and that would have, if you hadn't asked me. I'm glad you gave me a chance to clear it up. Poor Mom, she wanted out so badly at the end. It was no life for her once Dad died."

"I can see that from what she wrote."

They both fell silent for a moment, thinking about their parents, and then Michael looked at his brother across the desk.

"How was California?"

"The kids were great. And my soon-to-be ex-wife has a boyfriend," he said honestly. "That stung a little. It's hard to feel like a total loser. Money, career, and wife. Three strikes, I'm out."

"You've still got your kids," Michael reminded him, and Peter nodded.

"They're coming this summer, for three weeks."

"I can't wait to meet them. We have a lot of time to make up for," Michael said warmly.

"Yes, we do." Peter smiled and stood up. He knew his brother was busy. "I dropped by to see Maggie, by the way. She looks pretty good."

"She told me. Just be sure you don't put the make on her," Michael teased him, but he knew he wouldn't. Peter had always been honorable about things like that, more so than Michael, who had slept with several of Peter's girlfriends when they were young. "You've always been the handsome brother."

"Yeah, well, it didn't help me keep my

wife," he said as Michael walked him out. But Peter knew that was about money, not his looks, or even love. He still looked younger than he was, although Michael looked his age. "Fishing this weekend?" he asked on the way out, and Michael laughed.

"We're like Huck Finn and Tom Sawyer. Yeah, let me see if I can get away, if Lisa will stay with her mother. I don't want to leave Maggie alone all day. She has enough of that during the week when Lisa's in school." The two men hugged, and Peter left, feeling relieved by what Michael had told him. He had not euthanized either of their parents. It would make reading the rest of his mother's journals easier, despite his guilt over not coming home to see her more often. At least they had both died of natural causes. He would have been upset if Michael had done that without his consent, but even that wouldn't have been surprising, since the brothers weren't speaking to each other then. But all was well, and Peter was at peace.

He went back to the lake and started painting the boys' room that afternoon. He wanted it clean and fresh for their visit, and not some musty old room where everything was dark and dingy. He wanted them to love it here.

As he painted, he thought about what Maggie had told him about Michael and his son. He hadn't mentioned it to his brother. He knew it had to be a sore subject for him.

Peter didn't read his mother's journals again that night. They were too depressing, and he'd read enough for a while. Instead he answered some e-mails and went to bed early, and the next morning he was surprised to find an e-mail from an investment bank in London. He thought he had sent them a résumé a while back, but could no longer remember, he had sent so many. They were asking him if he would be willing to come to London for an interview, and he thought about it over breakfast. The real question for him was whether he was willing to live there. If he wasn't, there was no point going for an interview. His conclusion was that it didn't make much difference if his boys visited him in London or on the East Coast. They were no longer living in the same city. And he could still visit them in L.A. He answered the e-mail and said he would be willing to come. They answered

him an hour later, and suggested the following week. He had nothing else to do,
so he agreed. He didn't think it was a sure
thing by any means, but it was worth exploring, everything was, and it was a reputable firm.

He mentioned it to his brother when he
came out to go fishing with him that weekend. Michael wished him luck with it, but
Peter noticed that he didn't suggest that
Peter look up his nephew. Clearly, the two
were seriously estranged, and Peter didn't
say a word about it either.

"When are you going?" Michael asked
him as they divided up the day's catch.
They had a good time fishing together.

"Monday," Peter answered. And then Michael looked sad for a minute.

"I know it's selfish of me, but I hope you
don't get it. Not for a while anyway. I'm going to miss you when you leave here and
go back to the real world." They were catching up on so many years, and they were
both enjoying having their twin back, and
in a relationship they had never shared before. It was a blessing for them both.

"Yeah, I know. Me too. The last few
months have been great. But you know,

when I do leave, I won't stay away again. You won't get rid of me now."

"I hope not," Michael said, putting an arm around his brother's shoulders. They both smelled like fish, and he started to laugh. "Maggie won't let me back in the house." They both laughed like two kids as Peter helped him put the bucket of fish in the car. He couldn't remember being this happy in a long, long time. He stood there and waved with a slow smile as Michael drove away.

Chapter 12

Peter took a flight from Boston to London, and left his truck at the airport, as he had when he went to L.A. He didn't expect to be gone long. He had taken a day to travel, another for the interview, and two days after that in case anything else came up or if they wanted a second meeting. He had sent his résumé to several other investment banks in London since he was going to be there anyway, but so far no one had written back or asked to see him. Jobs were in short supply in the foreign markets too.

Peter watched a movie, ate dinner, and slept for two hours on the flight. A flight attendant woke him just as they were about to land. Peter looked at the familiar landmarks of London on their way to Heathrow, and wondered about his hotel. For years he had stayed at Claridge's, but needing to save money, this time he was staying at a smaller, lesser-known hotel. All he really cared about now was the interview. He tried to imagine what it would be like to live in London, as he took a cab into town, and he was satisfied with his room at the hotel. All he had brought was carry-on luggage, with a suit for the interview, a pair of jeans, two tweed jackets, some shirts, two ties, a pair of loafers, and running shoes. He had no social plans. And he took a walk in Hyde Park that afternoon, enjoying the May sunshine, as he sat on a bench and watched people wander by.

He had dinner alone in a pub that night, and thought about calling his nephew, but he didn't know what to say. He hadn't seen him since he was seven years old, and he was sure that Bill had grown up knowing that his father and uncle were at odds, not to mention the fact that finding a William McDowell in the London directory would probably not be easy. He could have called

Maggie for the number, but he didn't want to get her excited about his seeing Bill, and then disappoint her if he didn't. He decided to try it on his own the next day.

He had time on his hands in the morning, and he took the London phone book out of the drawer in the desk at the hotel. There were seven William McDowells, and he didn't know the neighborhoods well enough to identify which one was most likely. So Peter decided to try them all. The first two didn't answer, and on the third one an answering machine had an American voice. He knew it was his nephew immediately, because he sounded just like his father. There was no way he could be the wrong one. Peter left him a message saying that he was his uncle, hadn't seen him in a long time, but he was in London for a few days on business and would enjoy seeing him, if his nephew was so inclined. And he said that if not, he'd understand. He left him the number of his BlackBerry and the name of his hotel. He wondered if he'd return the call, and then he forgot about it when he went to the interview that had brought him to London. He met the managing partner and several others, one of whom had worked at Lehman Brothers in New York. They talked about the sad demise of a great firm.

It was after four o'clock when Peter left the building, and he thought the meetings had gone well. The managing partner had explained that they weren't hiring at the moment, but they were hoping to do so in the near future, and they had started meeting people to that end. He said that Peter was at the top of their list, if he didn't mind moving to London, and Peter said he was open to the possibility. They said they would pay for an apartment in London, which was appealing to Peter too. And after that, he went back to his hotel, took off his tie and suit coat, loosened the top button of his shirt, and lay down on the bed. The phone in the room rang almost as soon as he dozed off. The voice at the other end was the same one he had heard on the message machine that morning, and the man who asked for Peter McDowell sounded tense.

"I just got your message," he said in his father's voice. "I was surprised that you called. I've never heard from you before."

"I've seen your parents several times recently," Peter explained. "I'm living at Lake Wickaboag at the moment. I was with Whitman Broadbank when they folded, so I'm taking a break. I came over on business, and I thought I'd look you up." There was a long pause at the other end.

"How's my mother?"

"She seems all right," Peter answered. "About the same. I didn't tell her I was going to call," he said honestly. "I didn't know if I'd be able to reach you, and I didn't want to get her hopes up, or promise something I couldn't deliver. Would you like to get together for dinner tonight?"

The young voice hesitated again. He wasn't sure whether to trust Peter or not. He had been described as the enemy all his life, but Bill had always been curious about him, and he sounded sane and normal on the phone.

"Yes, I would," Bill finally responded. "I can pick you up at your hotel. I live nearby."

"There's a pretty decent pub downstairs. I had dinner there last night. Good steaks, warm beer, all the usual fare." They both laughed, and Peter could hear his nephew starting to relax. "I can meet you there. What time works for you?"

They settled on six o'clock, since Bill said he had studying to do, and he had to make it an early night, and at the appointed hour, Peter was there, sitting at the bar, nursing a scotch and water, as a young man walked up to him who looked shockingly like Peter himself. It was like looking in a mirror. They were the same height, had the same build, the same thin frame. He appeared much more like Peter than his father, which Peter suddenly realized must have made it even harder for Michael when they didn't get along. It must have been like battling with his twin brother all over again.

"You seem surprised," Bill said with a serious expression when he walked up to him. He had recognized Peter instantly, just as Peter had noticed him. The resemblance between them was remarkable. Neither Michael nor Maggie had mentioned it. Genes played funny tricks on people, especially with twins.

"You're all grown up, that's all." Bill slid onto a bar stool next to him and ordered a beer, and the two men looked each other over for a minute, while they tried to figure out what to talk about. Peter knew nothing about him except that he didn't get along with his father. And he could hardly open with that. But his nephew did.

"The only reason I agreed to see you was because I know you hate my father," he said, looking intensely at his uncle. "So do I." It was quite a start.

"That's a pretty tough statement. And I don't hate your father. We had some serious disagreements with each other when we were younger, but your mother encouraged us to make peace a few months ago. Fifteen years of the cold war between us seemed long enough. At our age, you start to realize life is short." Bill didn't answer and just nodded, and then looked at Peter with narrow eyes.

"Did my father ask you to see me?"

"No, he didn't," Peter said honestly. "He has no idea I called. I wasn't sure if I would. It's a little crazy calling someone you haven't seen since they were seven and saying here I am, let's get to know each other."

"Why did you call?" Bill had wondered about it all day.

"Probably the same reason you came to meet me. Curiosity. We're related. Your mother seemed sad when she said you won't come home. I did pretty much the same thing at your age. It was probably the right thing for me to do at the time. I needed to get away, from Ware, my family, your father, our fights with each other. I went away to college and business school, which was a good thing. But there are some things I regret now."

"Like what?" His nephew was curious about him. They both were. And Peter was wondering about the nature of his disagreements with his father, and if he could help in any way. It would have been nice if someone had done that for them years before. He was enjoying his brother now, and would never have thought it possible before.

"I'm sorry I didn't spend more time with my mother before she died. You don't get those opportunities back. But I was too angry to come home, except once," Peter told him quietly.

"That's why they left everything to my father."

"Except the lake house," Peter corrected. "That's not what I regret. I found some of my mother's journals recently, and I really made her sad. Michael was there with her, I wasn't. He was a much better son than

I was. I was too busy with my own life at the time, and too blinded by my fury at your father. I think your mother helped us both get over that. And maybe it was just time." Peter sat there looking peaceful as he glanced at his nephew, and took a sip of his scotch. The maître d' came to escort them to their table then, and the conversation was interrupted, but Bill took it up again as soon as they sat down.

"I'll go back and see her one of these days," Bill said quietly. "I know she misses me. I just can't stand what my father does to her. I can't stop him, so I left." He looked bleak as he said it, and Peter looked puzzled.

"From what I can see, he takes very good care of her. He treats her like a porcelain doll. I don't think she'd get better care anywhere in the world. She's never really been healthy since her accident when she was in college."

"My father convinces her of that so he can manipulate and control her, and isolate her. He has her terrified she's going to die any minute. A look, an expression, he takes her blood pressure, feeds her pills, keeps her loaded on tranquilizers and sleeping pills, and tells her she needs them. He makes her stay in bed until she's so weak she can't stand up. I used to argue with him about it, but it's pointless. He's a doctor, he's convinced her he knows what's best for her. It's only what's best for him. My father wants to control everyone around him. I think it's why he married her, because as an invalid, he has so much more power over her than if she were healthy. He isolates her completely. She doesn't see anyone but him and my sister, and he treats Lisa like his wife, while my mother lies in bed upstairs in their bedroom, and he assures her she's too weak to come down." Peter was startled by what his nephew was saying to him, and the spin he put on it. It had a ring of truth to it, and reminded Peter of their childhood. Michael had tried to control everyone and everything then too. Even if he had to lie to do it.

"Are you suggesting she's not as sick as he claims?" The thought had never crossed Peter's mind. But the notion of Michael needing to manipulate people was familiar to him.

"I'd be sick too, if someone kept me in bed for years, loaded on sleeping pills, tell-

ing me I was going to die any minute. I've
watched him do it to her all my life. I'm sure
there are some things wrong with her after
her accident. Head injuries can be dicey.
But from everything I know, and I've read
a lot about it, she made a good recovery,
and there's no reason for her to be as sick
as she seems to be. There's no valid explanation for it, except that my father tells
her she is. And he won't let any other doctor near her. He even took care of her when
Lisa and I were born. He put her on bed
rest for eight months to 'protect her.' From
what? She needs exercise for her stiff leg
from the accident, fresh air, a life, people.
He doesn't want her around 'germs.' He
doesn't want her to be part of the human
race. And this way, he runs her life. Isola-
tion is a form of abuse. And you're right, he
does treat her like a doll—his doll. My
mother is a prisoner, and she's totally controlled by him. He manipulates her subtly
with fear. It's going to kill her, and there's
nothing I can do to stop it. He does everything he can to convince her that she's sick.
It's mind power. My mother is a helpless
puppet, and he pulls the strings."

    "I think there must be more to it than

that," Peter said sensibly. Bill's theory sounded extreme to him. "It isn't easy for him either, to have an invalid wife. No one would want that." Even Michael at his worst.

"He loves it. He keeps her that way so he can tell her anything he wants. She believes everything he says, and does whatever he tells her. I think she's healthier than he acknowledges. The only diagnoses she ever gets are by him. Who knows if they're true?"

"I don't want to argue with you. I don't even know you, but I find that hard to believe. He is not Machiavellian. He's a man with a sick wife."

"You don't know my father. He's a very disturbed person. He's a pathological liar. Believe me, I've read a lot about it. I don't think he has a conscience about anything. Why do you think he takes care of all those old people? Because they leave him money. Five, ten, twenty thousand dollars. He acts surprised every time. He's not surprised. That's why he spends all his time making house calls to them, because he's waiting for them to leave him money, and he's sucking up to them so they do. Who knows if he doesn't kill them? I wouldn't put it past him." What Bill was saying was brutal, and Peter was totally shocked. Bill was painting a very frightening portrait of his mother's life, and the brother Peter had once loathed, but even to him, Michael's early lies and manipulations had seemed far more human scale. He was not the monster his son believed. And one thing Michael had never demonstrated was greed. He had very simple needs.

"Those are tough claims to make, especially against a doctor. You're accusing him of murdering his patients for financial gain," Peter said soberly. He didn't believe a word of it.

"I think he's capable of it." Bill reminded Peter of himself in his youth. He had believed Michael capable of anything, without a conscience, but he had come to know him better now, and he sincerely believed he was a good man. He was not after old people for money. He had everything he needed or wanted. Michael had never wanted a grand lifestyle, and had criticized Peter for his, and had the utmost contempt for it. He was happy with his life in Ware.

"I used to say things like that about him," Peter said honestly after they both ordered shepherd's pie and kidneys. It was the specialty of the restaurant. "I always thought he manipulated our parents to turn them against me, but the truth was that he was just easier to get along with than I was. I see that now. I was mad at someone or something all the time." Bill seemed a little that way too.

"Maybe you had good reason to be mad," Bill said, sounding convinced.

"I thought I did. I'm not so sure of that now. And I really think he's totally devoted to your mother. I am fully convinced of that. He knew what he was taking on when he married her. He adores her. There's nothing he wouldn't do for her."

"Except let her live like a healthy, normal human being. He talks to her about her 'nerves' all the time. He used to say it to us too. I don't think there's anything wrong with her nerves that a normal life wouldn't cure. My father won't let that happen. All he wants is to keep her debilitated and control her."

"Possibly, but it can't be much fun for him to have an invalid wife either," Peter said reasonably. "Why would he want to do that to her?"

"It's the only way he can feel good about himself. He's not as innocent as you believe. And now I think he's trying to kill her," Bill said, with a muscle working in his jaw. Peter could see that he was serious, and it broke his heart for him. He couldn't imagine anything worse than believing that your father was trying to kill your mother, but he could see that Bill was sincere. "I know that sounds crazy. But I really think he is. All my life I've watched him make her think she was weak so she has to depend on him. And now he wants her to think she's dying, and one of these days she will."

"It takes more than manipulation and suggestion to get someone to die, Bill," Peter said, speaking in a tone he would have used with his own sons.

"Maybe he's poisoning her. I used to think that too. It drove me crazy when I was home, just watching him with her. My father is a sociopath. I'm convinced of it, and you know it too." Peter was silent for a long time as he listened. He had hated his brother for years, but he had never put a label to it like this one. "He has no conscience, no integrity, he does whatever he wants, and he wants to control people."

"For what? What's in it for him?" Bill was as passionate about it as Peter had been at the same age. He had been certain his brother was the devil incarnate then, but now he seemed like a gentle, loving man. Michael had been demonstrating that since Peter moved to the lake. But listening to Bill now, Peter was confused. Which vision of Michael was true? Was what he had experienced with his brother recently just pure manipulation or sincere? Was Michael devil or saint?

"I think it's all about money with him, no matter what he claims," Bill said simply. "And control, of course. But there's always something in it for him. And I don't think it's an accident that my mother has had Parkinson's for the last two years, ever since my grandfather died. That seems like a weird coincidence to me."

"I don't think you can give someone Parkinson's with mind control," Peter said reasonably. What Bill was saying was just too unlikely. His theories about his father didn't hold water. Bill sat there and shook his head, as he saw Peter's skeptical expression.

"I don't know what he does to her, but

whatever it is, she gets sicker every year."
It was also possible, Peter knew, that Maggie truly suffered from ill health, ever since
her accident. "I think that's why he married
her," Bill went on. "All he had to do was
keep her alive long enough to inherit my
grandfather's money. My grandfather was
a great man. He never showed off, and he
was a hard worker. The mill was worth a
fortune. Do you know what my mother sold
it for? Ten million dollars. All my father had
to do was wait for my mother to inherit it.
That's worth waiting twenty-three years for.
He knew it was coming. I think he's going
to kill her one day. He knew she was sick
when he married her and wouldn't live forever. We'll never know how he did it, but he
will. All he had to do was keep her going
until she inherited Grampa's money. She's
been getting sicker rapidly ever since he
died two years ago. I think he's helping her
along."

The two men looked at each other sadly
across the dinner table, and Peter didn't
know what to say. What Bill was saying to
him sounded crazy and horrifying. But for
twenty years and until a few months ago,
he would have believed every word of it.

Now he no longer did. He wondered if Bill had ever been on drugs or had psychiatric problems. It sounded more like that to him. His theories were too wild and sounded like acute paranoia.

"I know what you're thinking," Bill said sadly. He could see it in his uncle's eyes as he looked at him. "You think I'm crazy. I can promise you I'm not. But he is. Mark my words, he'll kill her one day. I don't know how, but I'm sure he will. I think he influences her. He convinced her she's dying. And now that she has Grampa's money, I worry about her every day. That's why I'm here. He'd kill me too, if he could. He knows I'm on to him, and that I know what he is. That's why he hates me. And that's why he hated you. From everything my mother ever told me about you, you saw the same things in him I do. And now he's got you fooled. But I'll bet that he doesn't like you any better than he ever did. And he's got Lisa brainwashed too. She thinks he walks on water. He acts like he's married to her. It makes her feel important. She's his little minion. I was never fooled by him, not even when I was a kid. I've always hated my father for what he does to my mother. I'm the only one who sees it," Bill said sadly, "except for you."

"I'm not sure I see it either," Peter said sincerely. "He was rotten to me when we were kids, and he knew how to work my parents. They believed every lie he told them, and they never believed me. I was dyslexic, so everyone thought I was stupid. He was the smart one. And I used to get into rages and start fights at school. I was the troublemaker and the problem child, until I got to college and finally got some help with my learning disability. And Michael always set me up at home, but I think all he ever wanted was all of my parents' approval. He wanted them to love him more. Maybe he needed that. That makes him needy, but not a killer. Whatever he did, he saw to it I got blamed for it. And I always saw through him, just like you think you do. But I don't think he's as evil as we both wanted to believe. Maybe he was jealous of me in some way. But I honestly think the only thing he wants to do now is protect your mother and keep her alive for as long as he can."

"Until he kills her," Bill said grimly. "I know I can't convince you, but I'm right. I know

I am. And I can't stop him. I could never figure out why he would do that to her, until
my grandfather died, and I realized how
much he'd been worth." It had destroyed
his childhood worrying about her, and he
hated his father for it. He knew that his father had the whole world fooled. But Peter
couldn't see his brother being motivated by
greed. He had spent a lifetime taking care
of people. He was a dedicated doctor and
devoted husband, and he was a man of
modest needs.

Peter tried to change the subject then,
and he wished that he could reassure him,
but there was no convincing Bill of his father's innocence. Peter had seen a whole
other side of his twin brother lately. It had
convinced him that Michael was actually a
decent man, and Peter felt he had been too
harsh about him in his youth. But he could
do nothing to change Bill's mind, just as no
one could have changed his until recently.
Michael's solid life spoke for itself. It sad-
dened him that Bill had exiled himself to escape the agony of watching his mother
dying slowly. It made Peter suddenly remember something Michael had said, that
some people can't accept the death of

loved ones and have to find someone to blame. Bill was demonizing his father in order to brace himself for the inevitable with Maggie, that no matter what anyone did for her, she wasn't likely to live long. That was true and would have been whether she inherited her father's money or not. The accident she had at twenty had destroyed her health, and she had been spiraling down slowly ever since, whether her son was able to face it or not. Peter thought it far more likely that Michael had extended her life by years.

Peter turned the conversation to the financial crisis as they finished their dinner, and then ordered bread pudding for dessert. It wasn't Peter's favorite dinner, but it was hearty fare and typically British, and they ordered a glass of port for each of them afterward. In spite of Bill's suspicions about his father, it had been a pleasant evening, and Peter had enjoyed him. His nephew had a good grasp of economics, and they talked about the current banking crisis late into the night. Other than his paranoia about his father, he seemed like a rational, intelligent person. And Peter couldn't help wondering how many people had thought he was crazy when he talked about his evil brother when he was young. That kind of deep malevolence was impossible for normal people to believe. But in this case, Peter was convinced that Bill was wrong. Michael had undergone a deep and benevolent change.

They left each other outside the hotel, and Peter went back to his hotel room. He was planning to sleep in the next day. Instead, Bill called in the morning to thank him for dinner, and Peter spent the rest of the day walking around London, and visiting some familiar haunts. He had lunch by himself at the Maze Grill, and wound up in the bar at Claridge's for a drink in the late afternoon. And feeling tired from all the walking he'd done, he had room service that evening. He was flying back to Boston the next day. And he called Bill that night, just to check in before he left. He had already promised to stay in touch with him, let him know how his mother was doing, and warn him if she got any worse. Bill was convinced that with his father's help, she inevitably would. Peter urged Bill again to come home and visit her whenever he could. He didn't say so, but he knew from his own experience with his own mother, that it would spare Bill the agony of guilt later on. And Bill expressed the hope, before he hung up, that Peter would get the job at the London firm. He would have liked that too, but for now no offer had been made.

His flight back to Boston was uneventful, and with the time difference and the drive, Peter got back to Lake Wickaboag just after eight o'clock at night. And although he had done nothing all day except eat and watch movies, he was exhausted from the trip. He called Ben and Ryan as soon as he got in. They were excited about the end of school and the upcoming summer vacation. And after he talked to them, Peter went to bed.

When he got up the next morning, because of everything he'd heard from his nephew, Peter decided to visit Maggie that day. He wanted to see how she was. And contrary to Bill's dire predictions, when Pru let him in, he found her sitting in the living room with her walker standing near her, looking better than she had in months.

"Well, don't you look fresh and pretty today," Peter said, looking pleased as he sat down next to her. "I go to London for a few days, and you blossom like a flower."

"Michael put me on a new medication for the Parkinson's, the FDA just released it, and I haven't felt this good in two years," she said, looking pleased. It made Peter doubt Bill's fears even further. Michael was doing everything he could to extend her life and make her feel better, even researching new medications for her. It convinced him yet again of how off base Bill's accusations of his father were, and made him sad for him. He almost wanted to ask Maggie if her son had ever suffered from psychiatric problems, but he didn't want to upset her, and didn't dare. Clearly, Bill was suffering from severe paranoia, and all Peter said was that they had had dinner together, and the moment he said it, a cloud passed over her eyes. She knew about their dinner from an e-mail Bill had sent her, but she wondered if Bill had ranted about his father. She knew only too well how consumed with rage against him Bill was.

"Did he go on for hours about his father?" she asked, and when Peter hesitated, she knew he had. She hated it when Bill did that. Peter sighed in answer. Maggie obviously knew her son well.

"He sounds like me at his age," he said with a smile. "Maybe Michael just has a way of upsetting young males. Bill will calm down eventually. He says he's really enjoying the London School of Economics. He's very angry at his father. I told him how wrong I think he is. I hate to see him expend all that energy needlessly on that."

"I hope he doesn't take as long to get over it as you did," Maggie said sadly. It had torn their family apart. "I wish he'd come home one of these days."

"He will in time. To see you anyway. We hit it off pretty well." And then Maggie laughed.

"He looks just like you, doesn't he? Michael used to tease me about it. From his appearance, he could be your son."

"I hope to see him again sometime," Peter said sincerely, ignoring her comment.

"What happened with the interview?" She was interested in what he had to say.

"They're not hiring yet, so it was kind of a false alarm. Something will turn up at some point." She nodded, but she knew he was worried about what the next step would be. He couldn't stay at the lake forever, doing repairs on the old house. By the end of summer, he hoped to be back at work, hopefully in New York, which was his preference, or anywhere he could get a job.

He left Maggie after a while and drove to the lake. He had been reassured to see her in such good form. The new drug Michael had started her on had had miraculous results in a short time. And not in a million years did he believe that his brother would murder his wife for her money. He just wasn't that kind of man. He may have been a pain in the ass when they were kids, but that didn't make him a murderer now. And just because his elderly patients left him a few thousand dollars in their wills, it didn't mean he killed them. If Michael tended to them devotedly and made life easier in their final years, he had a right to their gratitude. He had seen in his mother's journals just how attentive Michael had been to her, visiting her several times a day. And he did the same for many of his patients, not just his parents. Michael had turned out to be a dedicated doctor and devoted son, and even a good brother now. He was absolutely certain that all of Bill's incredible theories were wrong.

Peter was thinking about him as he pulled into his driveway at the lake. There was more activity there now, and in the warmer weather, people were starting to take their boats out on weekends. Peter wanted to rent a small sailboat for the boys when they came out to visit. His parents had gotten rid of his old one years before.

As he got out of his truck, he was startled to see that there was a man sitting on his porch, waiting for him. He didn't recognize him, and his visitor was wearing overalls over a plaid shirt, and he had a tool belt around his waist. He looked like an electrician of some kind.

"Can I help you?" Peter asked with a curious expression. The man nodded and waited for him to approach. And for a moment, Peter was concerned. The house was isolated, and he had no idea why the man was there. He looked distressed, and Peter waited to hear why he had come.

"I want to talk to you about your brother," he said, sounding ominous for a minute.

"What about?"

"My father was a patient of your brother's. He died two weeks ago."

"What does that have to do with me?" Peter asked, and didn't invite him into the house.

"I want you to know what he did. Walt Peterson says you're a good man."

"Thank you," Peter said curtly. "So is my brother, and a good doctor." He was proud to say it now.

"He killed my father," the man said with a dark look.

"I doubt that," Peter responded, thinking again about what Michael had told him, that sometimes people who had lost loved ones needed to find someone to blame. And apparently, Michael was it in this case.

"I think my dad may have asked him to do it, but even if he did, that was wrong of him. My father had liver cancer, and he went out like a light the night your brother came to see him. He lived alone. I found him in the morning. He died in his sleep."

"Maybe it was just his time," Peter said, trying to sound calmer than he felt. He didn't like this man confronting him on his doorstep. There was something ominous about him, and threatening. He hoped that Michael wouldn't be in danger from him.

"No, it wasn't. I'm sure of that. We took him to an oncologist in Boston last month, and he said he had six months to a year. Two weeks later he dies in his sleep. I think your brother helped him out. And that ain't all." He waved a folded document at Peter. "He left everything he had to your brother. And he wasn't senile. I think your brother charmed him and made him feel so special that he wanted to give it all to him. He didn't leave anything to me or my sister, or our kids, just your brother. That ain't right. Everything he had. Forty thousand dollars."

It struck a chord of memory with Peter, remembering what his nephew had said. But you couldn't prevent old people from leaving whatever they wanted to their doctor. It was the only way they had to show their gratitude to the doctor who had been so attentive to them. And for a fraction of an instant, Peter remembered how he had felt when he had discovered that his parents had left almost everything to his brother. He had been just as angry as this man looked now. "I want an autopsy done," the man said with a look of fury. "I'm going to the police."

"How old was your father?" Peter asked with curiosity, taking the paper the man had stuck in his face.

"Seventy-nine. But he had been sick for two years. Your brother took care of him the whole time."

"Maybe your father was grateful he kept him alive that long," Peter said, looking non-committal. "Leaving him something in the will doesn't mean he killed him."

"I think he talked my father into cutting us out. My father would never have done a thing like that. He loved his kids and his grandkids. I think your brother is an evil man."

"You know, going after my brother isn't going to bring your father back," Peter said with a sigh. "It's just going to make trouble for everyone. What do you want from me?" Peter asked bluntly.

"I want your help. The police will really listen if you come with me."

"I can't do that," Peter said, looking out-raged. "He's my brother, and I have no reason to believe he killed your father, even if he did give everything to him in the will. That's not proof of murder, for God's sake."

"It's proof of some kind of influence on him. I want my dad exhumed for signs of foul play. I didn't know about the will until today." It sounded like sour grapes to Peter, and this man's anger over the money.

"I wouldn't do that if I were you. You're just going to upset a lot of people. And I'm sure my brother didn't kill your father."

"You don't know that," the man said angrily. "I think he did."

"You don't know that either," Peter shot back.

"Then we'll let the police figure it out. I thought maybe you'd help me."

"Why would I do that?"

"Walt said he screwed you out of your inheritance too. You ought to know how I feel. Besides, he killed my daddy," the man said with tears in his eyes. "I'm sure he did." He looked overwrought to Peter. He just hoped the man didn't have a gun and decide to shoot him instead. He hoped he didn't go to Michael's house and scare Maggie out of her wits, or Lisa.

"He didn't screw me. He's my brother. And he deserved what he got. That's nobody's business but ours."

"Fine, then. Don't help me. I'll go to the police." Peter said nothing as the man got into his car, revved the engine, and drove away, and he spat at Peter out the window as he drove past him, just missing Peter, who went into the house then to call Michael. He wanted to warn him that there was a nutcase on the loose. But Michael sounded unconcerned. He said he knew all about him and what he was saying. He was saying it all over town. Michael said he had already warned the police to keep an eye on the house. He told Peter that the man who had come to see him had a severe problem with alcohol and suffered from delusions, and his sister had had psychiatric problems for years. The whole family was nuts. And his father had been riddled with cancer before he died, "of natural causes," Michael added.

"I'm sorry he bothered you. I'll report it," Michael said calmly, sounding undisturbed. "It's one of those things I told you about. People who come unhinged when they lose a loved one. I feel bad that the old man left me his money, but it was the wish of a dying man. If they were decent people, I'd give it back to them, but their father wouldn't want that. They'll just spend it on drugs and booze. They're a bad lot, and their father knew it." Peter could see that they were. "That's why he left the money to me. He didn't have anyone else responsible to leave it to."

"Well, just be careful," Peter said, sounding worried. "I don't want them shooting you."

"They won't," Michael said, laughing. "I move too fast. And the police chief is my friend. He'll take care of me."

"Lock your doors tonight," Peter warned him.

"Thank you, brother," Michael said, smiling, and Peter shook his head when he hung up the phone. The man who had come to see him had really unnerved him. And Michael was right. He looked nuts. Poor Michael, that was all he needed, Peter thought, being accused of murdering a patient. But like Michael, Peter knew the accusation would go nowhere. Michael really was a saint. He would never do a thing like that. The man's accusations weren't worth a second thought. He just hoped that Michael would be careful for a while, until the lunatic calmed down.

Chapter 13

Peter didn't go into town again for a few days, and when he did, he stopped at the diner for lunch and saw Vi. She was a kindly, motherly presence in his life, and insisted he have a slice of fresh apple pie. It was delicious. She was busy and didn't have time to chat, and after lunch Peter stopped at the hardware store to pick up some things. He was replacing all the old screens before the summer. The house was looking better every day, and he wanted to finish all his little projects before the boys arrived. When he saw Walt, he was about to tell him about the irate man who had showed up at the lake, when Walt stopped him in his tracks with what he said.

"I'm sorry to hear about your sister-in-law," he said, looking sad. Everybody had loved Maggie since she was a child. Peter's blood ran cold at the words. If something had happened to her, surely Michael would have called him. He was suddenly terrified that she'd died, and she had looked so well the last time he saw her, on the new medication Michael had started her on.

"What do you mean?" Peter asked tersely, ready to grab Walt by the throat and choke it out of him. Peter stood looking tense as he waited for Walt to explain.

"I hear she's in the hospital, real bad. Pneumonia. She went in last night." It was a small town, and everyone knew what went on. Vi must not have heard it yet or she would have said something to him at lunch and she hadn't. And Peter knew just how serious pneumonia would be for Maggie. He literally ran out of the hardware store and called Michael from his truck. But the call went straight to voicemail. He drove to St. Mary's Hospital instead to see what was going on. And when he checked at the desk, they told him she was there. She was in a private room as a courtesy to Michael. And Peter went straight upstairs. Michael was sitting next to her bed, and Maggie had an oxygen mask on her face and her eyes were closed.

"What happened?" Peter asked him in a hoarse whisper. His brother looked devastated. Her face was gray, and she was either unconscious or asleep. It reminded Peter instantly of when he'd visited her after her skating accident and she was in a coma. She looked almost as bad as that now.

"She had a reaction to the medication we tried," Michael said in a whisper. "It paralyzed her breathing system. She did great on it for a few days. And now this." Peter looked grim as he listened, and his brother looked worse than his wife. Peter reached out and squeezed his shoulder and sat with him for a long time. Michael checked her vital signs regularly. The head nurse stuck her head in the door, but she knew Michael was with Maggie, so she left immediately. Maggie was getting the best care she could, with Michael attending to her. It was a long time before she stirred and opened her eyes. She smiled when she saw both

of them and looked groggy. She was se-
dated, and they had a breathing tube standing by in case she needed it.

"What are you two doing here?" she
whispered weakly.

"Just hanging out, we had nothing else
to do," Peter said with a lopsided grin. "How
do you feel?" He tried to look less worried
about her than he felt. But all their fear was
in Michael's eyes.

"I feel weird. Sleepy." She had taken the
mask off to talk to them, and Michael gently put it back. She needed the oxygen, and
there was a clip on her finger to check the
oxygen level in her blood. It had been frighteningly low the night before. He had called
an ambulance at midnight. He didn't want
to drive her himself in case her heart
stopped on the way there. She had been
in dire straits and barely able to breathe,
which was hard on her heart. And her heart
had been delicate for years. Lisa had been
panicked when they left, but Michael hadn't
wanted her to come. It was too upsetting
for her.

Maggie went back to sleep then, and at
seven o'clock Peter looked at his watch and
whispered to his brother, "Do you want to

get something to eat?" Michael hesitated, glanced at Maggie, and nodded. He had called in a young doctor from Warren to cover his patients all day. He had used him a few times before, but it was rare for Michael to take a day off. He had been at Maggie's side since midnight the night before, and only had some soup the nurses had given him. And he thought Maggie was stable enough for them to leave her for a short time now. And he knew Lisa was at a friend's. He followed Peter out of the room, and they walked the few blocks to the diner. Vi saw them as soon as they walked in. She had heard that Maggie was in the hospital by then, and asked how she was. The look on Michael's face said it all.

Michael's friend Jack Nelson, the chief of police, was there too, having dinner with one of his deputies. Michael stopped to say hello to him on their way to a booth. Jack looked instantly sorry. He stood up and shook Peter's hand when Michael introduced them.

"I heard about Maggie," he said with a look of concern. "How's she doing?"

"She's holding on for now," Michael said

with a hopeful look. He was visibly exhausted. "I think we got her to the hospital
in time." They lived from one crisis to the
next, and Jack Nelson felt sorry for him.
Peter thought he looked like a nice man,
and he seemed genuinely fond of Michael
and Maggie.

"Let me know if there's anything I can
do," the chief offered. "I'll have the boys
keep an eye on the house." He knew Lisa
would be there alone. "Tell Lisa to call if she
needs anything, even a pizza."

"Thanks, Jack. She's staying with a
friend," Michael said gratefully, and then he
and Peter went to their booth. Vi poured
them each a cup of steaming coffee the
moment they sat down, as they both slowly
started to unwind.

They both ordered the daily special at
Vi's suggestion. She said it was good, and
happened to be meat loaf and mashed potatoes that night. Peter figured Michael
needed the food, and he was hungry too.

"If Maggie's lungs give out, we'll lose
her," Michael said, looking desperate. "The
Parkinson's complicates everything and is
our worst enemy now. We have to wait and
see how she does in the next day or two."

"Have you called Bill?" Peter asked, and Michael shook his head. "I wanted to see how she did today. I don't want to bring him home for a false alarm."

Peter nodded. "I'll sit with her if you want, so you can go home and get some sleep." Michael had already told him that Lisa couldn't come to the hospital because she had a cold, and they couldn't take the risk.

"I don't want to leave her," Michael said wearily. "They can set up a cot in the room. I want to keep an eye on her." Peter understood, and he was suddenly reminded of his conversation in London with Bill. It was insane to think that this man would kill his wife. He looked like he was ready to give his own heart or lungs to save her life. He would have if he could. Peter could see that now.

They went back to the hospital after they ate, and Vi gave them a bag of snacks to take with them and a Thermos of coffee. Peter left him around eleven that night, with the admonition to call him if anything happened. Michael promised that he would. And then Peter drove back to the lake. It had been an interminable day, for everyone.

At least Peter had slept the night before, Michael hadn't and looked it.

He got back to the lake house at eleven-thirty, and checked his computer for e-mails. He saw that he had one from Bill in London and sat down to read it. He almost cried when he did, after the day they'd just been through. His nephew was insane. He had sent an article about a weed killer named paraquat, which, when ingested in minute quantities in liquid form, mimicked the symptoms of Parkinson's, and all of Maggie's other symptoms. It was used in underdeveloped countries for suicides. There were a few reports of poisonings, most of them fatal. It was sold in liquid form in the States with dye in it and a severe odor and vomiting agent added as safeguards, but in Canada and Europe it was sold without the additives, in pure form, with no color, taste, or smell. It was lethal if used in even small doses, and in minuscule doses, you could kill someone slowly over a long period of time. The accompanying message said that Bill was wondering if his father was using it on his mother. Peter didn't know whether to laugh or cry. His e-mail was the most ridiculous thing he'd ever seen, and reeked of paranoia.

He was asleep when Bill called him the next morning and woke him up.

"Did you see my e-mail?" were his first words, and Peter groaned. He was still half asleep, but Michael hadn't called him during the night with bad news, which was a good sign.

"Yes, I did," Peter said slowly. "Bill, you have to give this up. Your father isn't using weed killer to kill your mother. He's a doctor, for chrissake. If he wanted to kill her, which he doesn't, he'd use something a lot simpler than a weed killer he'd have to go over the Canadian border to buy. You have to let go of this." He had watched Michael's desperation to save Maggie the day before, which made Bill's suspicions seem even crazier now. Peter sat up in bed then and looked at the clock. It was seven o'clock in the morning, noon in London. Bill said he had been researching it for days, and the weed killer he'd found had to be it. All the symptoms described were his mother's. "Are you listening to me?" Bill shouted at him. And then he lowered his voice again.

"Your mom's sick, by the way. She's in the hospital," Peter interrupted. He hated to be the one to tell him, but he thought he might as well know. Peter had lost all patience with him and his insane delusions about his father.

"With what?" Bill sounded panicked about his mother.

"She had a reaction to a drug she was taking, for the Parkinson's. It did something to her lungs. Your dad is afraid it's pneumonia. But she's hanging in so far. I was with them all day yesterday until late last night. Believe me, he's not killing her. He's doing everything he can to save her. No one could do more."

"If he's been poisoning her all along, all he has to do now is sit there and cry and watch it happen. That's the best alibi he's got."

"You need therapy," Peter said seriously. "Or drugs. You're hallucinating."

"I know this is it. I know every poison on the Internet. I've been researching it for months. He's poisoning her, I know it. This stuff has been used before."

"Not by doctors on their wives," Peter said, feeling desperate. He couldn't get Bill to calm down. "Your mom's been sick since she was twenty. You have to face that, no matter how hard it is. She may not live through this. And if she does, there will be other times like this in the future. Bill, you have to grow up."

"You have to listen to me!" his nephew shouted back at him. "I know him. He's a sociopath. He's crazy. He has no conscience or morals."

"I know my brother. He's not as crazy as you think," Peter said, fighting to sound calm, although he wasn't. "He can be a jerk. I hated him just like you do. But I swear, he loves your mother. He'd give his life for her."

"My father doesn't give a shit about anyone. For all you know, he killed your parents, for their money."

"It wasn't enough to matter," Peter said quietly.

"My grandfather left her ten million dollars. Believe me, he would do it for that. If she leaves him half of it, that's enough. I swear he only married her for what he knew my grandfather would leave her. In the condition she was in then, no one else would have married her. She was an annuity for him."

    "That's a cruel thing to say about your mother."

    "I want you to do something for me." Bill sounded frantic, and Peter was sorry he'd ever met him. The last thing he needed was a lunatic on his hands. Now he thought he understood why Maggie had said it was better he'd gone to live in London. He was crazy, and she knew it. "I found a toxicology lab in Boston, from the Internet. They test for rare poisons. I called them yesterday. They said that if we can get them a few hairs from her head, they can tell us if this toxic agent is present. After that I'll leave you alone, I swear." Peter closed his eyes and shuddered as he listened. How was he going to get rid of Bill now? And Peter realized, listening to him, that Bill would go insane if his mother died. He might even try to kill his father, for a crime he had never committed and Bill had only imagined.

    "Look, I'm not going to go in there, in front of your father, who looks worse than she does, and rip a bunch of hairs off her head, and drive them into Boston to some quack you found on the Internet, so he can find out if your father is putting weed killer in her soup. Bill, you have to get real here."

"I'm begging you," Bill said, and Peter could hear that he was crying. He was about to cry too, out of sheer frustration. And Maggie might not even live long enough for him to do what Bill wanted. "I'll never call you again. I promise. Just do this one thing for me. For my mother's sake, if you care about her at all."

"I love her. And my brother." That was true now, he realized. He had formed a bond to his twin that he'd never had before, and it was important to him. "And I care about you. But I don't want to go on a wild-goose chase."

"Why not? What if I'm right and you save her life?" Peter sat staring into space as he thought about it. Bill was right, at worst he'd look like a fool taking three hairs to a lab in Boston to find out what kind of hair spray she used. And if what Bill said was true? . . . But it couldn't be. The whole idea was just too insane. The product of a sick mind, far sicker than the one he was accusing his father of having. There had been silence on the phone for a minute while Peter was thinking. It gave Bill hope when Peter didn't answer. "Will you do it? Just this one thing. For my mother. It won't hurt anyone if I'm

wrong . . . and if I'm right, we'll save her.
There could be permanent damage from
this poison, but if he kept the doses low
enough, she could recover, unless he's
stepping up the doses now to kill her. Just
tell me you'll do it. We may not have much
time." Peter felt as though he were being
sucked into the nightmare with him.

"I don't know why I'm doing this for you.
But if you're wrong, I want you to swear
you'll find a psychiatrist in London, and
never call me again. Your mother is a very
sick woman, and you'll just have to face
that."

"I promise you, I will."

"E-mail me the name and address of the
lab. I must be as crazy as you are."

"I sent it before I called you," Bill said,
sounding relieved, and then thanked his
uncle profusely.

"And how am I supposed to rip three
hairs off her head without your father thinking I'm deranged?"

"Stroke her head or something. I know
you can do it."

"I just want you to know that I think you're
wrong on this. A hundred percent wrong.
My brother is not a killer."

"Just do it," Bill said tensely.

"I told you I would. But I know you're wrong."

"Maybe I should come home today," Bill said, sounding pensive.

"Ask your father. But she doesn't look good to me."

"Let me know what the lab says."

"Whatever. I'll call you," Peter said, and was furious at himself for agreeing to do it. He hung up then, and an hour later he was at the hospital. Michael was dozing in a chair next to Maggie, who was sleeping soundly. Peter felt ridiculous when he remembered his mission. He walked over and stroked her hair, and without Michael noticing, he gently tugged a few hairs from her head. They came away easily, and he dug his hand into his pocket and clutched them. He left the room a minute later, before either of them woke up, and put the hair in an envelope he had brought with him. He was sure that no one saw him. And then he walked back into the room and sat down next to Michael. His brother stirred and smiled at Peter.

"How is she?" Peter whispered.

"About the same. She's running a low

fever." They both knew that wasn't good either. But she was still hanging on. "As long as her lungs don't get paralyzed, we have a fighting chance." She had the beginnings of pneumonia.

"I have to go into Boston today, to take care of some banking problems," Peter said, looking embarrassed, and feeling as demented as his nephew.

"Anything I can help you with?" Michael asked him with a look of concern. He was wondering if his brother was running out of money.

"No, I'm fine. You've got bigger problems here. I'll be back in about four or five hours. Call me if you need me." Michael nodded, the two brothers exchanged a smile, and Peter left the room as soundlessly as he had entered, and hurried to the parking lot, with the envelope in his pocket. He wondered if the lab in Boston even existed.

It took him an hour and a half to get to Boston. And he felt like a traitor all the way there. He was signing on for his nephew's fantasy, that his father was trying to murder his mother. Peter knew there was no way that could be true, but at least after this maybe his nephew would accept the truth, that his mother was dying. Peter didn't like it either, but it appeared to be reality. Maggie was holding on by a thread now. Her weak heart, kidneys, and liver combined with the Parkinson's and her earlier infirmities were more than any human could survive. Peter wondered if it was only a matter of days now, or worse, maybe hours.

He went to the address Bill had e-mailed him, and was surprised to find that it was a large, highly technical, space age, modern-looking lab. Several police officers were waiting, and the sign over the door said simply Forensic Lab. There were at least two dozen employees. Peter waited at the main desk and took the envelope out of his pocket. Five minutes later a lab technician handed him some forms.

"What are we testing for?"

"Paraquat," Peter said, trying to appear normal, but he didn't feel it. He felt foolish. "Human ingestion."

"You brought a sample?" He handed her the envelope with the three hairs in it.

"We need the results as soon as possible," he said, getting into it, as she wrote the word **Stat** in large red letters on the form.

"We'll have them for you tomorrow," she said coolly. "Are you a doctor?"

"Private investigator," he said, feeling not only stupid but dishonest as she nodded. "I'm investigating a criminal case," he added, and gave her the number of his BlackBerry.

"I spoke to your associate in London this morning," she said, and he realized that Bill had called them. "I'll call you tomorrow," she said, after asking him to pay four hundred dollars. It was a small price to pay for Maggie's life, if by some insane chance her son was right. Peter hoped not. He couldn't even imagine the consequences if the test came back positive, but he was sure it wouldn't.

He left the lab and started the drive back to Ware. As he got on the freeway, Bill called him.

"Where are you?"

"On my way back from Boston." Going to the lab had given reality to Bill's suspicions, which depressed him as he entered the traffic flow on the freeway.

"The hospital just told me she's in critical condition," Bill said unhappily. "I wish I could get her away from my father." Peter wondered if that was what this was all about. Some oedipal fantasy, where he wanted his mother and to kill his father. "Will you be with her today?" Bill asked him, sounding worried.

"Once I get back there. I won't be in Ware for two hours." Or less, if he drove faster.

"I'm coming in tonight," Bill said dully. "Can I stay with you?"

"Sure," Peter said, wondering what his brother would say if he heard about it. This was a royal mess from beginning to end. But if Maggie died, none of it would matter. "We'll have the results tomorrow."

"That's what they told me." All they could do was wait, but Peter was sure it was a futile expedition, and Maggie's unbalanced son would be staying with him. God only knew what he would do now. He clearly had an obsession. He almost wanted to warn his brother. If the test was negative, he was going to do that. Michael had the right to know that his son was out to get him. Peter suspected that Michael must know how disturbed his son was. After all, he was a doctor.

Peter thought about the test they were doing, all the way back to the hospital, and when he walked into Maggie's room, her eyes were open and she was smiling. Her breathing was labored, but she looked happy to see him. She took the oxygen mask off so she could talk to him for a minute.

"How are you feeling?" Peter asked her gently.

"Okay," she said bravely, but he could see how sick she was.

"Where's Michael?"

"He had to see a patient. She just came in with a heart attack. He can't totally ignore his patients," she said, as Peter motioned to her to put the mask on. He didn't want to wear her out. He thought about telling her that Bill was coming, but he didn't want to upset her, or give her the impression she was dying.

Michael walked into the room in his white doctor's coat an hour later. Peter was reading a magazine, and Maggie was dozing. He took her pulse and checked the heart monitor with pursed lips. Maggie opened her eyes when she felt him. She was checking his face for his reactions and saw him frown.

"I want to go home," she whispered, lifting the mask again. She was afraid that she was dying, and she had always told him she wanted to die at home, in her own bed. She had talked to Lisa that morning. She still had a nasty cold and was desperate to see her mother. Maggie knew that if she went home, she could see her, even if only from the doorway.

"We'll see how you are in a day or two," Michael said vaguely, and he told Peter, when they went out to the hallway, that she was safer here, with defibrillators and whole teams of people to revive her. She was still too fragile right now to go home, although he didn't like the risk of infection at the hospital either. He had to weigh the risks, and he was more comfortable keeping her at the hospital for now. Peter listened with a serious expression. It sounded like they were down to the wire, but he didn't want to ask him.

"How'd it go at the bank in Boston today?" Michael asked him warmly.

"It was fine. I had to sign some documents for Alana, for the house in Southampton." He tried to look annoyed about it, but he was angry at Bill anyway so it was easy.

"And you had to go all the way to Boston? She doesn't make it easy for you, does she?" Michael said sympathetically.

"No, she doesn't," Peter said, and then suggested they go to the diner for dinner. Michael hesitated but finally agreed, and they left when Maggie went back to sleep. Peter knew it seemed insane, but even though he didn't believe a word of Bill's theory about the weed killer, he was nervous now about leaving Maggie alone with Michael. He had told Bill where the spare key to his house was, and after dinner Peter suggested spending the night with his brother at the hospital. He couldn't imagine him having the guts to poison her here, or anywhere else for that matter, but staying seemed like a good idea. Michael looked at him gratefully when he said it.

"You don't need to stay. They're watching her closely. I was thinking about going home to Lisa. They'll call me if anything happens, and I can be here in five or ten minutes. I think Maggie will be okay here tonight. I'll come back, and call you, if anything happens."

"That sounds like a good plan. You need to get some sleep too," Peter told him.

Michael looked genuinely exhausted, and suddenly ten years older than Peter. Peter liked the idea of going home since Michael wouldn't be spending the night at the hospital either. If Bill was right, Peter wondered what Michael's plan was. To keep her as sick as possible in the hospital, and then let her go home and kill her? Or did he plan to deliver the coup de grâce here? Or had he already done it? Peter felt insane thinking about it. He was beginning to believe it. His trip to the laboratory in Boston had given serious weight to the theory. He knew it couldn't be true, but his mind was in a whirl now.

When they left the hospital for dinner, the nurse said Maggie's heart was doing better. For a while, the day before, all her systems seemed to be shaky. She was a little more stable now, except for her breathing and the ever-present risk of her lungs freezing, or a serious case of pneumonia, either of which would kill her.

After dinner, Michael went home to Lisa, and Peter drove to the lake and found his nephew on the couch as soon as he opened the door. He was drinking a beer, and looked as exhausted as his uncle and father. He stood up as soon as Peter entered, and he looked saner than Peter remembered. He didn't look crazy, but he had to be. All Peter could think of now was that they were testing Maggie's hair to see if her husband was trying to kill her by poisoning her with weed killer. How surreal was that? It sounded totally insane to Peter.

"Thank you for letting me stay here," Bill said humbly.

"I didn't think you could stay at your father's," Peter said matter-of-factly. Peter's head was reeling, and he had a massive headache. Without a word, he walked into the bathroom and took two aspirin.

"How's my mother?" Bill asked, looking worried. He had wanted to go to the hospital to see her, but had been afraid to run into his father.

"About the same," Peter said honestly. He didn't want to lie to him. She was still in critical condition. "I thought of spending the night there. But your father went home tonight. And we should know everything we need to know in the morning."

"What do we do then?" Bill asked him, and Peter stared into space, thinking about it for a moment.

"Hopefully nothing. With any luck, we won't have to."

"And if we do?" Bill persisted.

"We'll figure it out then. I'm too tired tonight to think about it. You can sleep in my sons' room." He pointed in the right direction down the hall. "There's a sleeping bag in the closet if you don't want to make the bed."

"Thank you," Bill said somberly, as Peter went to his own bedroom and closed the door. The nephew he scarcely knew had turned his life upside down ever since they'd met in London. And more than likely, he had led him on a wild-goose chase to save his mother from a danger that didn't even exist. Peter lay on his bed with all his clothes on, and was asleep five minutes later.

Peter awoke to the sound of his Black-Berry ringing at eight o'clock the next morning. "Mr. McDowell?" the voice at the other end asked him when he answered, and he responded with a deep affirmative rumble. "Tilton Labs here. We have the results for you on the paraquat ingestion." Peter shook himself awake and sat upright. He wanted to be awake to hear this clearly. "The results are positive for human ingestion. The subject has a heavy dose on board, possibly lethal. I'd say it's very close to lethal. The subject needs treatment immediately. I'll e-mail you the report this morning."

"Could you do it right now? We need to take it to the authorities this morning," he said, trying to sound official. His mind was reeling, and his heart was pounding. He wanted to cry.

"Of course. I'll have it to you in five minutes." Peter stumbled out of bed and saw it appear on his e-mail, just as Bill came through the bedroom doorway. Like Peter, he was still wearing his clothes from the night before.

"What is it?" his nephew asked him. He thought it was too early to be the lab, but Peter was looking at his e-mail with a grim expression, and hit the button on the printer. And then he turned to Bill.

"I owe you an apology," Peter said with a look of amazement. He still couldn't believe it. But there was no doubt anymore. Bill wasn't crazy. And it might be too late to save Maggie, but they had to try. "Your mother's hair tested positive for paraquat, a possibly lethal dose or close to it. We have to get back to the hospital right away. What the fuck do we do now?" Peter said with tears in his eyes. He hadn't expected this.

Bill stared at Peter when he spoke to him, frozen for a minute. Bill had been so convinced of it, but suddenly it was real. They knew that they had to act quickly, but neither of them knew what to do first. They hadn't eaten, and neither of them had showered or shaved. They stood staring at each other in disbelief for a long moment.

"Where do we go? The hospital?" Bill asked him nervously. "The police?" Peter considered the question. It was hard to know what to do next. Peter didn't trust Michael with Maggie at the hospital, but he wanted to get to the police and show them the lab report. He printed the e-mail, made two copies and held them in a trembling hand.

"Police first. Then hospital," Peter said as he sped into action, and both of them went to their rooms to shower and change. They were in Peter's truck in five minutes, speeding from the lake to Ware.

The two men hardly said a word to each other on the drive to town. Peter kept his foot on the gas, and Bill was staring out the window, as they both tried to absorb what had happened. Now that they knew for sure, Bill wasn't angry—he was frightened for his mother, more than he'd ever been in his life. Every fear and suspicion he'd ever had, had suddenly become real. And Peter had stepped into the nightmare with him. And there was no way out. With the positive lab report, there was no waking up from this.

They were at the police station in fifteen minutes, and Peter looked at his nephew long and hard. "Are you ready for this?" he asked him in a harsh tone. "They're not go- ing to believe us, you know. Your dad and the chief are good friends." The police were going to have to check it out themselves. Peter just hoped they didn't warn Michael. He was deathly afraid of what he would do to Maggie before he was stopped. And they had to stop him soon.

"I'm ready," Bill said in a shaking voice and followed his uncle out of the truck. Pe- ter strode into the police station with a se- rious expression and asked to see the chief of police. He declined to tell the sergeant on duty what it was about and said that it was an urgent personal matter and gave his name. Jack Nelson came out of his office five minutes later with a look of fear, recognized both men immediately, and was instantly afraid they had come to tell him Maggie had died.

"Maggie?" he said in a choked voice as Peter nodded.

"May we speak to you alone?" Peter said tersely.

"Of course," the chief said sympathetically, led them into his office, and motioned to the chairs across from his desk. "I'm so sorry," he said in a somber tone. "When did it happen?"

"She's not dead," Peter said clearly, "but she could be very soon. We've come to see you about a serious matter. I know this will sound hard to believe, and I have no explanation for it myself. My nephew has been convinced that his father was poisoning his mother. He's done considerable research on the Internet, and came up with a poison he was convinced my brother was using. I know it sounds like a crackpot scheme, and I thought so too. He convinced me to take some of Maggie's hair to a toxicology lab in Boston yesterday and have it tested. I did, and we just got the report. Maggie has been given a potentially lethal dose of a weed killer called paraquat. She has enough in her system to kill her." As he said it, he handed the lab report across Jack Nelson's desk, and the chief's eyes widened as he read it, and then he looked angrily back at Peter and then at Bill, who had been sitting there silently, looking distressed.

"Are you both crazy? That's ridiculous. Michael McDowell wouldn't hurt anyone, least of all his wife. I'd stake my own life on that." And then he narrowed his eyes as he looked at Peter and tossed the lab report on his desk. "I know you and your brother have had bad blood between you for years over your parents' will." Michael had told him all about it. "Maybe you're trying to get even with him now with a bogus claim that he's killing Maggie. I don't believe it!" he shouted at Peter.

"Neither did I," Peter said quietly. "I didn't want to believe it. I thought my nephew was nuts. He isn't. And Maggie is in grave danger."

"What makes you think Michael did it?"

"He's been keeping my mother weak and sick for years," Bill answered bravely. "And she's been getting steadily worse since my grandfather died. He left her a lot of money. I think my father wants it. I think that's why he married her. And now that she inherited it, he wants the money." Bill spoke up in a serious tone, as Jack Nelson met his eyes squarely. He could see that they were both convinced, but he wasn't, not by a long shot. He would never believe Michael capable of something like that, and he was going to prove it. He knew that Maggie's father had left her the lumber mill and that she had sold it for a huge amount of money, but not in a million years would Jack Nelson ever believe that Michael would kill her to get it. Their accusation was outrageous, but with a lab report sitting on his desk, he couldn't ignore it either. And he was furious about it. He hated the situation, and was convinced that Michael was being falsely accused and by his own son and brother, which made it even worse.

"You have to stop Michael and protect Maggie," Peter said seriously.

"Don't tell me how to do my job!" Jack shouted at him.

"What are you going to do?" Peter persisted. He was anxious to get to the hospital before Michael could poison her again, or just kill her.

"I'm going to run that test again, and make sure this lab report isn't something you two cooked up. And I'll get a search warrant on the house. I don't even want to mention it to Michael. He's got enough to worry about right now with Maggie so sick. I'm not going to accuse him of poisoning her too. He'll think I'm as off my rocker as you are." For now, he wanted to protect Michael as much as Maggie. "And we'll see what we have after that. And I'm warning you, if this is some kind of hoax to falsely accuse Michael, I'm going to bring charges against you both." Both Peter and Bill nodded. They believed him. "Don't either of you leave town." Jack Nelson sounded harsh.

"What are you going to do to protect Maggie?" Peter said, feeling desperate.

"I have no reason to believe she needs protection from her husband for the moment. Even if she's been poisoned, I have no evidence that he did it. I'll let the hospital know we have this toxicology report, in case they want to do anything about it medically, and I'll ask them not to tell Michael for now. That's all I'm going to do until we repeat the test and I search the house."

"When are you going to do that?" Peter doggedly persisted. He was not intimidated by Jack Nelson, and he knew the wheels of justice turned slowly.

"As soon as I get a search warrant," Jack said, in an angry tone. It was obvious he didn't believe Bill or Peter, but he couldn't ignore what they'd said either. He was planning to call a judge for a search warrant as soon as they left his office, and he was going to have the hospital provide another sample of Maggie's hair and send it to a police lab in Boston, and all of it without Michael's knowledge. Jack Nelson felt like a traitor, but he had to do his job. Even if Michael was his friend, Peter had come to him with a toxicology report from a reputable lab, claiming Maggie was being poisoned. He doubted it was true, but he couldn't just brush it off. Responsibly, he had to check it out. "I'll get in touch with both of you," he said as he stood up. They both gave him their cell phone numbers. Peter realized that he would be the only one protecting Maggie from Michael, until the police checked out his accusations. He hoped they'd do it quickly.

He and Bill looked somber as they left the chief's office. Jack had asked Bill if there was anyone at the house, and Bill said that Pru Walker was probably there. Jack had made no further comment. And Bill and Peter got into the truck feeling shaken.

"Now what do we do?" Bill said grimly as Peter started the truck.

"I'll sit with your mother, and you disappear, unless you want to see her too. It might be smart for your father not to know you're here for the moment. I don't want to make him nervous now and cause him to make any fast moves." Bill agreed. He said he'd go to a friend's house, who would keep quiet about it. Peter dropped him off and was at the hospital five minutes later. The scene there was peaceful. Maggie was asleep and a nurse was with her. She said Michael hadn't been there yet that morning and had called in to say he was visiting a few patients, and Maggie was about the same. No better. No worse, which was at least something. He settled quietly into a chair, his mind reeling from everything that had happened.

An hour later a lab tech came in and took a sample of blood from Maggie. She barely stirred, and then Peter saw him take a few hairs from her head, so he knew Jack Nelson had requested the test, and fortunately Michael wasn't there to see it.

When Michael did walk in an hour later, Maggie was awake and talking to Peter. She looked groggy, and a nurse had added something to her IV. Peter wondered if it was something to counteract the poison they now knew was in her system, but he didn't ask.

Michael appeared to be in good spirits, and Maggie was happy to see him. And he thanked Peter for keeping Maggie company. It was excruciating trying to appear normal. All Peter could think of was Jack Nelson and what he was doing to prove their story true. He wondered how soon Jack would search the house and what he would find there. Peter's mind was whirling, as Michael sat down next to him and Maggie went back to sleep.

"You don't have to stay, you know," Michael said gently, as he looked at his twin. "You look beat."

"I'm okay." Peter smiled at him. It was

going to be a long twenty-four hours waiting for verification of the first lab's report
and the police to search the house, if anything even turned up there. Peter couldn't
imagine it. Michael was too smart for that.
And Peter now knew that Bill's worst fears
were true. Michael had been killing Maggie, little by little, and all Peter could do
now was pray that he'd be stopped, and
Maggie would survive. For now, nothing
was sure, as Peter continued his vigil. Until Jack Nelson verified his story, Peter was
the only protection Maggie had. He hoped
it wasn't too late. For the rest of the day,
Peter never moved.

Chapter 14

Jack Nelson didn't know whether to scream or cry when Peter and Bill left his office. He didn't believe their story for a minute. They were obviously trying to frame Michael, and they both had had their issues with him, Peter over money and their parents' will, and Bill over some sort of father-son rivalry that had caused him to leave. And why would anyone want to kill Maggie? It made no sense. Jack had no intention of accusing Michael of trying to kill his wife, but he couldn't deny the toxicology report. He had work to do. Jack Nelson was above all a dedicated, conscientious cop, no matter how ludicrous the accusation seemed.

He called the hospital administrator at St. Mary's, as he had told Peter he would. He faxed him the report so they could act on it immediately if they needed to medically, and he suggested that they watch Maggie closely. If someone was trying to poison her, then Jack wanted a nurse in the room at all times. He was sure it wasn't Michael, and he didn't trust Peter or Bill. They were both under suspicion right now, as far as Jack was concerned. Why would they make an accusation like that against Michael? Maybe Peter had poisoned her himself. But why?

The hospital administrator agreed to say nothing to Michael. Jack didn't tell him that Michael had been accused of poisoning her, only that someone had been and that it was to remain confidential. Jack said that he didn't want to upset Michael further until they had more information, since Maggie was so ill. The administrator said he understood, and they would begin treatment immediately to try to administer activated charcoal and flush the poison from her system without alerting anyone that they had. There was nothing else they could do to counteract the poison anyway. There was no known antidote for it, which made Maggie's situation even worse.

Jack's next phone call was to obtain the search warrant on Maggie and Michael's house. He called a judge he knew well at the district court in Belchertown, since the courthouse in Ware had been closed for some time. And when the judge heard who it was for, he whistled through his teeth.

"Mike McDowell? That's insane, Jack. I went to school with him. My mother thinks he's a saint. Someone must be out to get him."

"I think so too," Jack said, sounding unhappy. "But I've got a toxicology report from a reputable lab in Boston that tells me she's been poisoned. We've got to do what we've got to do. I'm sure we won't find anything at the house."

"Has he got a motive?" the judge asked cautiously.

"According to their son, the money Maggie got for the lumber mill she inherited from her father."

"Mike's not after money. That's never

been his style," the judge said, sounding certain. And Jack was just as sure.

"I know that too," Jack agreed. "Let's get this over with, so we can figure out who really did it, if she's truly being poisoned."

"What about the kids?" the judge asked, seeming pensive. It was an ugly story and he didn't like the sound of it at all. But stranger things had happened. Crimes were committed every day.

"Their son hasn't been home for over a year, till now. He lives in London. He came back last night because his mother is so sick. He claims his father has been poisoning her for years. But the boy has had no access, he hasn't seen her. Their daughter is sixteen and a really sweet kid, and devoted to her mother."

"All right, I'll give you the warrant," the judge said with a sigh. "Send one of your guys over to pick it up. I'll have it for you in half an hour."

"Thanks, Tom," Jack said informally. They were good friends and worked together often.

"Let me know what you find," the judge said, sounding worried. He liked Michael too.

"You know I will," Jack reassured him.

Two hours later, Jack rang the doorbell at the McDowell home, and Pru Walker answered. She was vacuuming, and she looked startled when she saw the chief of police and the three police officers with him. Jack explained to her that he had a search warrant, and then he asked her not to discuss it with anyone, even Michael. He said he didn't want to upset him at this difficult time.

"But why would you want to search the house?" Pru asked, looking frightened. She couldn't think of a single reason.

"Just a crackpot claim we have to check out. We have to do something to earn our keep," he said with a smile, as she let them in, and the three officers dispersed around the house, while Jack waited for them in the kitchen. He was grateful that Lisa was at school, so she didn't have to see this, and he didn't have to explain it to her.

The officers quietly began a systematic search of the house. After searching Maggie's bedroom and bathroom, they came downstairs with large transparent bags filled with prescription pill bottles that were Maggie's, prescribed by Michael. They looked as though they had ransacked a pharmacy. The medicines they took as evidence filled the trunk of one of their cars. They searched both children's rooms and found no evidence of chemicals or poison, and then continued the search on the main floor. They found nothing alarming or unusual under the kitchen sink or in the pantry, as Pru Walker watched them, and Jack Nelson silently admitted to himself that he was relieved. This had to be some kind of terrible mistake or Michael had been framed. And then the officers went out to the garden shed behind the house. Jack was supervising the search himself to make sure that everything was done properly. He didn't want any accusations later of an improper search. His officers were wearing rubber gloves as they gathered evidence, and so was he, so as not to disturb any fingerprints.

The officers brought several bottles and cans out of the garden shed, carefully marked, in plastic bags. There were two bottles of a clear odorless liquid with no labels on them. Jack Nelson clenched his teeth when he saw one of his officers put them in a plastic bag. Privately, he was praying that they wouldn't prove to be the paraquat that had been found in Maggie's system. He didn't want it to be as simple as that. He wanted some other explanation for the accusations against Michael, and he hoped they hadn't found the evidence that morning. Or if they had, that it didn't have Michael's fingerprints on it.

The search took them two hours, and he thanked Pru for her cooperation, and then they left in two police cars, as Pru stood staring at them as they drove away. She had seen the enormous plastic bags filled with pill bottles, enough to supply an entire hospital, and the bottles and cans they had taken from the garden shed. She had no idea what they were doing or looking for. Jack had said nothing while he waited in the kitchen, quietly observing her.

And once back in the office, Jack signed a slip of paper to send everything from the garden to the crime lab, particularly the two unmarked bottles containing the transparent liquid. He called the lab himself and told them that he wanted the results of the tests immediately, and then he dispatched one of his officers to the lab. All he could do was hope that everything they had turned up was harmless and would lead to nothing. The last thing Jack Nelson wanted was to discover that Peter's accusations were true.

The scene at the hospital continued to be alarming. Maggie's condition seemed to have worsened, and she had a fever throughout the day. Nurses constantly came and went, and Michael checked her frequently. He told Peter, with a grief-stricken look, that her breathing was getting more labored, and Peter wondered if he should call Bill. He was hoping that charcoal and the flushing of her system would be able to counter the effects of the paraquat, but he couldn't know for sure. Bill had shown him on the Internet that it was the only neutralizing agent. Michael was out of the room when they administered the charcoal and Maggie seemed to be getting a large amount of fluids, mostly by IV, and Michael commented on it. They told him it was to bring her fever down, and he nodded. Michael looked devastated as the two brothers sat side by side all day.

Peter tried not to react as he looked at him. He realized now that Michael had fooled him yet again. He was just as evil as

Peter had believed him to be when they were young, and as Bill said. The last few months had all been an act to convince Peter that he was the saint that everyone believed him to be. But the demon lurked within. And all the while, he was poisoning his wife. It was truly beyond comprehension or belief.

"How's she doing?" Peter whispered late in the afternoon, and Michael shook his head.

"Not so well today." Peter was just praying that he hadn't found a way to give her another dose of the paraquat. It was going to be touch and go trying to save her as it was, with an almost lethal quantity of poison in her system. Peter wanted everything to happen more quickly and to get Michael away from her, but all he could do was wait. Peter felt the minutes dragging by interminably as Maggie slept. He wondered how long this had gone on, maybe years, if Bill was right. As Peter sat next to his brother, he had to do everything he could to restrain himself. He wanted to grab him and slam him up against the wall. Instead, he had to appear normal, as they walked down the hall to stretch their legs. It felt like the

longest day of Peter's life. He called Bill
from the men's room and told him nothing
had changed. They had to wait for the reports the next day. Peter had told Michael
that he wouldn't leave him alone that night,
and Michael thanked him with a grateful
look. And through it all, Maggie slept. Peter
never left the room unless Michael did.
And he watched him like a hawk.

Jack Nelson got the first report at six A.M.
It confirmed the one that Peter had given
him the day before. Maggie had been given
the weed killer paraquat in potentially lethal
quantities. It was identical to the report Peter had offered, which was accurate and
confirmed.

   Jack got the second call at noon. The
substance in the two unmarked bottles
from their garden shed was paraquat. It
had been purchased out of the country,
probably in Canada, since it met none of
the U.S. norms. There were fingerprints on
both bottles, the same prints that were
present all over Michael and Maggie's
room. Hers were on her hairbrush and her
laptop computer. They had gotten his from

his electric razor and a number of things on his desk. The fingerprints on the two bottles of paraquat were identified as his. They were the only fingerprints on the bottles. They were Michael's and no one else's.

Jack felt sick when he hung up the phone after the last report. Michael was his friend. He would have staked his life on him. He had wanted the accusations against him to be wrong. And maybe he had been framed, or it was some terrible misunderstanding, or accidental event. But the evidence was too strong. Maggie had been poisoned, and her husband's fingerprints were all over the bottles of the lethal substance that had been used to do it.

Jack picked up his hat and walked out of his office. He quietly asked his deputy to come with him, and have two patrolmen follow them in a separate car.

"Where are we going, Chief?" The deputy had never seen him look like that before. Jack Nelson felt heartbroken and betrayed.

"The hospital," he said grimly. He assumed Michael would be there. He just hoped it wasn't too late for Maggie and that

she could be saved. He knew they'd been
working on reversing the effect of the poison since yesterday.

The four men walked into the hospital
and got into the elevator together. Jack
knew the number of Maggie's room, and he
took the deputy with him when he walked
in and left the two officers in the hall. Michael looked pleased the moment he saw
Jack enter the room. He got up from the
corner where he'd been sitting with Peter
and went straight toward his friend in uniform. He assumed he'd come to offer his
concern and support. Jack instantly looked
pained, and Peter stiffened as he watched
the scene unfold.

"Thanks so much for coming," Michael
said with a warm smile, trying to put Jack
at ease. He could see that he was uncomfortable in the sickroom. Maggie was asleep
with a nurse standing at her bedside. Michael didn't know it, but Jack was the reason the nurse was there. Maggie hadn't
stirred in several hours, and her breathing
was still labored.

And before Michael could say another
word, Peter saw Jack stand up to his full
height, and when he spoke it was in a stern

tone, with eyes full of regret. He'd never been in a situation like this before, and he hated what he had to do.

"Michael McDowell," the chief said in a choked voice, "I'm placing you under arrest for suspicion of the poisoning and at-tempted murder of your wife. You have the right to remain silent . . ." He went on as he read him his Miranda rights, and Michael looked at him and laughed.

"Is this a joke?" he asked, looking vastly amused. He didn't even look mildly dis-turbed. Not nervous, worried, or shocked. He was innocence itself.

"No, it's not," the chief of police said to him, still standing in Maggie's room. She hadn't moved. "You can come with me qui-etly, or we can take you out in handcuffs," he said, touching the pair dangling from his belt. He hadn't used them in years. "It's up to you."

"This is the most ridiculous thing I've ever heard. I'm Maggie's doctor, and her husband. I'm not poisoning her."

"That's not what the toxicology reports say," Jack said quietly, wishing it wasn't true. His tone with Michael was an official one, but his voice was thick with emotion.

"Who ordered those reports?" Michael asked grandly.

"I did," he said, and then Michael turned and looked at his brother with narrowed eyes.

"You did this, didn't you?" he accused him. He could see that Peter wasn't surprised. He looked unhappy but relieved. "You're in love with her, aren't you?" Michael hissed at him. "How could you do this to me?"

"How could you do it to her?" Peter said sadly, as Michael literally snarled at him, and Jack reached out and touched his arm.

"Let's go, Michael." With that, the deputy stepped forward and put handcuffs on him, and Michael looked at him in outrage.

"You can't do this to me," Michael snapped at him.

"You're under arrest," the deputy said, looking embarrassed, and led Michael out of the room.

The chief stopped to speak to Peter for a minute before he left.

"I hope she makes it," the chief said quietly. He had spoken to the head of the hospital again before they came over, and he didn't sound hopeful, but he said they were doing all they could. They had been frantically researching treatments to counter the effects of the poison Michael had used on her. There were none. All they could do now was continue to flush it out of her system and hope the damage to her vital organs was not too great.

As the chief of police walked out, a medical team walked into the room. They gently moved Maggie and began working on her, while Peter went to call Bill and tell him his father had been arrested and now they would have Lisa to deal with. She knew nothing of what had gone on. Peter was anxious to tell her before she heard it somewhere else. He knew it would be on the news soon. And locally, the story would be huge.

And Bill wanted to see his mother. She had never woken up while Michael was being arrested. If she recovered, they would have to tell her too. They had hard days ahead.

Peter waited in the hallway for Bill to arrive. He came twenty minutes later, and they walked into Maggie's room together. This time her eyes were open, two doctors and a nurse were with her, and she looked at her son in amazement.

"What are you doing here?" she asked in a weak voice.

"I came to see you, Mom," Bill said quietly. He didn't want to alarm her and make her worse.

"Have you seen your father?" He shook his head. He and Peter had agreed not to tell her yet. She was still much too sick to hear such shocking news. They would have to stall her when she asked for Michael. But now that she was awake again, she looked more alert. Her system was beginning to clear of toxins, which meant he hadn't given her a dose of the poison in a while and she had survived the last one, so far.

Maggie smiled at Peter then. "Where's Michael?" she asked him.

"He left a little while ago," he said quietly. He didn't tell her he'd left in handcuffs. But she looked relieved to be able to see Bill, without dealing with the hostility between him and his father. She was glad that Michael wasn't there, at least for a few minutes, so she could thoroughly enjoy her son without the tension of his war with Michael. One of the doctors had just told her she was getting better, but seeing her son there told her just how sick she was.

"Did Daddy ask you to come?" she asked Bill, as she took his hand and held it.

"No. I decided to come on my own. He didn't call me." Bill thought that might reassure her. The two doctors left the room then, promising to be back soon, and the nurse took a discreet seat in the corner. She had seen all the events of the afternoon and was stunned when they arrested Michael.

Bill sat down next to his mother then and held her hand. He had to fight back tears of relief, hoping they had stopped his father in time, and he was grateful she was still alive and he could be with her.

They talked for a few minutes. He kissed her cheek and promised to come back soon. And then he and Peter left, and drove back to the house to wait for Lisa to come home from school. Pru was gone by then, still shaken by the search she'd seen conducted by the police the day before.

And as Peter and Bill walked into the house, Jack Nelson was sitting in his office with a devastated expression. He had lost a friend today, Bill and Lisa had almost lost their mother, and still might, and Maggie had lost her husband and didn't know it yet. It had been a hell of a day for them all. And unraveling how it had all happened had only just begun.

Chapter 15

After Bill and Peter left, two doctors came to see Maggie. They had come from Boston, were experienced toxicologists, and were satisfied with what was being done. The hospital administrator had asked them to come for a consultation, since this was such an unusual case. They'd never had anything like it in Ware.

The medical team that had been assigned to Maggie was working on her diligently. They were continuing to do blood tests, skin scrapings, X-rays, scans. Her fever had come down. And by later that night her breathing was better, but whenever she

woke, she couldn't imagine where Michael
was. He hadn't been there all afternoon,
and he wasn't answering her calls, which
was so unlike him. But after asking for him
weakly, she would go back to sleep every
time.

Later that night, a doctor from poison
control in Boston came in by helicopter and
explained to her that she'd been poisoned,
and at first Maggie didn't understand. She
was groggy, but she heard what she was
told, and asked several questions. How had
she been poisoned in the hospital? Had it
been an accident? How could this happen?
Did Michael know? She was told that it was
not an accident, but no one would give her
the details, and she was too weak to pur-
sue them.

They continued to force IV fluids through
her, and she heard two doctors discussing
dialysis if her kidneys showed signs of failing, which so far they hadn't. They gave her
oxygen to help her breathing. Her heart
was monitored closely, and their biggest
concern was her lungs. She was confused
and frightened by what they had told her,
and she felt sick from all the fluids, but her
color was already better than it had been

in several days. She lay in her bed exhausted that night, trying to absorb what had happened, but it was too overwhelming, and she finally went back to sleep.

After Bill and Peter left Maggie at the hospital, Peter pulled his truck into the driveway outside his brother's house. And he and Bill got out, as Peter looked up at the house bleakly. He was not looking forward to seeing Lisa. This was going to be one of the hardest nights of his life, and there were worse to come. Bill wasn't happy either. He and his sister hadn't gotten along in years. She always blamed him for fighting with their father and told him he was a bad son. He had had almost no contact with her in two years, only his mother.

Lisa was in her room when they entered. She walked out on the landing when she heard them come in. And she looked instantly shocked when she saw her brother. She suspected immediately that her mother was dying or already dead.

"Mom?" she said with a white face, looking from her brother to her uncle. Peter was quick to reassure her.

"She's okay, for now." She wasn't surprised not to see her father, since he would be at the hospital with her mother. She was only upset that she hadn't been able to reach him on his phone all afternoon. That had been the only unusual occurrence in her day.

"Then why are you here?" she asked her brother from the landing.

"Mom's pretty sick," he explained. "I thought I should come home." She nodded and came downstairs in jeans and bare feet. Her father had prepared her for a long time for this day. She knew it would be terrible, and had always known it, but in some ways she was ready. Particularly lately, her father had confided in her that her mother wasn't doing well. She was sad but not surprised or scared.

"How is she?" Lisa asked them both when she got downstairs. She had a platter of cold chicken ready for her father when he got home. She had cooked it while she did her homework. And there was homemade potato salad in a bowl.

"We're hoping she's going to get better now," Peter said quietly, as he sat down and motioned to her to sit. Bill was wandering around the room aimlessly, looking nervous. He had dreaded coming home, and now it felt as bad as he had feared. In fact, worse.

"I need to talk to you, Lisa. This isn't going to be easy, for any of us, but there are going to be stories in the paper tomorrow. Reporters may even come here," Peter said in a soothing tone.

"Why?" Lisa looked puzzled.

"Some bad things have happened, or at least we think so." He took a deep breath and jumped in. He had never expected to be delivering news like this to his brother's daughter when he came to live here, or uncovering a plot like the one his nephew had led him into. This didn't happen except in books. But it was all too real.

"What are you talking about? Why would reporters come here? Is someone trying to do something bad to Daddy?" In her eyes, her father could only be an innocent and a victim. He had formed her to believe only the best of him. The master manipulator at work.

"No. They're not trying to do something bad to your father." Peter proceeded with caution, trying to find the words that would mark his niece for the rest of her life. This was a moment none of them would ever

forget. Bill looked as though he were about
to crawl out of his skin. "Someone has been
poisoning your mother. We're not sure how
or why, but it's a very serious crime." She
looked instantly shocked when he said it.
He was certain they knew why and how,
but he didn't want to tell her yet. He had to
break this to her one step at a time. She
was only sixteen.

"Were they trying to kill her?" Lisa looked
shocked and panicked.

"We think so," Peter said, as he reached
out to her and touched her hand. He
wanted her to have some kind of human
contact before what he was about to tell
her next.

"Do they know who did it?" she asked,
still looking very worried, and Peter nodded. This was agony for him as well. The
last thing he wanted to do was hurt a child
her age, and she still was barely more than
a child, no matter how well her father had
trained her to stand in for her mother and
act like an adult.

"Your father has been arrested," Peter
said, measuring his words. "He's in jail.
There will be an investigation, and we'll
know more in the coming days. But right

now your father is the main suspect. He's the only one who's had that kind of access to your mother." Except Lisa, of course, which was absurd. She had no reason to poison her mother, and would have had no idea how to do it, with the sophisticated methods Michael had used. And psychologically, Michael had set the stage for the outcome.

"Daddy?" Lisa shrieked as she leaped off the couch and made a beeline for her brother, without waiting to hear more of what Peter said. "**You** did this, didn't you?" she accused him, pummeling her brother's chest with her fists and swinging wildly at his head. Bill grabbed her wrists easily and held her at arm's length. She was a small person like their mother, and Bill was a powerful young man, but there were tears in his eyes as he held her at bay.

"No, I didn't. Dad did. But I've suspected it for years." He was honest with her. He would have told her his suspicions long before, but she was still too young. He was six years older than she was, which made a big difference at their age. "He wants to kill her, Lisa, for Grampa's money."

"Daddy doesn't care about that money!"

Lisa screamed at him. "He told me so when Grampa died. He said it belongs to Mom, not him."

"Then he poisoned her for no reason, or he lied to you," Bill said miserably, still dodging his sister's fists as she tried to swing at him. She wanted to hurt him as badly as he was trying to hurt her father and her. "He's really sick."

"No, he isn't!" she bellowed. "You hate him. You always did. You're jealous of him because he's ten times the man you'll ever be. You're nothing!" she screamed at him. "And no one will ever believe you. Everyone in Ware knows that he's a saint, except you!" She spat the words at him as her brother shook his head.

"He tried to kill our mother. He's been doing it for years, convincing her she's sick, weakening her, and giving her pills. He keeps her drugged all the time, so she's too weak to get out of bed."

"She's sick!" Lisa screamed.

"No, she isn't. He wants her to think she is, and he wants us to believe it too, so when he kills her, everyone will believe she was dying for all these years." It was a clever plot, and it had almost worked, except for Bill.

"Daddy wasn't trying to kill her!" she continued to shout at him, and then out of breath and looking panicked, she turned to Peter. "We can't leave Daddy in jail. I want to see him."

"You can't right now," Peter said quietly, looking pained. "He has to be arraigned. He needs a lawyer. This is a very serious situation," Peter added ominously.

"The police won't believe it," Lisa said, looking frantic. "They'll let him go tomorrow. Chief Jack is his best friend!" It was all running through her head in a whirl, and for a minute Peter thought she might faint. The house of cards that was her life and the source of all her security and stability had just come tumbling down around her ears. She had a mother who had been dying for years, and still might do so at any moment, and the father she relied on for everything was in jail on suspicion of attempted murder. It was an overload of emotion and information for her.

"We'll have to see what happens in the investigation," Peter said somberly, but he could see where this was headed, given the toxicology reports.

"Can't we get him out of jail?" Lisa asked, sounding desperate.

"Not right now," Peter said reassuringly, as though there might be a chance of it later, which Peter didn't think there was, if all their suspicions proved to be true, and they appeared to be.

Lisa turned to her brother with a look of hatred then. "I'll never forgive you for this. You made this up to hurt Daddy." Bill just shook his head and looked away. He knew it wouldn't be possible to convince her of the truth. Even if their father was convicted and went to prison, she would always be convinced he was a saint. The entire town of Ware believed that too. It was hard to imagine a jury that would convict him in this town—the evidence would have to be indisputable, beyond any doubt.

"I know this is terrible news, Lisa," Peter said sympathetically. "It is for us too. It's going to be hard for all of us. Especially your mom."

"You used to hate him too," she accused him. "You didn't talk to him for fifteen years. You're just like him!" she said, pointing at her brother. "You both cooked this up to get rid of him. Maybe you want the money, because I know he didn't."

"This isn't about the money, Lisa," Peter said firmly. "This is about a crime that's been committed that almost killed your mother and still could." But her loyalty was to her father, not to the mother who had been an invalid all her life. Her father had seen to that too, and twisted the mind of an innocent child, making her revere him unreasonably. She was her father's adoring puppet, the little robot he had built to suit his needs and take her mother's place the moment she died. He had impaired her relationship with her mother, by treating Maggie as a nonperson, in order to strengthen his relationship with his daughter. It was frightening to think about. He had played with his own daughter's mind.

"My mother is going to die anyway. Daddy has kept her alive for years. She's lucky she lived this long because of him." They both knew there was no point in arguing with her. Her father's hooks were planted too deeply in her. The only voice in her head was his. She was going to take it hard if he went to prison, more so than she would have if her mother died. Michael had prepared her for that, but not for this.

Peter told her then that he and Bill were going to spend the night, so she wouldn't be alone, and she burst into tears.

"I don't want you here!" she screamed at both of them. "I want my father. I want you to get him out of jail." She leaped at Peter then and hit his chest too, and then she turned around and ran up the stairs and slammed the door to her room. Peter felt sick after what they'd just been through. And Bill looked no better as he let himself down on the couch with a beaten look.

"I knew it would be like this," he said to his uncle. "He did that to her. He's brain-washed her all her life. She doesn't care about anyone but him. She thinks he's innocent."

"So did I at first," Peter admitted. "I thought you were insane. She'll come around, especially once your mother comes home and starts getting better. Lisa will see the truth eventually." Peter was hopeful. She was a bright girl. And she had no other choice than to face the truth about her father.

"I don't think she will come around," Bill

said, looking discouraged. "She always hated me, because I called him a liar to his face. He lies about everything. He's just so good at it that he doesn't get caught at it very often, but sometimes he does. He twists everything around, and then he gets people to believe it." It was the portrait of a true sociopath, the kind of man who was sick enough to poison his wife and brainwash his own child for his benefit. And God only knew what he had done to the elderly people he took care of. That remained to be seen. Peter had doubts about that now too.

He felt like an intruder as he lay on the couch in his brother's house that night. He didn't want to sleep in Maggie and Michael's room. He went to the lake to pick up some clean clothes, and Bill's bag, and he was back an hour later, and stretched out on the couch. None of them had eaten dinner, and Lisa hadn't come out of her room. Peter had knocked on her door a couple of times to make sure she was okay, and he could hear her crying, and she told him to go away. He didn't want her to do something desperate, in honor of her father. And Bill had gone to bed in his old room, although even being there brought back a flood of bad memories for him. Having stopped his father wasn't entirely painless for him. Knowing he had a father who had done something so heinous had proven him right, but reminded him of the agonizing childhood he had had, at odds with his father, and always sensing that his mother was being abused in some way, and he and his sister too. Being lied to constantly had been painful for Bill.

The house was quiet that night, although none of them slept well. And Peter made breakfast for the three of them the next day. Lisa didn't say a word at the table as she played with her cereal and didn't eat it, avoided their eyes, and left for school. The paper had been on the porch that morning, and Michael's arrest had made the front page. Peter was worried about Lisa, but she said she wanted to go to school. She said no one would believe those lies about him anyway. She left for school then without saying goodbye.

Shortly after Lisa left, Pru Walker arrived to clean the house, and she looked stunned to see Bill and Peter sitting there. She had already been shocked by the police search two days before, and now this. And the minute she saw Bill, she was even more worried about Maggie.

"How is she?" she asked Peter in a hushed tone. He seemed to be in charge, and gave that impression as he sat at the breakfast table.

"About the same as yesterday. I'm going to see her in a little while. I hope she's better today." Pru hoped so too. She had read the newspapers and saw that Michael had been arrested for attempted murder. It had stunned her when she read it, and she didn't believe it. It had to be a lie. And she said as much when she put the dishes in the sink.

"Not a man like him," she muttered, and neither Peter nor Bill answered her. "It must be a mistake."

Bill went upstairs then. He had some e-mails to answer, and Peter got dressed to leave for the hospital. He had no idea what he'd discover there today, but at least Michael was no longer there. And Peter felt anxious as he walked into Maggie's room at the hospital half an hour later. He was pleased to find her sitting up in bed. She looked worn out, but she was awake. She seemed noticeably improved, although he knew from the doctor in charge of her case that she wasn't out of the woods yet. He wanted to tell her about Michael's arrest, but not before she was strong enough to hear it. The nurse left the room when Peter arrived, and told him to call her when he was ready to leave. The vigilance and tension around Maggie seemed to have relaxed a little, which Peter thought was a hopeful sign.

"Peter, what's happening?" Maggie asked plaintively with panic in her eyes. Everything they had told her about being poisoned was so confusing. She didn't understand. And Michael was nowhere to be found. It had been almost twenty-four hours since she'd seen or heard from him. And no one had given her the newspaper that morning, so she had no idea. Peter was relieved they hadn't. He was very much afraid that her reaction would be as vehement as Lisa's the night before.

Peter sat down in the chair the nurse had vacated next to Maggie, trying to decide where to begin. For the second time in two days, he knew he was going to break someone's heart, and tear their life apart. And he knew just from looking at Maggie in her weakened condition that it was too soon to tell her about Michael. She wasn't strong enough to hear it yet. One thing at a time.

"They found poison in your system, Maggie," he said with a look of sorrow in his eyes as he started. "They're doing everything they can to counter its effects." The doctors had told her that the night before, so it wasn't a surprise, although she didn't fully understand it. No one did just yet. "They don't know how long it's been there, or how it got there. Most likely, it was put in your food," he said solemnly. The doctor from poison control had explained to him that she had probably been given a drop or two regularly on an ongoing basis. More than that would have killed her immediately or within days. As Peter watched her, he saw that her hands were no longer shaking, and he realized that the symptoms of Parkinson's were less obvious now as she was slowly recovering from the poison.

And one thing was sure, this was no accident. Everyone agreed. Tests were being run now to see if she really had Parkinson's disease. The toxicologist felt it more likely that the symptoms had been caused by the poison, and not a disease.

Everything that was happening was frightening Maggie, understandably, and she was terrified by Michael's disappearance. She had been totally dependent on him for years.

"Where is Michael?" she asked insistently again, with wide eyes. She couldn't face this without him. "Is he handling all this?" And why hadn't he explained it to her? He was the only doctor she had total faith in. Peter looked away to avoid the questions in her eyes.

"He's not here," Peter said vaguely, and Maggie looked even more frightened as she laid her head back on the pillow. He was her protector and savior and had kept her alive for years. She had an even more alarming thought then.

"Was he poisoned too?" Maybe he was sick, or worse. Her eyes flew to Peter's, and he shook his head.

"The police are doing an investigation of how this happened" was all Peter said. He could see that she was already worn out by his visit.

The doctors had no idea how long it

would take to clear the poison from her system, after being poisoned over an exten-
sive period of time on a regular basis. But
they agreed with her son. This was not a
single event; nor had it occurred only recently. Her neurological symptoms suggested that it had gone on for a long time.
They had also asked her about what medications she took regularly, and she didn't
know. She had told them to ask Michael,
but that she knew that he gave her sleeping pills and tranquilizers for her nerves,
and several different pills, she had no idea
what they were. The paraquat and the
medications could have kept her bedridden
for years and in deteriorating health, and
already had. The records from her skating
accident were being brought out of the ar-
chives to be compared with the symptoms
she had now and had been experiencing
for years. Few of them were related to her
fall, or even the coma afterward, except for
her stiff leg, and headaches she had had
within the first year and never since.

"Where's Michael? Why isn't he here?"
she asked again, starting to cry then. She
wanted to know. And Peter knew he couldn't
avoid the subject forever.

He didn't want to tell her yet that Michael had been arrested. She was in no condition to hear that her husband had been trying to kill her, maybe for years. Like Bill, he no longer believed that Michael had only done this since she inherited the money from her father. He had been preparing for this for a long time, destroying her psychologically and physically so he could control her, just as Bill had said, perhaps intending to kill her once she inherited her father's money. This had been a long-term plan, Peter felt sure. He was a monster, just as Peter had known when they were young, and as his own son had discovered later. Peter had believed him to be a different person now. He wasn't. If anything, he was infinitely worse.

Maggie's breathing became more ragged, as she became agitated asking for Michael, and a nurse came in and put her oxygen mask back on, with a warning look at Peter. It was clear that they weren't going to be able to tell her about Michael's arrest today.

She dozed for a little while, and then Bill came in to see her while Peter was still there, sitting quietly in a chair.

Maggie opened her eyes a few minutes after Bill got there.

"Hi, Mom, I love you." He smiled gently at her.

"I love you too," she said, choking on a sob, and squeezed his hand. Her grip was stronger. "Have you seen your father?" She echoed her question to Peter. Bill shook his head.

"All you have to do is get better. Why don't you try and get some sleep now?" She closed her eyes, and Peter and Bill exchanged a look, and then Maggie opened her eyes again.

"I'm so worried about your father," Maggie said to her son, and then her eyes drifted to Peter. She could tell that they both knew something she didn't. "Is he hurt?" Maybe he'd been in an accident on the road. No one would tell her.

"You're going to get better now, Mom," Bill promised her. And if his father hadn't done too much damage, that would be true, better than she'd been in years. He had weakened her with bed rest, medications, and their side effects, and brainwashed her into believing she was sick and frail. The drugs alone that he had administered had weakened and confused her for years, along with the psychological games and fears he instilled in her about infection, accident, and germs that could kill her at any time, and comments about her "bad nerves." He had shut her away from the world so he could control her, and he had played mind games with his children, inflating Lisa's role to one of greater responsibility and importance than she should have had at her age, to diminish her mother further, and he had tried to control Bill and never succeeded. He wanted to break him and punish him for his clear vision of his father, and instead Michael had driven him away, which worked for him too, and tried to convince his mother that he was crazy. Maggie hadn't known what to believe, but looking into Bill's eyes now, she could see the strong, healthy man he was.

"Are you staying?" she asked hopefully.

"For a while." He had sent an e-mail to school that day saying that a family emergency had called him home for several weeks. He had requested that his assignments be sent to him electronically. It was the best he could do, but he was prepared to drop out for the semester if he had to. His mother was more important than anything else in his world, and he had no idea how long it would take now to restore her. No one did.

Maggie remained agitated whenever she talked to Bill and Peter about Michael, and finally she seemed to wear herself out and settle down. They both felt guilty for being dishonest with her, and their excuses for Michael's absence were thin. Peter finally told her Michael was home with Lisa, and Maggie accepted that with a peaceful look. She wasn't clear on how long it had been since she had seen him. They had claimed an emergency for him earlier that day—a patient who had had a stroke, and he needed to be with him. Maggie had accepted that as well. Peter had no idea when she would be strong enough for them to tell her that Michael was under investigation, in custody at the jail, and about to be arraigned on charges of attempted murder.

It was late afternoon when Bill and Peter were able to leave her. She had finally fallen into a deep sleep, holding her son's hand. They knew they had a hard night ahead of them with Lisa, and Jack Nelson had called to say that reporters were buzzing around the police station like flies, and were likely to turn up at the house.

The chief of police called Peter on his cell phone as they left the parking lot.

"I want to speak to you and your nephew tomorrow," he said sternly. He hadn't had a case that upset him this much in years. Michael was someone he would have trusted with his life. He was still hoping that it was some kind of mistake, maybe an accidental poisoning of some kind. Everyone in town knew how much Michael loved his wife. They had evidence of it for years. He had been totally dedicated to Maggie.

Twice in his career, Jack had dealt with crimes of passion. One of them had been a friend who found his wife in bed with someone else, and he had shot them both and then himself. It had been terrible, and Jack had been first on the crime scene. He had been a young policeman then and had answered the call when a neighbor heard the gunshots. Jack had cried afterward. But if this was true, it upset him even more, because he and Michael were so

close. This was attempted murder, premeditated, with malice aforethought, the
work of a dangerously sick mind. He was
praying for some other explanation, but
there was none so far.

Chapter 16

Jack Nelson stood outside Michael's cell at the police department before he turned the key and let himself in. They had a few holding cells in Ware, and Jack was keeping him there intentionally instead of transferring him to the house of corrections in Northampton. He'd have to move him there for the arraignment. But he kept him in Ware for a few days, so he could discuss the matter further with Michael. He wanted to do all he could to help him. This had to be some kind of terrible mistake.

Jack needed to talk to Michael without drawing attention to either of them. He had helped himself to the keys to Michael's cell during lunch. Michael was sitting on his bunk, looking unaffected, and smiled when he saw his old friend. Jack looked far more distressed than he did. Michael was astonishingly calm and undisturbed despite the depressing surroundings. The jail cells at the station were old and grim, and there was a toilet next to the bed.

"Thanks for the visit," he said to Jack, as though he had dropped by his office for a chat, which Jack often did when he drove by. And other times they met at the diner for lunch or dinner, on one of the rare occasions Michael went out for a meal. He usually stayed home with Maggie every night.

"This is pretty ridiculous, isn't it?" Michael said with a rueful smile, making room for Jack on the bunk.

"I hope so," Jack said, looking miserable. He seemed in considerably worse spirits than Michael. He had been awake all night, thinking about it, trying to find a rational explanation for the two reports. "Christ, I hope so," Jack answered. "What do you think happened? This is off the record," he reassured him, and then felt he owed him

a warning, "but if you did it, tell your lawyer, don't tell me."

"I don't have one. And I didn't do it. I don't
know what the hell happened. Maybe a
mistake at the lab. Some crazy chemical
circumstance that mimics something else.
Maggie's on a lot of medications. Sometimes things work together and make
strange composites and reactions. The
only thing I know for sure is that I didn't
poison her. I love her," Michael said innocently, as Jack patted his shoulder. He
hated what was happening, and wished he
could change it for him. Michael didn't deserve to be in jail. He was a great guy. He
had spent an entire life helping people, and
Jack just knew that Michael wouldn't try to
kill his wife. But he offered no explanation
for the weed killer they had found in his garden shed and the fact that his fingerprints
were on it. That was a tough one to explain
away. Jack looked deeply concerned. And
then Michael suddenly looked up, as if he
had a dark thought he hated even to put
words to. "Maybe my brother tried to frame
me. He's my brother, but he was rotten as
a kid. I thought he'd straightened up when
he came back here. Maybe he didn't.

Maybe that's why he showed up, to get even with me about my parents' wills and what they gave me. Or maybe he came back for Maggie." Michael looked sad and disappointed as he said it. "He's always been in love with her."

"Do you think she's in love with him?" Jack asked. A love triangle was certainly another motive. Peter had shown no sign that he was in love with Maggie when he had seen Jack the day before. But Jack assumed Peter was smart enough to conceal whatever he felt, and Michael looked dismayed as he made accusations about his brother.

"Maybe she's in love with Peter. I'm not a very exciting person," Michael smiled shyly, "and he's always been the handsome one. They had a fling in high school. Sometimes women go back to guys like that years later, to put a little excitement in their lives, and Maggie has a lot of time on her hands. She spends hours on the Internet, and I've been thinking. Maybe they've been e-mailing for a long time, and set this up. Maybe she broke up his marriage." He was implicating his wife and brother, but he looked like he sincerely believed it was possible and the idea upset him. "And Bill's always been just like my brother. The bad seed. I tried to fight it and straighten him out. I never could. Bill's been a liar all his life, just like Peter." Jack nodded. He knew that Michael had had trouble with his son for years, and was sad but relieved when he left, because he constantly upset the family, and he and Michael were eternally engaged in battle. He had said it to Jack many times.

"I hope we get enough evidence to clear you," Jack said sincerely. "I don't want you in here." He smiled sadly. "I want to send you home where you belong." He believed that Michael was the victim of a sinister plot, and Jack was determined to get to the truth. Maybe Michael's brother and son had conspired against him. He still believed Michael to be as much the victim here as Maggie. He was an innocent man. And Jack didn't want him to go to prison for a crime he didn't commit.

"You won't find the evidence to convict me. It just isn't there," Michael assured him. Jack was glad to hear it, and he believed him. He was sure Michael was telling the truth and that he couldn't understand what had happened any more than Jack could. Knowing Michael as he did, the two bottles of the poison and the toxicology report just made no sense.

"You know, I read up on that paraquat stuff on the Internet last night," Jack volunteered. "It said that it's used in underdeveloped countries for suicides, because it's cheap. Do you think Maggie might have been trying to do herself in?" Jack had thought of it the night before. She was a desperately sick woman, and led a miserable life as a shut-in. Maybe she was just tired of it, and wanted out. And maybe inadvertently, she was taking Michael down with her. And maybe Peter had taken advantage of her. Everyone knew he was broke. He needed Maggie's money far more than Michael. Jack had Googled him too.

"It's possible," Michael admitted reluctantly. "She's dying and she knows the Parkinson's will get her sooner or later. Maybe she wants to end her life, and she wouldn't say that to me, because she knows how hard I fight to extend it." And then, as though confiding a deep secret, "She's had psychiatric problems for years, ever since the accident. It's understandable, given her life and what she has to look forward to. I try not to think about it, but she's probably suicidal. She may have been poisoning herself without my knowledge." It sounded like a viable explanation to the chief of police and far more credible than Michael poisoning her, which was ridiculous and truly impossible to believe. But then why weren't her fingerprints on the two bottles of poison instead of his? Or maybe his brother had framed him. Jack was more than willing to believe that too. He was willing to believe anything, but not Michael trying to murder his wife. And he looked like an innocent man as he sat there, talking to his friend. Jack Nelson was proud that he had a nose for liars and criminals, and Michael McDowell wasn't either one. He was dead sure.

"You'd better get yourself a lawyer," he reminded Michael grimly.

"I don't even know who to call," Michael said glumly. He'd been thinking about it all morning. Jack gave him the names of lawyers in Northampton, Hadley, and Springfield, and Michael thanked him.

"Take it easy," Jack said, touching his

shoulder again. "We'll get you out of here, and get to the bottom of this yet. I promise." It was a mystery Jack just couldn't fathom.

"Thanks, Jack," Michael said gratefully as the chief of police let himself out of the cell. He lay down on his bunk after that and went to sleep. He was feeling reassured by the chief's visit. None of the police in the station believed he was guilty. They had been talking about it since the night before. He took care of them, their families, their parents. A guy like Dr. Mike didn't go around killing people, and surely not his sick wife. They all believed it was a mistake, or that he had been framed, and so did their chief. He was certain of it. Given the evidence, Jack had had to arrest him, but he was positive that Michael was innocent.

Peter and Bill went to the station that morning to be fingerprinted and to meet with Jack before they went to the hospital to see Maggie. They had agreed to do so to cooperate with the investigation. They were wiping their hands clean when the chief asked them to come into his office. He had just left Michael in his cell, and he questioned Peter and Bill about their relationships with Michael. Both readily admitted that they had been difficult, although Peter said that he and his brother had grown close in the past several months and had spent a considerable amount of time together.

"And did he ever give you the impression that he was unhappy with his wife, or tired of taking care of her?" the chief asked him pointedly, and Peter shook his head.

"No, he didn't. He always seemed very devoted to her, which is why I didn't believe this at first either. I thought my nephew was crazy." He smiled apologetically at Bill.

"Are you in love with her?" Jack asked Peter directly then in a stern voice.

"With Maggie?" Peter looked startled. "Of course not. She's Michael's wife. I love her like a sister, I always have."

"What's your own marital status right now?"

"I'm in the process of divorce," Peter said with a stony look, wondering if he was becoming a suspect. It sounded like the chief was trying to find a motive, but he didn't have one, except that he didn't have any money and had lost all of his, and Maggie had inherited ten million dollars two years before when she sold her father's mill, so maybe it did look to the police like he had a motive.

"How long have you and Maggie e-mailed each other?" the chief asked harshly. Peter looked startled. "We never have."

"Employed?" the chief asked him. He already knew the answer from what he'd read on Google, but he wanted to hear what Peter would say.

"Not at the moment. I'm looking for a job. My firm folded in the market crash last October." The chief nodded and didn't say more. And then Peter gingerly brought up another subject he wanted to bring to the chief's attention. He had discussed it with his nephew before they came in. "A man showed up at my house recently, sent there by Walt Peterson. He claimed that my brother had influenced his father into leaving him, Michael, all his money. He suggested that he might even have killed him, or euthanized him. I think it's worth looking into," Peter said politely, and Jack shot him an evil look.

"You really don't know your brother, do you? And don't tell me how to run my

investigation!" Jack said bluntly. "Your
brother takes care of most of the elderly
in the county. I don't think he's killing all of
them, or any of them. But thanks for the
tip," he said sourly, clearly annoyed by the
suggestion. Peter could see that he was
on Michael's side and believed him innocent. He had also implied that Peter might
be involved with Maggie, but he wouldn't
poison her if that was the case. But he obviously thought Peter might frame Michael
to get him out of the way. It was a Machiavellian idea, and Peter wondered if Michael
had suggested it to him. It sounded like
pure Michael to him.

The chief ended the interview a few minutes later, and Peter and Bill talked about
it on the way to see Maggie.

"It sounds like he's trying to pin it on me,"
Peter said, understandably upset.

"Or me," Bill added, as he looked at the
paper. The story of Michael's arrest was all
over the front page, and it didn't sound like
the reporter believed it either. Michael was
a hero in three counties. All the article
talked about was his good deeds and ac-
complishments, and the alleged poisoning
of his wife got a lot less attention. It said

the matter was under investigation, and Michael was being held for arraignment in a few days. It said that Maggie had been poisoned and Michael was the prime suspect. The nature of the evidence had not been disclosed. And the article said that the possibility of other suspects had not been ruled out. It made a tremor run down Peter's spine.

"I'm going to be pissed if I wind up in prison because of you," Peter said to his nephew with a nervous laugh, and Bill shook his head.

"That sounds like my father's work. He'll get us both hanged if he can."

"They'll have to have hard evidence for that, and they don't. We didn't poison her. He did," Peter said simply. "We have truth on our side."

The chief of police was Michael's best friend, and he wasn't doing either of them any favors. It was obvious that he would have liked to attribute the crime to them, and not Michael, if there was any way to do it. And he clearly hadn't liked hearing Peter's implications about his brother's elderly patients. He had looked outraged by the suggestion, but legitimately he couldn't ignore anything, and he was an honest man. He had to add up the evidence they had and follow procedures. For now, Michael was his prime suspect, with his fingerprints on the two bottles of poison from the shed. He wouldn't falsify an investigation, even for a friend. But it was clear to him that Michael McDowell was an innocent man. He'd been framed, and falsely accused. He was sure the truth would come out soon, and he was going to do all he could to make it happen. It was the least he owed Michael, his old friend. He had had an obligation to arrest him, given the evidence, but he did not believe him guilty.

Peter and Bill decided to go to the diner on the way to see Maggie, and the place was buzzing with the news, and everyone had another angle, explanation, or theory. But almost no one believed Michael did it. And Vi commented as she poured their coffee. She was a brutally honest woman.

"I never liked your brother. You were a little pain in the ass, always getting into fights, and trouble. But you were a sweet kid underneath that. Your brother was different. He always reminded me of that kid on **Leave It to Beaver,** Eddie Haskell. He was always polite, but it never felt real. I see your brother in here all the time, usually with Jack Nelson. But when I read that about him in the paper today, I wasn't surprised. I know everyone else loves him, but he never struck me as an honest guy." Peter looked at her in amazement. He didn't know a single other person in town who would say something like that about Michael. Vi had Michael's number and always had, even now, with the astonishing discovery that he'd been poisoning Maggie.

On the way to the hospital, Peter told Bill he wanted to tell Maggie what was happening. It seemed entirely wrong that she was the only person in town who didn't know Michael was in jail, and worse yet, for attempting to kill her. But she had been too sick for them to say anything to her yet.

But when they walked into the hospital late that morning, Maggie looked considerably better. The doctors had run blood tests on her again that morning, and the nurse said the toxic levels were coming down. Her breathing had improved, although they were still monitoring her closely, but her eyes looked brighter, and she looked happy to see Peter and her son. The one thing she couldn't understand and kept asking them was where Michael was. He had never disappeared this way before, she couldn't reach him on his phone, and everyone's excuses for his absence sounded like lies to her. She asked Peter and Bill about it again the moment they walked in. And this time Peter could see that she expected a real answer, and she looked ready to hear it. She had been waiting anxiously for them for hours.

They both knew they had a hard task ahead of them, just as they had with Lisa. Peter was well aware that this was going to be even worse. But now that she was more alert, they had to tell her, just as they had agreed on the way to the hospital. They couldn't lie to her forever. The story of Michael's arrest was all over town. The whole hospital was talking about it too, but not in Maggie's room. Most people believed in his innocence, and that he would be cleared soon. People were saying that charges like that just wouldn't stick, not against a man like him. Only his brother and son believed different. And possibly Vi at the diner.

"Tell me the truth, Peter," she begged.

"Did Michael have an accident?" she asked him with worried eyes. Something was wrong, and she knew it, and she knew she'd been poisoned, and had no idea by whom. She assumed it was accidentally, and wanted Michael to explain to her how it had happened. He was the only one she trusted. She had worried all night that he might be dead and they didn't have the heart to tell her. She wanted the truth. Not knowing was worse.

"No, he didn't," Peter said, and looked like he was telling the truth. Maggie seemed less tense after he said it.

"He's not answering his phone." Nor was Lisa. Peter and Bill had insisted she not tell her mother yet. She wasn't strong enough to know. So Lisa texted her, but hadn't told. Maggie studied Peter with a worried expression, as he approached her bed and took her hand in his own, and her son stood at the foot of it, watching her. They were about to tell her some very tough stuff, and Peter had no idea how she would take it, or how it would impact her health. It was an awesome responsibility delivering such bad news to a woman who was so ill.

"You know you were poisoned, Maggie," Peter said slowly, and Maggie nodded.

"I know that." She wasn't out of danger yet, particularly with her breathing, but she felt stronger and she looked it. "I want to talk to Michael about it. I don't understand how it happened. Was it some kind of mistake in my medications? An error at a pharmaceutical company who made them?" She had gone over all the reasonable explanations in her head. And when she got home to her computer, she wanted to do some research on it herself.

"It wasn't a mistake, or at least that's not likely. You were poisoned with an extremely toxic, lethal weed killer, probably in your food. It was intentional, Maggie, not an accident." They had talked about it the day before, but she was clearer-headed now.

"That's not possible. Who would do that?" She looked shocked and frightened.

"We don't know yet. But not a lot of people have access to you, and given the symptoms you've manifested for several years, it looks like someone has been doing it for a long time." Peter spoke in a low quiet voice, carefully choosing his words.

"What did Michael say about all this?" she asked. It made no sense to her. She didn't want it to. And Peter could see that she was still in denial. He had been at first too. It was the kind of thing you just didn't want to believe.

"Michael's in jail, Maggie," Peter said softly. He didn't want to hide it from her anymore. "On suspicion of poisoning you and trying to kill you." They were terrible words, and they hit her like bullets. She sat straight up in bed and stared at Peter.

"Are you serious?"

He nodded in answer. "We got the toxicology report back that you were being poisoned. And Michael had access and motive. He's in jail pending further investigation. But with the evidence they have, they're going to charge him with it in a few days. He has a lot of explaining to do if he didn't do it. They searched the house a few days ago. They took a lot of stuff out but they didn't tell us what it was. Pru says it was mostly prescription medications and some things from the garden shed." Maggie looked speechless for a moment, and then thought instantly of her daughter. "Oh my God, how's Lisa?" She was suddenly panicked for her and the effect this would have on her.

"About the way you'd expect her to be. She worships her father. She blames me and Bill for all this, and she's convinced he didn't do it." Bill nodded in agreement. Peter had said everything pretty much the way it was.

"So am I," Maggie said loyally, lying back against her pillows. "Can I call him?" Peter shook his head. And he understood her reaction. This was enormous for all of them to accept, and especially for her to learn that the man she had trusted for twenty-three years, and loved presumably, might have been trying to kill her, and could easily have succeeded in the near future. He almost had this time.

"You were dying, Maggie," Peter spelled it out for her. "Someone was doing it to you. It wasn't an accident." Tears slid down her cheeks as she listened. She didn't want to hear it.

"That can't be. Michael wouldn't do a thing like that." She was sure of it, but she could see in Peter and Bill's eyes that they believed it, which was horrifying to her.

"People do strange things sometimes,"

Peter said philosophically. "I used to think he was dangerous. He convinced me otherwise since I came back here. Maybe I was right in the beginning. We'll have to see what the evidence looks like, but it's not looking good for him at the moment. He's the only one who could have done it. It was a pretty sophisticated substance to use, and well thought out, and carefully dosed, or it would have killed you a long time ago. Your doctors say you don't have Parkinson's. The disease was mimicked by the effects of the poison." And Michael had insisted she had the disease. She fell silent as she lay in bed, with her face turned away, as tears rolled down her cheeks. It was the worst moment of her life, and Peter's heart ached for her. He wanted to put his arms around her but didn't dare. Things were complicated enough as they were. And with the chief's inferences that morning that he might be in love with her, he didn't want to give the wrong impression now. He loved her as family and friend, but they hadn't been having an affair. Neither of them was that kind of person, and Peter was still hurting after Alana and the pain of the divorce.

"What does Michael say?" she asked,

turning back to Peter with a look of terror, her voice barely audible.

"That he's innocent. But the paraquat in your system says he isn't. Or someone isn't," Peter said, looking grim. And no one else had access to her, except Lisa, which was unthinkable. There really was no one except Michael who could have done it, or would have wanted to, and they all knew it. And he would have known how to dose it. Michael had the opportunity, the skills, and the motive, if Bill's theory about his grandfather's money was correct. Peter didn't mention her inheritance out of respect for her, but it could have been a major motivating factor. Ten million dollars was a lot of money, and Michael must have wanted it very badly, no matter how modest he appeared. Maybe he wanted it enough to kill her for it. Stranger things had happened. The news was full of things like that all the time.

"I just can't believe he did it," Maggie said, deathly pale again and shaken to her core. But despite her allegedly "bad nerves," according to Michael, she was handling the terrible news he'd given her with grace and reason, as she handled everything else.

But she looked desperately upset and hurt. She wasn't sure what to believe, faced with the news, and no word from him.

The rumors at the police station were not encouraging for Michael. Aside from the evidence they'd gotten from his garden shed, with his prints all over it, and the lab reports about Maggie, the chief had gotten a call from the family of an elderly patient Michael had recently taken care of, and who had left him some money. The family was suddenly convinced that he had killed their father, after reading the account in the paper of his poisoning Maggie. And they wanted their father exhumed and examined. There were three calls like it the next day, from families who had been suspicious of him. And in each case, Michael had inherited money from the deceased. The cases were too reminiscent of what Peter had mentioned to the chief, and Jack Nelson couldn't ignore them. Dreading what was happening and what might come next, he filed for permission to exhume. By then, he had to transfer Michael to the detention house in Northampton for the arraignment. Michael had contacted an attorney, one of the ones Jack had recommended, and he had agreed to take the case. Michael pleaded not guilty to attempted murder in the first degree, and he was bound over for trial, for the poisoning of his wife, and the local papers reported it again. He was held without bail.

Michael's fingerprints on the two bottles of paraquat from their garden shed, and the fact that no one had had access to Maggie and her food except him and their sixteen-year-old daughter, were both very damning. And Pru Walker had no reason or motive to poison her. And Maggie's remarkable recovery over the next week, when she was not being poisoned, was additional evidence. She looked and felt better than she had in years. A police detective had come to the hospital to ask her who prepared her meals every day. She said that her daughter usually made dinner, her husband made lunch for her when he had time to do it, or Prudence Walker, if no one else did. The detective asked a few other questions about her medications, and then he left.

And Michael still hadn't called Maggie, which she couldn't understand. Suddenly,

the man who had been a constant presence and never left her side for twenty-
three years had disappeared. She knew
where he was, but he wasn't calling her, although he had the right to one call a day.
And she couldn't call him. She had had no
word from him since his arrest, and she
didn't know what to think, and didn't want
to believe the worst. She wanted a better
explanation, and only Michael could give it
to her, but he didn't. He was silent.

Not hearing from Michael was almost as
upsetting to her as the charges against him
and the fact that he was in jail. After living
with him, day and night, relying on him in
every way, trusting him completely, he had
literally vanished out of her life, and was
being accused of trying to murder her. She
still didn't believe he had done it, and she
wondered if he was too ashamed to call her
from jail. This had been a terrible blow to
him too, and she felt deeply sorry for him.
She wasn't angry, because she still didn't
believe it.

And within a week, Jack Nelson had nine
geriatric corpses waiting to be exhumed
and examined. It was turning into a very
ugly case, and Jack didn't know what to

think. Michael still said he was innocent and looked it, but it had become impossible to pin it on either Peter or Bill. All the evidence pointed to Michael, more so every day. Jack just hoped that the people they were about to exhume had died of natural causes. And Maggie did too when she heard about it. She didn't want Michael to go to prison, nor did his daughter.

Lisa begged her mother to take her to see her father as soon as she came home from the hospital, but Maggie wasn't up to it yet, and she didn't think it would be good for Lisa. Maggie felt that visiting him in jail would be too traumatic for her. And Maggie wanted to see him too, but since she had heard nothing from him, she didn't want to embarrass him by visiting him in jail. She had written him two letters, full of love and support and her faith in his innocence, and he hadn't answered. She wondered if they withheld his letters at the jail. Michael had not contacted Maggie from the day he was arrested.

One afternoon after visiting Maggie at the house, Peter decided to stop in at the county clerk's office on Main Street. Just out of curiosity, he wanted to do some of the research in Michael's case himself. He wasn't sure if what he was looking for would show up. He wanted to see if there would be a record of all the wills Michael had been named in, where he had inherited money from patients. Peter wondered just how many there were.

And as he walked into the county clerk's office, he had a surprise. The clerk was the older brother of a boy he'd gone to school with, and he smiled as soon as Peter walked in. They chatted for a few minutes, and Peter was sorry to hear that the man he had gone to school with had died in an accident several years before. Bob, the county clerk, then offered his sympathy for the difficulties Michael was in. He had been as stunned as everyone else.

And with that, Peter explained what he was searching for. He was wondering how many people Michael had inherited money from over the years. It might establish some kind of pattern that would confirm his guilt with his elderly patients, or even uncover new ones.

"We wouldn't have a record here of cash bequests he inherited," Bob explained, "only if he inherited land or property, like a house. But I can certainly take a look and see what I find. And if you talk to the bank manager, he may remember some of the bequests Michael got from his patients. If you want, I'll call him. He's my wife's uncle." Peter smiled at the convenient incestuousness of a small town. He was taking full advantage of it.

But he wasn't prepared for the answer he got from Bob a few days later. As it turned out, the deeds to four houses had been left to Michael over the years, which was considerable, and he had sold them all. They were small and not of immense value. And Bob's wife's uncle at the bank remembered distinctly several bequests Michael had gotten, some larger, some smaller, but in his estimation, over the years, Michael had inherited between two and three hundred thousand dollars from elderly patients. It was a considerable sum of money, particularly added to the proceeds from the houses he got too, and it was certainly not proof of murder, but it was an area that merited looking into.

Bob promised him an informal written

summary, which Peter wanted to give Jack Nelson for the police investigation. Peter couldn't help wondering how many of his geriatric patients Michael had killed, but it was clear to him now why he had done it. It was about money. Michael's son Bill was right, his father had been trying to amass a fortune of ill-gotten gains. He had no idea what Michael was planning to do with it, but he had quite a lot of money put aside, and if he had succeeded in killing Maggie, he would have had a great deal more. But it really was all about greed and money, which seemed unlike Michael. Bob promised to do a full report on whatever he found and give a copy to Jack Nelson. But it was clear to Peter that Michael had been a stranger to them all. Peter was trying to absorb it and figure out just who Michael had been, and Bill was too, but Peter was shocked to realize that even after Maggie was out of the hospital, she was still in the grips of powerful denial about her husband and her marriage. Maggie just couldn't accept that Michael had tried to kill her. She refused to believe it. It was shocking for all of them, and Maggie just denied it and found a thousand implausible excuses to explain what had happened. She could not accept the truth.

And Lisa was not much better. She was still not speaking to her uncle or brother. She insisted that they had framed her father. And when Maggie wouldn't take her to see her father in jail, Lisa took the matter into her own hands.

She got a bus to Northampton one day after school, after checking on visiting days and hours. She left her mother a message that she was doing homework with a friend, and Maggie believed her. She was deeply worried about her, and worried about the trauma to her. And Maggie had wanted to be present for her. She had begun walking with her walker, and almost didn't need it now for support. Her left leg still dragged a little, as it always had, but she felt steady on her feet now, and had regained her balance, which had been shaky for years. She was working with a physical therapist to strengthen her legs. She no longer took sleeping pills at night, tranquilizers for her nerves, or any of the mystery pills that Michael had fed her for years, assuring her that she needed them and she needed to entrust him with her care and treatment. But with each passing day that she felt stronger, she became more anxious about Michael. Without the medicines he had given her, she felt like a new person, or the old one she had been before they married. There was no remnant of her old head injury, only the stiff leg, which she could live with, and her limp was even less pronounced than it had been, thanks to the exercises she was doing, and she no longer felt so unsteady. And once she was ready, she had Bill put her wheelchair and her walker in the garage. She walked everywhere on her own two feet now. But she continued to insist that none of her improvement had anything to do with what Michael had been doing to her. She couldn't bear knowing that the accusations were true about him, even though both her better health and his silence said it all.

When Lisa went to see her father in jail, she showed her student ID card, wrote her name on a list, and sat in a waiting room full of scary-looking people. It was raucous and rowdy. Women with no teeth and men with tattoos were shouting obscenities at each other in a crowded waiting room that smelled bad with overflowing garbage cans, and she was shaking when they called her name. She was led into a cubicle, and for the first time in weeks she found herself face-to-face with her father. He was wearing dark blue pajamas that looked like a surgical suit. He was clean-shaven, looked immaculate, and his hair was perfectly combed. He could have been sitting in his office. They were separated by a thick wall of glass, and they had to communicate via a phone on either side of the glass. And the moment Lisa saw him and sat down, tears exploded from her eyes, and she choked on a sob. Michael smiled at her immediately, and the kindness and love in his eyes overwhelmed her. He pointed to the phone, and she picked it up, still crying as she looked adoringly at her father.

"Don't cry, baby," he said soothingly, "everything's going to be fine. This will all be cleared up soon, and I'll be out of here in no time." He looked totally convincing and unworried, and Lisa gazed into his eyes and found everything she had always loved there.

"This is all nonsense," he continued. "I'm sure it won't even go to trial. How's Mom?"

His eyes clouded a little when he asked her, and she wasn't sure why.

"She's okay. She looks good. She says you haven't answered her letters. We miss you."

"I've been busy," he said with a broad smile that reminded her of better times. When she looked at him, it was as though they weren't in a jail. She could imagine herself sitting across from him in the kitchen, he looked that normal, which was a relief to Lisa. Being here at the jail was scary, with all the other visitors, who looked as bad as the people in jail, or worse. Her father certainly didn't belong here. You could see that instantly. "I've been meeting with my lawyer to get this whole thing taken care of. It should get dismissed," he said with an easy smile, to reassure his daughter. "I didn't poison your mother, Lisa. You know that."

"I know, Daddy. The stuff in the newspapers is awful. It's about some of your patients too."

"Don't read it. It's not true," he said, and she nodded. "I think this is something your uncle Peter cooked up to get rid of me and go after your mother and get his hands on your grandfather's money now that he's lost his own. It's a vicious thing to do. And very sick. He always was a bad apple, even when he was a kid. My parents knew it too. That's why he hates me. This is his vengeance against me."

"I know. I hate him," she said fervently, and she hated her brother too. They both believed her father guilty. But at least her mother still believed in his innocence.

"Has he been around a lot?" Michael asked her casually.

"Yeah. Kind of. He checks on us. Bill is home," she volunteered, and something flitted across her father's eyes again. She could see he didn't like that.

"He belongs in a psychiatric hospital, but your mother would never let me put him in one. I only agreed to let him go to London to get him away from you. I didn't want him to hurt you."

"Do you think he would?" Lisa looked surprised. Even from jail, he was manipulating all of them, and pitting them against each other, and he had abandoned Maggie completely after trying to kill her. But he still had Lisa's total loyalty and faith in him. And he intended to keep it that way, whatever it took. She was his, just as Maggie had once been, but now she had betrayed him. She no longer needed him. She was free, and would testify against him. But above all, she no longer trusted him blindly. He knew that Lisa would never do that to him. She would belong to him forever, she was his flesh and blood. He wasn't even sure Bill was his, he looked too much like his uncle, although Maggie had always denied it.

"I think your brother is capable of anything." He planted the seed of terror in her, and dissent. Divide and conquer had always been his style, just as it had been in his youth. "And so is your uncle. Be careful of them, Lisa, don't trust them. Or even your mother. She means well, but she's a deeply disturbed woman, with serious psychiatric problems. That's where Bill got them. You're the only healthy one in the bunch."

"And you, Daddy," she said devotedly. Anyone hearing their conversation would have retched. And her brother and uncle would have wanted to kill him for what he

was doing. Now, using only his mind and
his words, he was poisoning her, just as he
had her mother. He had to control her, and
make her his puppet, even from jail.

"Just don't worry, baby. I'll be out of here
soon. Will you come to see me again?" She
nodded as tears sprang to her eyes. "Don't
tell Mommy. She'll worry about you." Lisa
nodded and knew it was true.

"I'll come back soon. I promise." A buzzer
sounded then and the phone went dead
in their hands. The visit was over. They
mouthed "I love you" to each other, and
Lisa stood up to leave. A door opened then
behind her father, and a sheriff's deputy
escorted him from the cubicle as he waved
at her, and Lisa left the jail. Her heart was
singing. She had seen her father.

She took a bus back to Ware then, and
went straight to her room when she got
home. She didn't tell her mother she had
seen him, and that night, when her mother,
brother, and uncle had dinner in the kitchen,
she refused to come downstairs. Maggie
was having dinner in the kitchen every night
now, and she had started cooking again.
She was taking her rightful place that she
had been robbed of for years. It made Lisa

feel as though there was no room for her now, but she didn't care. She had seen her father, and she believed him. Everything was going to be fine, because he said so. And she was totally convinced that he never lied to her.

Chapter 17

Jack Nelson sat looking at the autopsy reports on his desk in despair. Nine bodies
had been exhumed. Each of them had a
puncture mark on their upper buttocks that
no one had seen before they were buried.
Michael had examined each of them when
they died—they were his patients, and
he had signed the death certificates. The
cause of death was listed as heart attack
in all nine cases. And the coroner said that
the puncture wound with a tiny needle was
consistent with succinylcholine, a muscle-
relaxing drug used to paralyze the respiratory muscles either in surgery or to insert

a breathing tube. Only a competent anesthesiologist would know how to dose it, and
Michael had been one in the early days of
his career, before he joined his father in his
practice in Ware. In overdoses of the drug,
death results as the patient suffocates, but
the cause of death presents as a heart attack. The drug was virtually untraceable,
while the patient was alive, but the telltale
giveaway was the injection site, which each
of these bodies had in precisely the same
location. And the drug the coroner tested
for was present in the tissue of all nine victims. The evidence was conclusive, much
to Jack Nelson's horror.

It was impossible to know now if Michael
had euthanized them at their request, or
had simply killed them. But every single
one of them had left him money, in most
cases everything they had. There was no
way he could spare Michael now. The tide
had turned irrevocably. No matter how innocent he seemed, or how much Jack had
liked him, it was beginning to appear that
he had committed wholesale murder in the
geriatric community. And his poisoning of
his wife had been even more vicious. She
was a young woman, and he had made her

an invalid, destroyed her life, and nearly killed her. Jack had begun to think that he had a sociopath on his hands. The evidence was overwhelming.

Michael was arraigned again, this time on nine counts of murder. It would be a tough rap to beat, along with the attempted murder charges relating to Maggie. Jack felt sick about it, and he couldn't look his friend in the eye at the arraignment. Michael appeared totally calm and undisturbed, and pleaded not guilty to all charges.

Jack was sitting in his office feeling depressed, when his lieutenant told him that Peter McDowell wanted to see him, and escorted him in a minute later.

Jack sighed deeply at his desk. "It looks like I owe you an apology," he said unhappily. "I think there's a side to your brother I never knew." But sociopaths were deceitful and insidious, as he was well aware. He had never suspected Michael was one. They committed horrendous crimes without batting an eye, showing no guilt or any kind of remorse later. In some ways, they were subhuman, robots of some kind, humans gone awry.

"I always knew that," Peter said quietly.

"Thank you. It's a hard time for Maggie and Lisa." Jack Nelson nodded, sorry for both of them.

"Lisa's been visiting her father at the jail twice a week," Jack said sadly. "Does her mother know?"

"I don't think so. I'll tell her. I don't think that's a great place for her to be, and God knows what her father is telling her." Jack only nodded. He agreed. He didn't think it was a good idea, she was an innocent young girl, and Michael had proven himself to be a dangerous man, psychologically as well as physically.

"What brings you here today?" Jack said with another sigh, and Peter matched it. It had taken him weeks to reach the decision. And now he believed his mother's journals, and not Michael's explanation of them. Nothing Michael said was true.

"I want my parents exhumed," Peter said unhappily. "I think he killed them." It seemed more than likely now. And they had found vials of the incriminating succinylcholine in Michael's office. He had felt so secure that he had hidden nothing, neither the drug he used to kill his geriatric patients, nor the paraquat he had used to poison Maggie.

The evidence against him was overwhelming. And even Maggie was no longer claiming his innocence. She was having a hard time admitting to herself that the man she thought she had been married to had never existed. But she could no longer deny it. She knew that now.

"Half the town wants their parents exhumed," Jack said as he slid the forms across the desk. There was no reason to refuse, it was a reasonable request, and it was potential evidence against a man who was accused of nine murders, and an attempted one. Peter filled out the forms and slid them back across the desk, and then he left Jack's office. They had never been friends when they went to school. Jack's lifelong friendship with Michael had precluded it. And Peter felt sorry for him now. He had been duped like everyone else. Even Peter had been fooled in the last few months, although he knew better. Michael was a master of deceit and manipulation.

After he saw Jack, Peter stopped in to see Maggie and told her what the police chief had told him, that Lisa had been visiting her father in jail. Maggie looked upset about it, especially that she hadn't told her. It made her feel strange too that Lisa had been seeing Michael but she herself had heard nothing from him, and hadn't seen him in the weeks since he'd been arrested.

She confronted her daughter about it when she got home, not in a hostile way, but she asked her if she'd been visiting her father. Lisa immediately exploded—her secret had been exposed.

"Yes, of course I have!" she shouted at her mother. "Do you think I'd let him sit there all alone? How could you do that? You haven't been to see him once!" She was entirely overlooking the fact that her father was accused of trying to murder her mother, and he had made no contact with her since his arrest. It was awkward for Maggie, and she had waited for him to reassure her, and convince her of his innocence. He hadn't. He had disappeared in silence and answered none of her letters. Nor had he called her. It was as though she had never existed in his life. It was a frightening feeling for Maggie. She didn't even know now who she had married, or even worse, who he had become. The man she had loved had disappeared.

"I don't think he wants to see me," Maggie said, looking pained.

"Of course not," Lisa explained for him. She knew that she understood her father better than anyone else. He said so. "He's accused of poisoning you and trying to kill you. Why should he want to see you? He's in jail because of you." Lisa was venomous as she said it, and Maggie looked stunned by her words.

"This is my fault? What about the old people he supposedly killed? Is that their fault too?" Maggie realized now that Michael was twisting Lisa's mind, he was using every opportunity to brainwash her, just as he had Maggie. But she was not going to let that happen to her daughter. "I don't want you seeing him at the jail anymore," Maggie said firmly. "You're too young to go to a place like that. Someone could hurt you." She didn't want to say that her father was doing her more damage than any of the criminals she might be meeting, but it was obvious to Maggie what Michael was doing to their daughter, manipulating her. He was an incredibly evil man, and it was impossible to believe in his innocence anymore.

"You can't stop me!" Lisa shouted at her, then ran upstairs into her room and slammed the door.

Maggie talked to Bill about it that night over dinner in the kitchen. Lisa never ate with them anymore. She helped herself to what she wanted out of the fridge and took it up to her room to eat alone. She was isolating herself, just as her father wanted her to do, filling her with distrust for her mother and brother and convincing her that they were deeply disturbed, when in fact he was. It was all a mind game, and Lisa was his victim, just as Maggie had been, and Bill, and Peter. It was the only relationship you could have with him, or any sociopath— that of victim.

"I don't think she should see your father in jail," Maggie said to Bill in a whisper, and he agreed with her totally, as had Peter when he told her about Lisa visiting her father. Even the police chief didn't seem to think it was a good idea. Michael had revealed himself to be a highly toxic, dangerous person, to say the least. He had murdered multiple people, tried to kill his wife, and was toying with his own child's mind.

"I have to go back to school soon," Bill said pensively. "Why don't the two of you come with me? I only have a month left of the term before summer vacation. Maybe we could go somewhere in Europe. It would be good to get Lisa away, and then she can't see him. She can go to school in London in the fall. It might be better for her."

"I'm not sure she'll think so," Maggie said, looking worried. She herself hadn't traveled in years. She would have loved to, but Michael had told her she wasn't healthy enough and it was too risky. Now the whole world had opened up to her, and when she thought about it that night, she liked the idea. They all needed a change of scenery, to get away from the awful stories about Michael in the paper. It hung over them like a storm cloud. And they had been told that Michael wouldn't go to trial until December or January while the D.A. and his lawyer prepared the case. Getting out of Ware sounded like a wonderful idea to Maggie. All she had to do now was sell it to Lisa, or maybe she just had to tell her they were going. She was removing her for her own good, whether she liked it or not, as far from her father as they could get.

She told Bill about it in the morning. He was planning to leave the following week to finish classes and exams before the end of the semester. And he had six weeks off over the summer. Maggie was thinking she could rent a house somewhere, in Italy or the South of France.

She called Peter and talked to him about it, and he liked the idea for her too. He couldn't think of anything worse than her continuing to live in the house where she'd been an invalid for twenty years, and lived with a man who had tried to kill her, little by little, every day. He endorsed the plan immediately.

"What can I do to help?" He was always kind to her, and he had very little to do now. Their whole life had been taken up by the investigation and their discoveries about Michael for the past month. Peter was also acutely aware that his sons were arriving soon, and he was no longer sure if he wanted them there, in a town where his brother was the local scandal and was all over the papers every day. It worried him, and no matter how nice the lake was, he didn't think it would be good for the boys to be the object of scrutiny and whispers.

He had been trying to figure out somewhere else for them to go. But he thought
it was important now for Maggie to get out
of town, and even more so for Lisa to get
away from her father, whether she wanted
to or not.

"All I have to do is pack," Maggie said
practically. "I don't have to be here till the
trial, whenever that is. And I like Bill's idea
to put Lisa in school in London in the fall. I
can figure it out when we get there." If she
wanted to leave with Bill, she had a week
to get ready, and she thought she could do
it. She e-mailed Claridge's, where her parents used to stay, and made reservations
for her and Lisa. She had gone there with
them several times when she was in college. Bill had his own studio apartment.
And they would be together. Suddenly, the
world was opening up. Maggie thought
about seeing Michael before she left, and
then decided against it. His silence said it
all. And she knew he was guilty. She no
longer had any doubt. And the way he was
manipulating their daughter confirmed it,
and how desperate he was.

Predictably, Lisa went berserk when her
mother told her they were going to London

with Bill. And Lisa was adamant that she didn't want to spend the summer in Europe, much less go to school there.

"We can't stay here," Maggie said sadly. "We're going to be besieged by the press. Every time there's a new story about your father, they'll be all over us."

"I'm not going to abandon him," Lisa shouted at her mother, and finally Maggie lost her temper, which was something she rarely did, especially with her children, or even Michael.

"He abandoned us! He tried to kill me!" she said with such force that it frightened Lisa.

"No, he didn't!" Lisa shouted back in tears. She was fighting for denial, and her mother knew it would be agony for her when she finally let it go, and she wasn't ready to do that. Michael had pulled her in too close, and for too long. But her mother was determined to free her. Her psychological well-being and survival depended on it, if she was to recover from her father's emotional abuse and influence. He was a criminal to his soul, and a destroyer of people, not just with poisons but with his very, very sick, twisted mind.

"Lisa, at some point you have to face this," her mother said gently. "I loved your father too. But he's guilty of terrible crimes. We need to get away to get some perspective, and it will be good for us to be together in London."

"I won't go," she said, looking like a petulant five-year-old as she crossed her arms.

"You have no choice," her mother said clearly. "This is what we're doing." And as she said it, she realized that there was more to it for Lisa. She had not only lost her father, but she had lost her "job," her "position" as his almost-wife, that he had created for her in order to shut Maggie out and make her feel useless. Now it was Lisa who felt she had no role. She had forgotten how to be a sixteen-year-old kid, and Maggie had let it happen because she was always so sick. They had a lot to make up for, and a long way to go to get back to a normal life.

Maggie packed for both of them in the next week. And it wrenched her heart when Lisa begged her to let her see her father one last time. Against her better judgment, she finally gave in, but this time Maggie went with her. She didn't go in to see him, she sat in the waiting room while Lisa went in for a visit. Jack Nelson saw her and came to sit with Maggie. He had been in Northampton to file some papers. Suddenly the entire room became subdued because he was there.

"I don't think this is good for her," he said in an undervoice, and Maggie agreed with him. Who Michael was really frightened him now.

"Neither do I, but she wanted to say goodbye. We're leaving for London tomorrow." He was relieved to hear it. Their life in Ware, as it had been, was over forever. The damage couldn't be repaired. People all over town were mourning their lost doctor, the saint they had known, and others were mourning lost parents, whom he had killed. Demon or saint, he was both. But this was no longer a healthy place for his wife and daughter to be. He was glad that Maggie knew it.

She was surprised when Lisa came out of the visiting area a few minutes later. She could have stayed for ten minutes, but she didn't. She only stayed for two or three. And she was crying. Jack told Maggie somberly that he would be in touch with her about progress on the case and to be sure and leave her numbers. She promised to do so, and then escorted Lisa out of the building. She looked shattered.

"What happened?" Maggie asked her as they stood in the sunlight. Lisa's eyes looked glazed with grief.

"I told him we were leaving, and he said I'm just like you and Bill, liars and cheats and people who don't stand by the people they say they love. He just hung up the phone and walked away. I pounded on the window, and he wouldn't even look back." Maggie pulled Lisa into her arms then as she sobbed, but Maggie was relieved. By rejecting his daughter, Michael had freed her. He had thrown her away, and now she could heal. They all could. Lisa said not a word on the way home, and when she went upstairs, she finished packing her last few items in her suitcase. Maggie knew she had done the right thing. Letting Lisa see her father one last time had given her daughter a glimpse of who he really was. A man who rejected and killed and destroyed and had no idea how to love. He hadn't loved Lisa or Maggie, he had controlled them.

Lisa came downstairs to have dinner with Peter and her brother that night, for the first time in a month. She didn't speak to either of them, but she sat quietly and listened, still looking very shaken, but no longer hostile. Peter drove in from the lake to join them. He told them how much he was going to miss them, but he was glad they were getting away. Peter wanted to leave soon too. His time in Ware was over. He had come because he had nowhere else to go. It had been a time of healing, but now there was nothing for him here. He had given his mother's journals to Jack Nelson as evidence. He didn't want to read them again. It was over. All of it. It was the end of innocence for them all.

Chapter 18

It was lonely for Peter at the lake, once Maggie and her children were gone. The weather was beautiful, and he had gotten the house ready for the boys, who were due in a week, but he still had mixed feelings about having them come here, since Michael's arrest. A pall had been cast over it now for Peter, but he couldn't think of where else to take them. He had wanted to show them where he spent his boyhood summers, but that seemed grotesque now since his brother had turned out to be as dangerous as he'd always believed him. In fact, worse.

He was sitting on the deck one afternoon, reading, when Jack Nelson called
him. He hadn't expected the call and was
surprised to hear him.

"I have bad news," Jack said in a serious
voice.

"Now what?" He was sure it had to do
with his brother. These days, bad news only
related to him, and there had been a lot of
it recently.

"Your parents," Jack said, and Peter understood immediately. "They both show
traces of the same substance as the other
people we exhumed. I assume he used the
same drug on them." He had killed them.
They were dying anyway, but it was a terrible feeling knowing that his brother had
killed their parents. Peter felt sick when he
heard it, and then thanked Jack and hung
up. It was the last straw for him. He was
ready to leave. It was time. Too much had
happened here now. All he wanted was to
get out.

He spent that night trying to figure out
where to take the boys, and came up with
an idea that he liked. Maggie was in London for two more weeks before they left for
Italy. She had rented a house in Tuscany

for a month. But before that, he could take the boys to London for a week, and maybe spend another week or two with them in Europe. It was more money than he had wanted to spend, but he needed a breather now. And his children had never met Maggie and their cousins. And Maggie was their aunt after all. Lisa was only two years older than Ryan, and Bill would be fun for the boys, although he was older. And it would only be for a week, then he and his boys could travel around Europe. He liked the idea of going to Spain with them, and it wouldn't be too expensive, if they stayed at small hotels and ate at neighborhood restaurants.

He called Maggie in London the next morning and told her, and she loved the idea. She said she wanted to meet Ben and Ryan. He called the boys that afternoon. He hadn't told them about their uncle's arrest yet, but he had hinted at family issues that he would tell them about when they came.

"Well, we've had a change of plans," Peter announced when he talked to Ryan. "Things have been a little dicey here. I was going to tell you about it when you got here."

He told them a slightly cleaned-up version of Michael's arrest and his crimes, without going into too much detail.

"That sounds really scary, Dad," Ryan said, sounding impressed. "Do you think Uncle Michael will go to prison?" he asked in a subdued tone.

"Yes, I do. For a long time." Hopefully forever. Michael deserved it for what he'd done. He hadn't told Ryan that his twin brother had killed the grandparents he had never known. That was just too much at his age. He could tell him when he grew up. Peter hadn't digested it yet himself, although he had told Maggie when he talked to her. Nothing surprised either of them anymore. Michael had become a stranger to them all. The husband she had known and loved had never existed. All the while, he had been killing his elderly patients, manipulating money out of them, and poisoning her, after killing his own parents. His crimes were heinous, and it seemed like a miracle to them both that Maggie was still alive.

"So what do you think?" Peter asked his oldest son, who liked the plan.

"London sounds like fun, Dad. And maybe

we can go fishing in Spain." He had been looking forward to the lake, but he was a good sport, and three weeks in Europe sounded great to him, and to Ben too when they told him. He liked the idea of meeting his cousins, although he was sorry Bill was so old. Peter assured them they would like them both. And he hoped that Lisa was in better shape than when she left. She had been through a lot.

Peter said he would meet them in London, and he spoke to Alana after that to arrange to have her put them on a plane from L.A., and he would fly over the night before. She sounded businesslike and impersonal on the phone. He promised to get the boys back to her three weeks later in Southhampton. And after that, he was going to come back to the lake and put the house on the market. He was done. He didn't want to own anything there anymore. He was going to look for a small apartment in New York, and start beating on doors again for a job. He was hoping things would loosen up by the fall.

Peter spent a quiet night before he left, and sent Jack Nelson an e-mail about how he could be reached if anything came up.

He hoped nothing would. Michael was accused of eleven murders now.

Peter watched the sun come up over the lake. There was going to be a regatta that day. As he stood there, he thought about the times he had gone fishing with Michael recently, and the times they had swum out to the raft as boys. It was all part of history now, a history he wanted to put away.

He drove to Boston in his truck, and left it at the airport. He flew to London and checked into the hotel he had stayed at before, when he first met Bill, and he called Maggie that night. She invited him to dinner with Ben and Ryan the next day. They were staying at Claridge's, which was a grand hotel and fun for Ben and Ryan to see. Ben had already said that he wanted to see the changing of the guard and the stables at Buckingham Palace, and Ryan wanted to go to the Tower of London and see the rooms where they had tortured people. And the wax museum would be fun. It was going to be a nice holiday for them.

"How's it going?" he asked Maggie when they talked. "How do you feel?" She had gotten stronger every day. Without the paraquat in her system that Michael had been administering along with all the tranquilizers and sleeping pills, she was feeling great. "How's Lisa doing?" he asked with concern.

"She's struggling. She still can't believe what Michael did to her. He really confused her in the cruelest way possible in order to control her." And he had for a long time. He had turned her against her mother and brother, and even Peter, before he let go. But she was young, and she had her mother and brother now. "It's still hard for her. We went to look at schools yesterday."

"How does she feel about that?" Peter asked her.

"Not great. But I think it will be good for her. I'm not going back to Ware, except for the trial. I've decided to sell the house. I want to rent an apartment here." She never wanted to see the house again where she had been an invalid for so long and almost been killed by her husband.

"I want to sell the house on the lake too." She wasn't surprised. "I'm going to move back to New York." A lot had changed for both of them, and particularly for him in the past eight months. But her life was changing too.

And he was thrilled to see Ben and Ryan the next day. Ben threw himself into his father's arms, and Ryan was beaming from ear to ear. They both commented that he had lost weight—the last months had taken a toll. He took them back to the hotel, and they showered and put on clean clothes for dinner, and then took a cab to Claridge's to meet Maggie, Lisa, and Bill. They were waiting for them in the lobby in jeans and T-shirts, and Maggie had made a reservation at a restaurant nearby recommended by the concierge.

"What's wrong with her leg?" Ben asked his father in a stage whisper, when he saw Maggie limp as they walked outside.

"I fell skating on a pond a long time ago," Maggie turned to explain to him with a smile. She had no trouble talking about it now.

"That must have hurt," Ben said sympathetically.

"It did. I bumped my head and was out cold for five months," she said as she took his hand in hers, and Ryan and Lisa talked

about the bands they liked. Ryan had been
to concerts given by most of them, and Lisa
was impressed. Bill walked along with the
adults and chatted with Peter about his exams. He was writing a paper about the demise of Lehman Brothers.

The six of them had a good time at the
restaurant. Lisa was more talkative than
she'd been in months, and Ben entertained
them as he always did. Ryan and Lisa
seemed to have struck up an easy friendship, and Maggie and Peter looked across
the table at each other, proud of their kids,
and Peter couldn't help thinking how far
they'd all come. Maggie was thinking that
too. And what a miracle it was that she'd
survived.

Lisa was telling Ryan about the house
they'd rented in Italy, that they'd found on
the Internet, and Peter and Bill were talking about Spain. Bill had been there several times since he'd moved to Europe. And
Peter invited Lisa to go with them to see
the Tower of London and the changing of
the guard the next day. He asked Maggie
if she wanted to come along. He wasn't
sure if she was up to it, but she said she
was game. And after that they walked Mag-

gie and her brood back to Claridge's and then took a cab back to their hotel. The boys were exhausted after the long plane trip, and they were sound asleep in their hotel room, as Peter tucked himself into bed. It was wonderful to be with his children again. Suddenly life felt normal to him, for the first time in a long time.

They met up with Maggie and Lisa the next day, and took a double-decker bus to the Tower of London. The kids loved the ghoulish exhibits and the explanations of what had gone on there. And Maggie and Lisa loved the jewels.

They were all in great spirits when they went to lunch. It had been a perfect morning. They were planning to go to the stables at Buckingham Palace after that.

They were finishing dessert when Ben commented that he liked his mother's boyfriend Bruce, and his older brother shot him a dark look.

"That's okay," Peter was quick to reassure them. "I'm happy if he's nice to you guys."

"He is," Ben said simply with ice cream on his chin. "I like his Ferrari and his dog." They all laughed at that, and Peter noticed that Lisa had gotten quiet. She still seemed to go in and out of being sociable, and she was chattier with his boys than with him. She was lost in thought for the rest of the afternoon, and Maggie noticed it too. She asked her if she was okay when they went back to the hotel. The two families were dining separately that night, but had promised to get together the next day. Everyone seemed to be enjoying it, and the cousins were having a good time together. It was working out better than they had all hoped. It was easy and fun and relaxed, which was exactly what they all needed.

"Are you and Dad going to get divorced?" Lisa asked her mother as Maggie lay down on her bed to relax for a while. It had been a long day, and she wasn't used to walking that much, but she wanted to get strong. She needed the exercise.

Maggie hesitated for a long moment. She knew she'd have to, but she hadn't wanted to face it yet. "I haven't thought about it. Maybe." She was more concerned about the trial, but Michael was going to be away for a long time, and she was never going back to him again. "I guess it would make sense," she said simply, and Lisa nodded. She couldn't defend her father anymore.

"Would you ever get remarried?" Lisa asked her nervously, and Maggie laughed.

"You're way ahead of me. I can't even imagine it." She just wanted to get through the coming months and the trial. And the thought of dating again, at her age, sounded horrifying to her. Her experience with Michael hadn't made her anxious to trust anyone again.

"Dad said you and Peter were in love with each other and having an affair. Is that true?" It had troubled her since she'd heard it and made her suspicious of Peter.

"Of course not." Maggie looked horrified at the suggestion. "I was in love with your father until our last day."

"But not anymore?" Maggie shook her head. She was in love with the man he had pretended to be to her, but not who he really was. And looking back over the last twenty-three years, she realized that what she had thought was love was really control. It hadn't been loving at all, just like what he had done to their daughter, turning her into more of a wife than a daughter when she was only a child. And Maggie had still never heard from Michael, and suspected she never would again. That said it all. She had ceased to exist for him.

They had room service that night, and Bill stayed at his own apartment, so he could finish writing his paper. They had a quiet night, and Peter and his boys did too. They went to a movie after dinner, it was pure science fiction with robots attacking each other, precisely the kind of thing they loved. And then they went back to the hotel and watched TV.

The two families got together again the next day. And the rest of the week flew by. They were leaving for their trips to Spain and Tuscany on the same day, and the night before Peter took them all out to dinner at a nice restaurant. And afterward, Peter and the boys walked them back to Claridge's. They all hugged on the sidewalk and promised to stay in touch with each other. Ryan and Lisa had been texting each other all week when they weren't together, and Ben gave Maggie a big hug when they left her. They liked their new aunt, and the kids had had fun together. Ben said he was sorry they didn't live in L.A.

And the next day Peter and the boys left

for Spain. They went to Madrid and Seville
and Toledo, and then lay on a beach on the
Costa Brava, and they spent the last few
days in Mallorca, and they all loved it. He
called Maggie a couple of times to see how
they were doing, and she loved the villa
they had rented.

"You like her, huh, Dad?" Ryan commented one night after he heard his father
talk to her, and Peter looked startled.

"Yes, of course. She's my sister-in-law
and I've known her since we were kids."

"I mean like a girlfriend," Ryan explained
as though his father were stupid, and Peter
laughed.

"No, not like a girlfriend," he corrected
him. "We're just friends."

"How come you don't have a girlfriend?"
Ryan asked. All his friends' divorced
fathers did, and usually pretty jazzy ones
who were a lot younger than they were.
That wasn't Peter's thing. He didn't know
what his "thing" was. He hadn't dated in fifteen years, since he married Alana.

"I don't know. I'm still getting over your
mother. I liked being married. I don't feel
like a bachelor yet. I feel kind of like . . . a
nothing. I just want to hang out with you

guys." But his brother was going to prison for life, he had just found out he had killed their parents, and his sister-in-law had been poisoned. He wasn't in the mood to date. And eight months before that, his whole life had fallen apart and his wife had left him. It was a lot to absorb. And when he talked to her about it, Maggie said she felt the same way. She was just starting to live again after twenty-three years. They had talked about it while walking around London with the kids. Neither of them could imagine dating again. At least not yet. And all Peter wanted now was a job.

His wish came true when they were in Madrid. He checked his e-mails when he got to the hotel. And he was startled to see that the firm he had interviewed with in London had offered him a job. It had taken them a while, but it was a great offer. He just didn't know if he wanted to live in London. He really wanted to go back to New York. He was ready for Wall Street again. But no one had offered him a job there so far. And this was an excellent offer, worthy of him, with a partnership in the firm within two years, profit sharing, benefits, stock, and they were willing to pay for an apartment for him, big enough for his boys when they came to visit. It was everything he wanted, just not in the right town. He didn't know whether to accept it or not. And he talked to Ryan and Ben about it over dinner.

"So what do you think, guys? How would you feel if I took a job in London? For a few years anyway." If something better came along in New York, he would take it. But this was it for now.

"I like it," Ryan said sensibly. He knew his father needed to go back to work. He wasn't happy just hanging around, not like their mom, who got her nails and hair done, and had lunch with her friends every day.

"Would you still come to see us in L.A.?" Ben asked, looking worried, and Peter was quick to reassure him.

"Of course I would. And you can come here. We could go skiing in Switzerland over Christmas or New Year's. It's not a bad flight from L.A." The boys agreed. It wasn't that much farther than New York, if Peter went to live there.

Peter thought about it for the next few days and then sent an e-mail to the firm in London, and accepted the job. They wanted him to start on September 15, which sounded good to him. It gave him time to close the lake house, make a quick trip to L.A. to see the boys, and start work in the fall. And with a shiver down his spine, he realized he would be divorced by then. His divorce would be final in September. Brave new world.

He told the boys he had taken the job, and they were happy for him. Ryan sent a text to Lisa about it that night: "My dad is moving to London. He took a job there. We'll visit. See you soon. Ryan." Lisa responded immediately: "Cool. L."

Chapter 19

Their trip to Spain was a success, and Peter delivered the boys to Alana in Southampton in the third week of July, as promised. She was having a big birthday bash for herself, and she wanted them there. And of course, Bruce was with her. He was a permanent fixture these days.

They were sad to say goodbye to their father, but they were looking forward to the month in Southampton with their friends. It was part of their old life and familiar to them. And Peter had promised them he'd fly out to California to see them before he left for London, so they knew they'd see him soon.

He drove back to New York after he dropped them off, and flew to Boston, where he had left his truck, and drove back to the lake. The place looked dreary to him now, and he was lonely without the boys, after spending three weeks with them in fun places.

For the next month, Peter swam in the lake every day, and lay on the raft. And the rest of the time, he packed up the house. He was surprised at how much paraphernalia he had collected in the six months he'd been there. He threw most of it away, and the rest he packed to send to London. He met with the realtor and arranged to put it on the market, for a reasonable price, and hoped that someone would buy it quickly. He wanted it off his hands now, and this chapter of his life closed.

It was upsetting knowing that his brother was in jail nearby, awaiting trial. Peter had no desire to see him. And he wanted to get as far away from Ware now as he could. Jack Nelson drove out one afternoon with an investigator to interview Peter. The interview was peaceful. They wanted to know his impressions about his brother. Peter was honest with them and said that he thought he had been a sociopath, a man without a conscience, since his youth. He gave them some examples of the lies he'd told, his manipulation of their parents and constant lies to them. Peter didn't paint a pretty picture.

"Why doesn't he just plead guilty and make a deal?" Peter asked Jack, who knew him well, and the police chief shook his head.

"I suggested it to him. He refused. He wants his day in court and a jury trial. It's going to be a circus, with reporters from all over the state." Peter was dreading it, and he knew Maggie was too. She would have to testify against her husband.

They chatted for a little while afterward, and then Jack left. Michael had become a mystery to him too, as he was to so many now, but not to Peter.

He only drove into Ware once, to stop in at the diner to see Vi and tell her about his plans. She told him how sorry she was about everything that had happened and gave him a warm hug. She said she was sorry she hadn't met his boys. And he ran into Jack Nelson as he was leaving. They shook hands, and he hurried out. Everything about the town depressed him now, more than ever before. Too many bad things had happened.

Peter was anxious to get to work. The vacation had gone on too long. It had been ten months since October. And he was delighted to close the house on Labor Day weekend, and hoped he'd never see it again, when he handed the keys to the realtor. He had sold his truck back to the used-car lot in Ware the day before, and he'd gone to say goodbye to Walt Peterson at the hardware store, and had a last cup of coffee with Vi at the diner.

"Looks like the prodigal son is leaving again," Walt teased him.

"I'm not sure which one of us that would be," Peter responded.

"You'll be back for the trial, I guess," he asked, and Peter nodded. So would Maggie and Bill. She wanted to leave Lisa in London. She didn't want her anywhere near it. It would be traumatic enough for them. "He was a good doctor," Walt said in defense of his brother, and Peter didn't comment. He could no longer say that about him, nor could the other people whose parents he had murdered. Michael had left a trail of bodies behind him, including their parents'.

Peter left then and drove the loaner that the used-car lot had given him for his last day. He dropped it off the next morning and took a shuttle to the airport in Boston. It was a long ride and he had time to think on the way. He was reflecting on his brother in jail in Northampton. As much as he had loathed him at times in his youth, he had never thought it would come to this.

With the time difference, he got to L.A. in the early afternoon, and the boys seemed subdued to him when he got to the house. He couldn't figure out what it was, and Ryan was particularly uncommunicative with him. Ben finally spilled the beans.

"Mom's getting married. Ryan's mad about it." It gave Peter a strange feeling when he heard it. There was something so final about it, even though he knew Alana had been dating Bruce for nine months. But somehow their getting married made him feel as though he had never existed.

"He's a jerk, Dad," Ryan said glumly.

"I thought you guys said he was nice to

you and your mom." Peter's radar was up after what Ryan had just said. "What kind of jerk?"

"He's a show-off," Ryan said with a look of disgust. "All he cares about is money." Peter didn't say it, but he had that in common with their mother. It was her priority too. She had proven that to him amply in the last year. She had learned it from a master, her father. All that mattered to either of them was money, although he had to admit she was a decent mother. But she had been a lousy wife to him when he needed her. She had bailed at the first opportunity.

"When are they getting married?" Peter asked with curiosity.

"Christmas," Ben supplied the information again.

"Good. Then let's go skiing when they're on their honeymoon," he suggested, and Ryan broke into a grin.

"Maybe Lisa can come with us," Ryan suggested. The two cousins had been texting a lot. He thought she was very sophisticated because she was two years older, and he felt sorry for her because of her father. She never talked about it to him, although that didn't surprise him, from what his father had said.

"I'll ask Maggie," Peter offered.

They went out to dinner that night, and bowling afterward. He hated playing the role of the divorced dad who had to find entertainments for them. He preferred being at home with them, but there was no home he could offer them here. He was going to London to look at apartments that week and promised he'd find something they'd like. It was easy now with the firm paying for it, and a big salary coming his way again. In some ways, he hadn't minded the simplicity of the past year. It had taught him about what mattered to him and what didn't, and that he could live simply and enjoy it. It had been an odd time, he had lost a brother forever, but he had gained a sister and friend, and a niece and a nephew. Ryan and Ben agreed with him. They loved being with their aunt and cousins since their mother was an only child.

Peter stayed in L.A. for three days to see the boys, and then flew to London. Alana had agreed to let them come to him in London for Thanksgiving and Christmas, since she was going away with Bruce for

Thanksgiving to his family in Baltimore, and they were going on their honeymoon in the Caribbean over Christmas and New Year's. The boys were a little disappointed that she was going away for both holidays, but thrilled that they'd be visiting their dad in London. And he had promised to organize a ski trip over New Year's. Peter was feeling good about his life as he left for London. And he had arranged for some of his things to be sent to him from storage. He was going to have a real home again, a place where he could be with his kids.

And he hit the ground running when he landed. He saw five apartments the first day, and three the second. And the last one he saw was perfect. It had three bedrooms and was a duplex in a beautiful old building across the street from Regent's Park. He could throw a football there with his boys. And the apartment was comfortably decorated with masculine-looking furniture, big comfortable leather armchairs, and a cozy den with a giant flat screen in it. He called Maggie after he signed the lease and told her all about it. She invited him to dinner to celebrate. He still had a few days to get organized before he had to start work. And he arrived with a large bunch of flowers when he showed up at the mews house she had rented for herself and Lisa. Bill wanted to keep his apartment. He had a new girlfriend and liked his freedom. Everyone was happy. And he had come over to her place for dinner to see Peter. There was an instant atmosphere of celebration, as everyone talked about their summer, and their plans for the fall. Lisa had just started school that week and said it wasn't so bad. She was at the American School in London, and she liked the kids, and there was a boy she had her eye on. It looked like she and Maggie had made the adjustment. And the mews house suited them to perfection. It was owned by a woman who had moved to Hong Kong, and everything in it was flowery and cheerful. Maggie looked totally at home there, and so did Lisa.

"It looks like you guys have really settled in," Peter commented as he and Maggie talked after dinner. Lisa was in her room on the phone with one of her new friends.

"It's the perfect house for us," Maggie said, smiling.

"You have to come and see my apartment."

"How were the boys when you saw them?"

"A little ruffled, but fine. Alana is getting married over Christmas. Ryan isn't too happy about it. Alana has known the guy forever. I think he's probably a decent guy, but kind of an L.A. show-off. That suits her. I'm going to take them skiing over New Year's while she's on her honeymoon," he said casually, and then saw Maggie's face cloud over. The trial was immediately afterward. They were both anxious for that to be over. The prosecutor had recently sent her a page of questions to answer, and some of them were pretty ugly. She wanted to show them to Peter but hated to talk about it, and she didn't want to deal with it that night.

Maggie and Peter were happy to see each other. They sat and talked for a long time, until Peter finally left. He had a lot of unpacking to do at his apartment. He invited her and his niece and nephew to dinner there the following weekend.

"I warn you, pizza and takeout, or 'takeaway' as they say here." There were a lot of new things for him to get used to, like driving on the wrong side of the road, which Maggie had no intention of trying, particularly since she hadn't driven in twenty-four years. She wasn't about to start here.

"I'm glad you're here," Maggie said to him warmly, as she walked him to the front door. "It's nice having family around, isn't it?" They had turned into a good support system for each other, especially now, with everything that had happened, and living three thousand miles from home in another country. It was a fresh start for them all, especially her and Peter.

He was thinking about her as he took a cab back to his apartment. She looked pretty and relaxed. She had gone shopping and bought new clothes, and she seemed younger again. Peter knew he felt better than he had in years, after his vacation with the boys, and healthy life at the lake. He was ready to start his new job, and a new life in London.

And as Peter and Maggie thought about the pleasant evening they'd just shared, they had no idea how close their kids had gotten, and how comfortable with each other. They really enjoyed their cousins. As soon as he left, Lisa sent a text message to Ryan.

"Your dad was here for dinner."

"Nice. What did you eat?"

"Pizza. And Chinese takeout."

"Wish I were there."

"Me too. Hurry up and visit. Or you should move here," Lisa wrote easily and meant it.

"My mom and grandfather would have a fit."

"They'd get over it," Lisa assured him.

"Yeah. Maybe. Don't think so." It made him homesick for his father when he wrote it. "Hug my dad for me when you see him," Ryan answered. She sat and stared at the keyboard on her BlackBerry for a minute before she answered. She still had mixed feelings about Peter. She knew he had exposed her father, and all her life she'd been told he was the enemy. She wasn't sure what he was or how she felt about him, but she loved Ben and Ryan, almost like brothers. She started texting again then.

"Sure," she said in response. "See ya soon. Love, L." And with that, they both went back to what they were doing.

Chapter 20

Peter's new job got off to a good start. He liked his colleagues and associates and the broad base of their clients. They gave him a handsome office, and within weeks he felt as though he had been there forever. It was different from New York, but in a nice way. London was a big, bustling city, and in some ways it was like a more sophisticated, more charming New York. He was happy.

And on Sunday nights, he and Maggie took turns having the whole family over to dinner. They loved his apartment, and Bill enjoyed coming over to watch sports on the giant TV. In some ways, Peter had become the substitute for the father he'd never had. And Peter liked him. It made him less lonely for his boys, and he took Bill to sports events when he had time. He was a bright young guy, and they enjoyed each other's company. Maggie was grateful that Peter was so generous about spending time with him, and often said so.

"It's not a sacrifice," Peter reassured her. "I have fun with him. He's going to do well." Peter was growing closer to him.

"I hope so. His father always gave him such a tough time." It was no surprise, and Peter and Bill both liked the fact that whenever they went out together, they were mistaken for father and son, they looked so much alike.

They were all having dinner together in his spacious kitchen one night in October. Peter happened to look at the date on his watch and realized it was October 10.

"A year ago today, I had lost everything. I was out of a job, the stock market was in the toilet, and so was my life, even more than I knew at the time." Alana had left him shortly afterward. But he had adjusted to it now; it no longer hurt, even if it felt strange.

He had just recently gotten his final decree of divorce from California, and he was less upset by it than he had expected to be. Alana felt like ancient history now, and he could no longer imagine their marriage. The best part of it had been their boys. He didn't miss the rest anymore. A year later, he was fine, and she was about to be married to someone else. Sometimes life was really strange. A year ago it had seemed like a tragedy. Now it just felt like history.

"Should we celebrate your survival and rebirth into a new life?" Maggie asked cautiously. They both had new lives now.

"Definitely," Peter said, pouring her a glass of wine. Bill had already helped himself to a beer. He knew his way around, and had spent several nights in the apartment, in his uncle's guest room, when they shared a rowdy sporting event or a late night. They had fun together.

The kids went to watch something on TV after dinner, and he and Maggie cleaned up the kitchen. It was always easy, since he ordered takeout and didn't cook.

"Do you want to go to the theater sometime?" he asked Maggie as they put the dishes in the machine. "Apparently my office has a great ticket agent. Ballet, theater, whatever we want."

"I'd love that," she said, looking pleased. He was a wonderful addition to their life.

"I'll check it out," he promised, and they went to sit in the living room. "It really is amazing. I wasn't kidding at dinner. My whole world fell apart a year ago. I was at the top of my game before that, and I thought everything was over a year ago. And Alana going back to L.A. with the boys was the final blow. And now, to be honest, I'm enjoying myself." He felt free as a bird and he liked it. And she was having the same experience. She could do whatever she wanted, and she was no longer a prisoner of her health. Everything had changed. Some terrible things had happened to both of them, but blessings had come of it in the end. Although for her, the agony wasn't entirely over, and it was all more recent. Her world had fallen apart four months before, when they had discovered what Michael was doing to her. But she had made great strides in four months, and she knew it had been the right decision to be in London. It had all worked out as it was meant to. Peter often thought that if he hadn't come to

London to interview for the job, he never would have met Bill, Bill wouldn't have sent him the e-mail about the weed killer, and Michael would have still been poisoning Maggie. Or by then he would have killed her. He nearly had. It was a chilling thought. Peter often thought about the strength of the human spirit and its ability to prevail.

Maggie and her children left a little while later, and he called her on Thursday. True to his word, he had gotten tickets to a play that was opening, and she was excited to see it. She hadn't been to the theater in years. Not since she married Michael. She used to go to New York with her parents as a young girl. But once she was married, Michael kept her close to home, told her she was weak and sick, and wouldn't let her go out at all.

Peter suggested they have dinner afterward, since the theater was early in London. They had a seven-thirty curtain. And he made a ten o'clock dinner reservation at Harry's Bar. They'd gotten him a membership through his office. And he used one of the office chauffeured cars to pick her up and drive them for the evening. She felt very spoiled as they left for the theater in

the West End. And the play was even better than expected. They both loved it.

She had bought a new short black dress
for the evening, and Lisa had frowned when
she saw it.

"New dress? Going on a date?" she
questioned her.

"New dress, but not a date," Maggie responded. "Just Peter. We have fun together."
Lisa nodded and didn't comment.

Maggie looked very pretty when she
took off her coat at Harry's Bar, and Peter
saw the dress. She had worn dressy flat
shoes, since her stiff leg didn't allow her to
wear heels. But even her leg was doing
better now as she moved around more,
and she was continuing her physical therapy and taking yoga classes. Her limp was
much less pronounced.

And the dinner was delicious. They both
ordered pasta, and Peter ordered champagne. It felt like a celebration, and it was.
They had both seized hold of life again.

"To our renaissance," Maggie said, lifting
her glass to him, "our rebirth."

"That's a nice way to put it," Peter said,
smiling. "I hadn't thought of it that way, but
it's true. I'm enjoying my work more than

ever. I really like it here, and I lucked out with this firm." And then he had another thought. "And I found you again." And they both knew what that had led to, his saving her life. In great part that was thanks to Bill and the research he had done on the Internet, convinced that his father was poisoning her. Only Bill's dogged pursuit of his suspicions had saved her. But Peter had helped.

Peter had another idea during dinner. He wanted to explore Europe. He loved living there and all the places they could go that were so nearby. "Do you want to go to Paris sometime? We could take Bill and Lisa. Or even the boys, when they come."

"I'd love it." Maggie looked thrilled at the idea. Everything was new now, and fun. The only thing that made her sad sometimes was when she thought about Michael. It was almost as though he had died. And in some ways, for her, he had. Peter had seen the shadow cross her eyes, and gently patted her hand. It brought her mind instantly back to the present where it belonged. The past was too dangerous for them both, a minefield where neither of them wanted to venture.

"Let me know when you want to go, and I'll arrange it." He had a wonderful new secretary who seemed to be able to organize anything.

"Anytime," Maggie said happily. "Lisa will love it. Paris is such a wonderful city." She wasn't sure how Lisa would feel about going to Paris with Peter, but Maggie thought it would do them all good. They were family after all.

"What about in two weeks?" Peter suggested. "I'm going to a soccer match with Bill this weekend. And he'd kill me if we cancel." She laughed. Paris would be far less appealing to her son than soccer.

And once again Peter made all the plans. He told them about it that Sunday night when they had dinner at her place. They were taking the Eurostar to Paris, which would arrive right in town. He had made a reservation for three rooms at a charming little hotel on the Left Bank. They only served croissants in the morning with a café au lait in bowls, Peter explained. They were going to eat dinners in little bistros and do enough shopping to keep the ladies happy. And on Sunday night they'd come back. Maggie beamed as she listened, and

Lisa was smiling too. And even Bill thought it sounded like fun, as long as Peter went. A shopping weekend in Paris with his mother and sister was his idea of hell. But Peter assured him they'd find something male to do, maybe a soccer match one afternoon while the women shopped.

"Okay, I'll come," Bill conceded.

And the following weekend, the four of them went. They loved the little hotel he'd found in the sixth arrondissement. He had made reservations at restaurants that were fun for the young people. He managed to find a soccer match on Saturday afternoon for him and Bill. Peter had done his homework, and made an excellent tour guide. They strolled around the Place Vendôme, and the Faubourg St. Honoré. And on Saturday night after dinner at a restaurant called Market, he and Maggie sat in the Hemingway Bar at the Ritz in cozy elegance and relaxed. It had been a busy day.

"Alana must be crazy," Maggie said happily as she sipped a glass of champagne.

"No. Just spoiled. Why?" He didn't know what she meant.

"Because you're the most attentive man

I've ever met. You see to it that everyone has a good time. You made all the plans. You made sure Lisa and I had shopping time, you got Bill to a soccer game so he's happy. You took us to a restaurant we loved. The hotel is fabulous. You think of everything. How could she ever let you go?"

"I never said she was smart," he said, and then laughed. "I'm just kidding. She'd rather be in L.A. than anywhere on earth, near her father. It suits her. It's all rhinestones and flash. And don't forget, I lost my job and all our money. That wasn't what she had in mind. I'll make it again one day," he said, looking serious for a moment. And he was being handsomely paid in London. They had offered him a partnership in two years, maybe sooner. But he knew he had a long climb back up to where he'd been, if he ever got there. It wasn't quite as easy at his age as it had been in his twenties and thirties, and it was a different era. Money had been free and easy then, and it no longer was. Times had changed. "I'm not sure it matters to me as much anymore," he said honestly. He was always honest with Maggie. She was easy to talk to. "Maybe it would have fallen apart with

Alana anyway, even if I hadn't lost my money. Looking back, I'm not sure how much we had in common, other than our kids. I never had time to think about it. I was too busy working."

"And I wasted twenty-three years of my life being sick," Maggie said sadly. She'd never get back those lost years.

"You had help. He **made** you sick, or think you were, so he could control you. What does it say in the Bible, something about you'll get back the years the locust hath eaten? That's true for both of us. We lost a lot, but look what we have now." They were both enjoying their lives more than ever before, and they had someone to do it with, even though they no longer had partners or spouses. Friendship was perfect when it was as comfortable as this. Neither of them wanted more than that for now.

They talked for a long time at the bar, and took a cab back to their hotel at two A.M. Peter kissed her on the cheek, and she thanked him again. And she was surprised to find Lisa still awake in the room they shared. She had waited up and greeted her mother with a look of interest.

"Did he kiss you?" she asked, sounding more like mother than daughter.

"Of course not!" Maggie laughed at her. "Don't be silly. Why would he kiss me? We're friends. Besides, he's my brother-in-law."

"So what? He's divorced. And you're . . ." They both knew that her marriage was over too, even if she was still legally married to Michael. But she wouldn't be forever. She and Peter were both free. "Besides, he likes you. Can't you tell? Why do you think he brought us to Paris?"

"So we'd all have a good time. Not to kiss me, you goof." She ruffled her daughter's hair and unzipped her dress and stepped out of it, and she saw that Lisa was looking worried. She had no reason to.

"You looked pretty tonight, Mom." She'd worn another new dress. She'd bought three for the trip to Paris. And new shoes.

"Thank you, sweetheart. Don't worry about Peter. Honestly, we're just friends." Lisa was quiet for a minute.

"Maybe you should kiss him," Lisa said pensively. "I guess Daddy's never coming back." She looked sad.

"No, he's not," Maggie said as she put

her arms around her. "I'm not ready to kiss anyone, and when and if I am, it probably won't be Peter."

"Why not?"

"Because sometimes being friends is better, and I wouldn't want to spoil it." Lisa nodded, reassured, and a minute later, they slipped into bed together. She lay thinking about what Lisa had said for a long time. Maggie hadn't lied to her, and she believed what she had said. Sometimes friendship was better. She was just grateful for her new life, and she felt like she'd been born again. Paris was just the icing on the cake. And Peter was exactly what she had said. A friend. And a moment later, she was asleep.

Chapter 21

When the train pulled into the St. Pancras Station in London on Sunday night, they had all had a fabulous time, thanks to Peter and his impeccable arrangements. He had been thoughtful and generous to them all weekend. They didn't make dinner plans that night because they had eaten on the train. And in the cab on the way home, Peter said he thought they should do that in a different city every weekend. He was teasing, but they had certainly had fun. They had spent so much time exploring the Marais on Sunday afternoon that they almost missed the train and had to hurry to catch it. And they had played several rowdy games of cards on the trip back. Peter was good company, and so was Maggie. She said she hadn't laughed so much in years. She had forgotten what being carefree felt like.

He dropped Maggie and Lisa off first with the cab, and then took Bill home, and then went home himself.

Maggie called him as soon as he got in. "I don't know how to thank you for such a wonderful weekend. We loved it."

"So did I," he said generously, and he meant it. "You have wonderful kids."

"So do you," she said, and meant it too. She loved his boys, and they were so sweet, just as he was.

"That's because we're such wonderful people," he teased her. "I'm glad you had fun. We'll have to do it again. I'm trying to organize a ski trip for the boys, by the way. Maybe the three of you should come with us. We'll make it a family vacation." And it would be an important one. They all needed some fun before the trial, which was scheduled for early January.

"I don't ski," she said, sounding embarrassed.

"Neither do I. I blew out my knees playing football in college. I'm strictly a hot toddy at the fireplace guy. We can play cards." She had to admit, she liked the idea. They were providing each other the family and adult companionship that they both lacked. "I'll let you know what I come up with. I'm thinking Switzerland or France."

"Bill would go nuts. He's a big skier."

"So are the boys. I'll figure out something. We can talk about it when they come out for Thanksgiving. Do you want to join us for that, by the way? It's not a holiday here, so we'll have to create it ourselves."

"I was thinking about that too." And they didn't have friends here yet, although Lisa was meeting Americans at school. "Why don't I do it at my place? Lisa and I can cook."

"That's good. Otherwise we'll be having Chinese takeout, or curry, for Thanksgiving, and the boys might be a little upset."

"We'll do it," Maggie volunteered, sounding happy. "Anyway, thank you for a fantastic weekend in Paris."

The next day she sent him two very good bottles of Bordeaux to thank him, and he called to scold her:

"You don't have to do that. We're family."

"Are you kidding? We had a ball." He had treated them to everything and even paid for the train. He had spoiled them. "You're very good to us, Peter," she said kindly.

"We're good to each other, Maggie," he said gently. "That's what life is all about." They were both nice people. He was right about that. And they had both been badly bruised before this. It made them grateful for the good times. "I loved it too." He had to leave for a meeting then and he promised to call her on the weekend. When he did, the kids were busy with friends, and he took her to a movie and a simple Indian dinner afterward. And on Sunday night, they had their usual dinner at his apartment. It was becoming a routine they all enjoyed. And she noticed that Lisa seemed more relaxed with him after her reassurance in Paris, or maybe she was just more used to him. Lisa was finally coming out of her shell after all she'd been through, and so was Maggie.

And when the boys came to London for Thanksgiving, it felt like a party. The four kids had pillow fights, played wild games of cards, played monopoly and cheated liberally, went to the movies, and Maggie and Lisa cooked a superb Thanksgiving dinner. Everyone was so stuffed they could hardly move. And the next day, they drove out to the country for the day.

"What's happening with your mom and my dad?" Ryan asked Lisa, as they walked in the woods, with their parents trailing behind them, enjoying watching them and talking.

"Nothing. Why?" Lisa looked surprised, wondering if he knew something she didn't.

"I wish something would. They're nice together," Ryan commented. "I'd hate it if he got together with some woman we don't like. It would ruin everything."

"I guess it would," Lisa said thoughtfully. "My mom says they're just friends."

"Yeah," Ryan said, looking disgusted. "They're both stupid. It would be cool if we were brother and sister instead of cousins," he said wistfully, and Lisa smiled.

"Maybe it would," she conceded.

"If they stay like that, she'll end up with some creepy guy you'll hate one of these days, and my father will end up with some bimbo, and we'll all be screwed," Ryan said, and Lisa laughed.

"My mom says being friends is better."

"That confirms it," Ryan said unhappily. "We're screwed. Are they dating anyone else?" Ryan asked her, looking worried.

"She's not. My mom's still married to my father."

Ryan nodded. "We're already divorced."

"I guess we will be too." They both knew what had happened with her father and never talked about it.

At dinner that night, Peter reminded Maggie about the skiing trip he was planning with the boys after Christmas.

It was another wonderful weekend that they all hated to see end when the boys flew back to L.A on Sunday. And they were due back in three weeks for Christmas vacation, right after their mother's wedding in L.A. Neither of the boys was enthused about the wedding, and Bruce seemed to be wearing a little thin, but Peter still had the impression that he was nice to the boys, which was all he cared about. And he wished Alana well. He was no longer in love with her, and his ego had recovered after being dumped. And he was having a wonderful time in London with Maggie and her kids. They satisfied all his needs for companionship for the moment. There was a very pretty woman in his office, but he didn't have time to take her out, and then he heard she was engaged. He took some woman out a few times and was bored with her, so he stuck to Maggie and her kids. And all of them were looking forward to the holiday in Courchevel. The photos of the chalet looked terrific, and all the kids had approved. Maggie was touched again by his kindness to them.

By the time the boys came back, there was snow on the ground in London, it was freezing cold, and Peter had put a tree up for them. Maggie and her children had helped him decorate it, and he and Maggie had talked endlessly as they strung up the lights and hung the decorations. It was the first time Maggie had decorated a tree since she was married. She and Peter did most of it, since Lisa and Bill were watching something special on TV in the other room. Decorating the tree, or even watching someone else do it as she had had to for years, always brought back memories of her childhood. And it did for Peter too, though his weren't as pleasant.

"My brother knocked the tree over one

year, and blamed me of course, and then I got punished for lying when I said I didn't do it. I think I was about seven. Michael was always doing things like that to me."

"He can't stand being blamed for things," Maggie said, looking pensive. She didn't like thinking about him now. It always upset her. Peter could see it and changed the subject quickly.

"Do you remember when you and I were dating, and we hitched Mrs. McElroy's pig to a sled?" he said, and she started to laugh until tears ran down her cheeks.

"It was the funniest thing I've ever seen."

"I got in a shitload of trouble for it with my father," Peter said, laughing, "but it was worth it. He said the pig could have gotten hurt." But it hadn't. They had had good times in those days, before things got complicated. Before her accident, and everything that came later. And then suddenly, he remembered when he kissed her on the raft at the lake. She had been beautiful, and they were both so young, fifteen and seventeen. Life was just beginning. He looked a million miles away, and Maggie noticed it and asked him what he was thinking. "You'd laugh if I told you."

"Try me."

He looked sheepish when he said it. "I was thinking about when I kissed you on the raft at the lake." She looked nostalgic as he said it.

"Life was so simple then, wasn't it? Nothing had happened yet, and everything was easier and happier. You were a good kisser too," she said, smiling shyly.

"How would you know? You were fifteen, and you probably don't even remember."

"Of course I do," she said, looking mischievous, as he moved closer to her, suddenly tempted to remind her, and just as he leaned toward her, Bill walked into the room and asked if Peter wanted a beer.

"No, thanks," Peter said cheerfully, and turned to hang another string of lights on the tree. The moment passed after that, and they talked of other things. But for a single moment, a current of electricity had passed through them like lightning. It was the first time Maggie had felt like that in years. And she smiled when they left, and she kissed him on the cheek.

"I remember the raft perfectly," she whispered to him as she hugged him, and Peter grinned.

Chapter 22

Christmas in London was magic. Store windows were festive, trees were put up and decorated everywhere, people strung up lights on their houses. The weather cooperated and it snowed repeatedly, and people in costumes wandered through the streets singing Christmas carols. It was everything Christmas should be.

Ben and Ryan arrived from L.A. fresh from their mother's wedding. Lisa knew that Ryan had been upset about it, and she inquired as soon as she saw him at one of their Sunday-night dinners.

"So how was it?" she asked cryptically.

He knew what she meant, and shrugged appropriately for his age.

"Dumb. Too much food. Too many people. Cheesy music."

"Where was it? Like the Rose Bowl or something?" Although she was older, Lisa was always impressed by the fact that Ryan lived in L.A., and she thought he led a glamorous life, instead of a small town like Ware, and now she lived in London.

"No, it was at my grandfather's house. They had gardenias everywhere and I coughed all night. I hate them." Lisa laughed at the description.

"Sounds like a typical Hollywood wedding."

"Yeah, I guess. I've never been to one before."

"Did she wear a white dress?" Lisa wanted all the details.

"No. She wore pink. But she looked nice. So how are they doing?" He nodded toward their respective parents, sitting in the living room near the tree and talking. They did that a lot.

"Still friends. They have a nice time together." Lisa had relaxed about Peter. She had gotten used to him. He never crowded

her and never came between her and her
mother. He was nice to have around, and
Bill was crazy about him. He finally had a
father figure.

"I think they're hopeless," Ryan said,
looking discouraged. But everyone was
having fun, despite the lack of romance
between their parents. It was just Ryan's
fantasy because he loved Maggie and
his cousins, but they staunchly remained
friends, with no sign of romance between
them.

The six of them spent Christmas Eve together, and went to midnight mass. And
on Christmas Day, Peter took them to Claridge's so Maggie didn't have to cook dinner. They all exchanged gifts, and had
bought each other small, thoughtful things.
Maggie had bought Peter a beautiful cashmere scarf and leather gloves. And Peter
bought her mink earmuffs and a mink collar that she loved. All the gifts were just
what the other person wanted, and after
dinner at Claridge's, they all went back to
Peter's apartment and watched movies and
played games. It was a warm family Christmas. Peter said it was the nicest one he'd
had in years. It was light-years better than

his last one in L.A., on their way to a divorce.

And two days later, they left for Courchevel. They flew to Geneva, and then took a van to the little village in the French Alps, nestled between three valleys. It was snowing hard when they got there. And the chalet looked like something in a fairy tale. It had six bedrooms, and they only used five since Ben and Ryan shared a room. Ben didn't like to sleep alone. And every morning, Peter took them to the ski lift, where he had arranged for private instructors for the group, to take them to the various locations on the mountain. They had a choice of all three valleys and several mountains and could ski all day. And after dropping them off, Peter went back to Maggie at the chalet. She had brought some knitting with her, and they sat by the fire and relaxed, and then went for long, easy walks. She had gotten much stronger, and the yoga had helped her. At night, they had the kids, but the days were all theirs.

Peter and Maggie explored the shops in the town, some of which were luxurious, and others were quaint. They had lunch sitting outdoors in the winter sunshine, and afterward she would tuck her hand into his arm and they'd walk, until they got tired and went back to the chalet to sit by the fire again.

"I wish we could stop time and stay here forever," Maggie said wistfully. She was dreading going back to Ware in two weeks for the trial. They were both trying not to think about it, but it crept into their minds anyway, whether they talked about it or not. Peter had had several e-mails from the district attorney, and everything was on track. Michael had claimed his right to a speedy trial instead of trying to postpone it, which was something of a relief. None of them wanted the trial hanging over their heads all year. And apparently, he wanted to get it over with too.

"Thank you for sharing your vacation with us," Maggie said to Peter as she handed him a mug of hot chocolate one afternoon after their walk. He was sitting in a comfortable chair with his legs stretched out in front of the fire, reading a book. And he smiled at her as he took the mug of hot chocolate.

"It wouldn't be half as much fun without you here." He was finding that that was true of most things. He enjoyed Maggie's company everywhere. He'd been thinking about it a lot recently, and he gently touched her hand as he took the mug. Maggie looked surprised.

"My kids love being with you," she said, and sat down on the rug near his feet, enjoying the warmth from the fire.

"I love being with you, Maggie," he answered. "Do you ever think about what it would have been like if we'd wound up together?"

"I wasn't glamorous enough for you," she said as she laughed. "You were destined for stardom in New York. I was just a small-town girl."

"As I recall," he reminded her, after a sip of the steaming chocolate, "you were the one who dumped me, for some hot football player. I think he was the captain of the team."

"He was on the basketball team," she corrected him with a grin.

"So what was so hot about him?"

"I don't know. I can't remember. I was dumb in those days, and that was before I hit my head," she teased, and he gently touched his fingers to her cheek.

"You were never dumb. You were smarter than I was, even then."

"If it's any consolation, I was sorry after I dumped you. I broke up with the other guy in two weeks. He was a jerk. He practically tore my sweater off at the movies." She giggled.

"Smooth move. We were all so sophisticated then," he said, and she laughed.

"I was always pretty square," she said, comfortable with him. She could say anything to Peter. And after all they'd been through recently, even more so.

"I remember how square you were," he chuckled.

"Come to think of it, maybe that's why I dumped you. You wanted to go further than I did."

"I was two years older. It makes a big difference at that age." She nodded.

"And then you went off to college after that summer, when you kissed me on the raft."

"I should have taken you with me." He looked down at her sitting next to him, and their eyes met, and without thinking, she reached up and rested a hand on his knee. He gently took her hand in his and stroked her fingers. "What do you think about us now, Maggie?" He had been wanting to ask her that question for months, especially lately.

"What do you mean?" She looked startled.

"Do you ever think about our being together?"

"We are together," she said simply.

"I mean more than this."

She lowered her eyes then. She had thought about it too. "I don't know," she said shyly. "I don't want to spoil anything."

"I don't think we would. I don't want to scare you, Maggie," he said gently. But he didn't. He never had.

"You don't," she said, looking up at him again. "You couldn't." He was nothing like Michael. He hadn't scared her either. He had overwhelmed her. Peter never did. She knew she was totally safe with him. That was important to her now. And she enjoyed what they had, and the time they spent together with their children.

"Should we put it to a family vote?" he teased her. "I think I know what they'd say. My kids are crazy about you."

"So are mine." She smiled up at him, and

then with a sad look she added, "Maybe we should get through the trial before we think about it. That's going to be so hard." He nodded and squeezed her hand. It was going to be the first time she saw Michael since the hospital.

"I'll be there with you. I won't let anything bad happen to you ever again," he said with a serious look, and she knew he meant it, as much as anyone could ever promise that. But Peter would have done anything he could to protect her, and he had.

"I love being with you," she said softly. He nodded, and then just so she would have something to remember until after the trial, he leaned down and kissed her, and she kissed him back. Thirty years faded between them when he did it, and it felt just like being on the raft. She was smiling when they stopped. "See, I told you, you're a great kisser," she said, laughing, and he kissed her again, just to prove it. Kissing her was exciting and he wanted more. For the past year, he had felt nothing, and now a lifetime of emotions were welling up in him and pouring into her. She could feel it too. It gave them both something to look forward to, and to hope for, after the trial.

They were sitting quietly by the fire, talking to each other, sitting close together, when the kids came home from skiing, and Ryan gave Lisa a knowing look. When they got upstairs to take off their ski clothes, he whispered to her.

"I think he kissed her."

"How do you know?" Lisa whispered back.

"I can tell. They look like they have a secret."

"You're crazy," she said, laughing at him. "Maybe they're just having a nice time."

"Yeah," he said, shrugging. "Maybe you're right." And when they came back downstairs, Maggie was in the kitchen, getting dinner ready, singing to herself, and Peter was smiling into the fire, remembering the day on the raft. He had something to compare it to now.

Chapter 23

Maggie, Bill, and Peter flew back from London together for the trial. Peter had arranged for a car to pick them up in Boston. And Peter was going to be staying at their house in Ware. There was nowhere else that made sense for him to stay, and he didn't want to commute from the lake. And Maggie and Bill were grateful for his support. It was hard for both of them to be back in their house again. Maggie hadn't wanted Lisa there, and she was staying with a friend from school in London, without explaining the reason for her mother's trip. It was too painful for her.

Their first night in Ware, they had dinner together at the diner. And it gave Maggie the creeps when they walked into the house afterward. It was all she could do to force herself upstairs to the bedroom, and see the room where she had been sick for so long. But there was nowhere else for her to sleep, since Peter was in Lisa's room, and Bill was in his own. The house felt like a graveyard to her now. She was planning to put it on the market after the trial, and file for divorce. She was dreading the trial, and her first sight of Michael in all this time, eight months.

They had a meeting set that night with the DA, after dinner. He was coming to the house. He wanted to prepare each of them for their testimony and for cross-examination by Michael's attorney. Maggie wondered why he had insisted on a jury trial when he was so clearly guilty. She wondered if he thought he'd be acquitted at a jury trial. He was still pleading not guilty. Jack had tried to talk him into changing it to guilty, but Michael had just laughed.

The whole town was talking about the trial. At the diner, several people had told Maggie it was nice to see her back. And everyone was friendly to Peter. There was no question who the good brother was now. When they met the DA at the house, he went over their statements with each of them. He was there till after midnight. He told them they were starting jury selection the next morning. None of them had to be in court for that. They only had to be in court for their own testimony. And he was planning to put Maggie on last. He thought her testimony would be the most powerful for the jury. And the most shocking. Of the three of them, he was going to put Bill on first, then Peter, and last Maggie. The families of the elderly people Michael had killed were going to be his first witnesses, and would set an early emotional tone for the trial, since many of their relatives were terribly upset, like the man who had come to see Peter at the lake.

The DA explained that he also had several expert witnesses, mostly about poisons and medications. He expected the actual trial to last for about two weeks. He estimated two days to select the jury. And there was no predicting how long it would take for the jury to reach a verdict. He just hoped it wouldn't be a hung jury. And he was anxious to do all he could to avoid a mistrial so they wouldn't have to do it all over again. Maggie trembled at the thought.

They all went to bed after he left. Maggie lay awake in bed for hours, thinking about the things the DA had said. They would be sequestered in a private room at the courthouse during the proceedings, away from prying eyes and the press, but readily available when they were needed. It was going to be a long week or two while they waited to testify.

The three of them shuffled around the kitchen the next morning, scrounging up breakfast from a few things they'd bought the night before, and Vi had given them a bag of cinnamon rolls, but none of them were hungry.

They left for the courthouse at eight-thirty, in a squad car Jack Nelson had sent for them, and they drove to Northampton and walked into the courthouse through a back door. A horde of reporters had anticipated that, and were lying in wait for Maggie. Peter and two policemen hustled her into the building quickly, and she looked frightened and pale as they got into the room that had been set aside for them and locked the door.

"Are you okay?" Peter asked her tersely, and she nodded and sat down, but he could see that she was shaking. She had her hands folded tightly in her lap. She wasn't looking forward to reliving her entire marriage to Michael, on the witness stand.

It took two days to select the jury, as the DA had predicted. There were eight men and four women, and two additional women as alternates. The DA had expected Michael's attorney to ask for a change of venue, but he didn't. In fact, he had advised it, but Michael had insisted that he was comfortable being judged by twelve of his peers in his own hometown. He was expecting his reputation as a saint to serve him well. It was a little late for that.

On the third day, the trial began. The judge addressed the jurors, explained what the case was about and told them what their duties were. He spoke loudly and clearly and sounded stern. Maggie could hear him from their little room off the courtroom. And then the two attorneys made their opening statements to the jury. The

district attorney described Michael's heinous crimes, not only murdering eleven
people, including his own parents, and manipulating all of them out of their money,
but poisoning his wife and trying to kill her,
controlling her and convincing her of her ill
health for twenty-three years.

Michael was being charged with eleven
counts of first-degree murder with deliber-
ately premeditated malice aforethought,
and one count of premeditated attempted
murder. The prison sentence for first-
degree murder was life imprisonment without parole, since the death sentence had
been declared unconstitutional in the Commonwealth of Massachusetts, and he was
facing twenty years for attempting to murder Maggie.

Michael's attorney walked slowly down
the courtroom, strolling back and forth past
the jury box, looking each juror in the eye.
He said that he understood how serious
the charges were, and so did the defendant, and he said that they could only convict beyond a reasonable doubt. He said
that expert witnesses would explain to them
later that the substance Michael was ac-

cused of using to murder eleven elderly, very sick people could have been used merely to relax them in their final hours. All of them had been dying, and no one could say that he had murdered them. He had made the last moments of dying people easier. Michael McDowell had **not** killed them, he assured the jury. The district attorney might try to convince them it was murder, but clearly it was **not**. The anesthetic in question had been found in his medical supplies at the office, but as a general practitioner, it was entirely reasonable that he might have this medication among his supplies. In fact, his attorney stressed to the jury, Michael McDowell had not killed anyone. He was a revered, much respected, dedicated doctor who did everything in his power to keep his geriatric patients alive. And if they chose to leave him money in gratitude, in their last wills and testaments, that was an entirely respectable circumstance. It is not a crime, the attorney pointed out, to be named in someone's will, and Michael did not extort or manipulate anyone to get that money. These were the grateful gifts of adoring patients. He pointed out that Michael was regarded as a saint in the community, and saints do not kill their patients.

And in the case of Michael's wife, he went on, she was a mentally and physically impaired woman who had been an invalid for all of her adult life, and here again, Michael had kept her alive, despite over-whelming odds. And the toxic substance found in her bloodstream eight months ear-lier was most commonly used for suicides, and he intended to prove to the jury that Mrs. McDowell had in fact tried to end her own life while Michael fought to save it. Of course, Michael McDowell's fingerprints were on the bottles of weed killer, since he tended to the garden. And what if she had handled the same bottle to poison herself while wearing gloves? All Michael's attor-ney needed was reasonable doubt. He had just raised it. At no time, he assured the jury, did Michael McDowell poison his wife or try to kill her. And he assured the jurors that by the end of the trial, they would acquit his client for being the innocent man that he was. And with that, he thanked them and sat down. It was a lot of high drama, and smooth courtroom style, to try and ex-

plain away some very ugly facts. All the evidence was against Michael. And all the
defense attorney had to do was try to cloud
the issues enough to create a "reasonable
doubt" in the jurors' minds. It was Michael's
only hope.

Jack Nelson was glad that Maggie wasn't
in the courtroom to hear what had been
said about her. It was the usual perfor-
mance of a well-trained defense attorney,
but it still made Jack feel sick to hear it, so
he was relieved that Maggie hadn't.

And with that, the proceedings began. It
was the commonwealth's responsibility to
present their case first. And the defense attorney's to defend his client afterward.

The commonwealth's first witness was
an expert from a toxicology lab in Boston,
testifying on medications normally used
in anesthesiology, succinylcholine being
one of them, which he believed could have
been administered in the geriatric deaths.
And with training as an anesthesiologist,
Michael would know how to dose it and
use it. When dosed to excess, it was an
extremely lethal substance. The expert
droned on for two hours, explaining various
medications and their effects and chemical

makeup in minute detail. But essentially, he agreed with the coroner's presumed cause of death of the victims, that they had received lethal doses of succinylcholine, the same substance found in Michael's medicine closet in his office, so he had easy access to it. And after the expert's testimony, they recessed for lunch.

The afternoon was taken up by another expert witness from the poison control center in Boston, to explain the properties of the weed killer paraquat to the jury. They were told this was the substance Michael had used to try and kill his wife, since she had a nearly lethal dose of it in her system, and showed signs of prolonged exposure to it.

Both experts were cross-examined by Michael's attorney, and he asked the man from the poison control center if paraquat was used most frequently in suicides. The expert agreed that was sometimes the case, but usually only in underdeveloped countries because of the low cost. Michael's attorney sat down after that question. Everyone in the courtroom was ready to fall asleep after the expert testimony, and the judge adjourned for the day, after admonishing the jurors not to discuss the case with anyone, or he would sequester them for the remainder of the trial. They all nodded agreement and left the courtroom like sheep. And then the district attorney explained to Maggie, Peter, and Bill what had gone on that day. It sounded tedious to them, but nonetheless important, in order to establish Michael's guilt, since he had access to both substances, and his fingerprints had been all over the bottles of the poison used on Maggie. From what the DA described, it was going to be a long trial.

The rest of the week was taken up by the emotional testimony of the relatives of the nine geriatric patients who had allegedly been murdered. And in his testimony, Peter would have to talk about what he had read in his mother's journals, where she mentioned that Michael had euthanized his father, which he had denied when Peter asked him about it. But now Peter had no doubt that he had, and when his parents had been exhumed, the test results had proved it.

There were tears and accusations from the relatives of the elderly people, and

Michael sat expressionless throughout. He was led out of the courtroom at the end of the day, in handcuffs and leg irons, after the jury left so they wouldn't see it. And he was wearing a suit, a white shirt, and a tie. He looked impeccable and totally calm. He was the image of an innocent man—or one without a conscience.

By the end of the week, Maggie looked exhausted and so did Peter. Bill had kept distracted by texting people on his cell phone, and had given them several messages from Lisa, who he said was doing fine. He had also brought some of the reading for his homework with him. And his mother and uncle seemed considerably more on edge than he did as the days dragged by.

They spent every day sitting and waiting, and there was nothing else they could do. And on the weekend, Maggie and Peter decided to drive up to the lake and take a walk there. They both smiled when they saw the raft, but he didn't kiss her. This wasn't the time or place for them to think about romance. They sat side by side, in silence, looking out at the lake and thinking about the trial.

They checked on Peter's house and found everything in order, and then they went back to Maggie's house, and tried to pass the time. It was difficult to go outside, because there were frequently reporters waiting, and television camera crews, hoping to catch a glimpse of them. It was easier to stay inside, with the shades drawn, until they left for court again on Monday morning. Vi brought them food from the diner and refused to let them pay. They filed quietly past the reporters then on Monday morning and made no comment.

There was more expert testimony that day. And finally, on the seventh day of the trial, they called Bill to the stand. The district attorney led him through his Internet search for a poison that matched his mother's symptoms, and his desperate call to Peter, which led to the first toxicology report. They had him identify it in court.

"And why did you think your father was poisoning your mother?" the DA asked him, blocking his view of his father as he stood there, so that Bill wouldn't be intimidated by him.

"Because I think he's a pathological liar, a sociopath, and a very dangerous person," Bill said, visibly shaking. On cross-examination, Michael's attorney asked him if he was a psychiatrist, or had psychiatric credentials, and Bill said he didn't.

"Then on what basis do you make that diagnosis of your father? With what credentials, sir?" he asked Bill contemptuously with a smug smile.

"Because I grew up with him and I saw what he did to my mother," Bill said in a choked voice, as everyone in the courtroom sat riveted. And Peter watched him from the back of the courtroom with tears in his eyes. They excused Bill from the witness stand after that.

Peter was the next witness. He described the call from Bill, getting the three hairs from Maggie's head, and the trip to the toxicology lab in Boston, and the condition he saw Maggie in at the hospital. It was emotional for him too, but he got through it. And then the attorney for the defense took him by surprise.

"Did you date Margaret McDowell when you were growing up? I believe her maiden name was Higgins."

"Yes, I did," Peter answered easily.

"How old was she at the time?"

"Fifteen."

"And you were?"

"Seventeen."

"Did you have intercourse with her?"

"No, I did not," Peter answered calmly.

"Did you have an affair with her later on, when she was married to the defendant?"

"No, I didn't." Peter remained undisturbed throughout.

"Is William McDowell your illegitimate son?"

"No, he isn't."

"Have you noticed that he looks just like you?"

"If that's the case, it's unfortunate for him," Peter said, as a ripple of laughter swept through the courtroom, which broke the tension for a minute.

"Were you jealous of your brother?"

"Sometimes," Peter answered honestly.

"Do you hate him?"

"I did at one time." Honest again.

"Enough to try to send him to prison, so you could start a life with Mrs. McDowell?"

"Of course not." Peter frowned.

"Did you have an affair with his wife when you came back to Ware last year?"

"No, I didn't."

"If you could have gotten your brother out of the way, would you have made advances to his wife?"

"I never thought about it. She was his wife. And I believed they loved each other."

"What changed your mind about that? Did she say something to you about being unhappy with your brother?"

"Never. I realized he didn't love her when he tried to kill her, and I realized he had been trying to do so for some time." Peter's eyes were like ice as he looked at the attorney.

"The witness is excused," the defense attorney said just as coldly. "You may leave the stand." His attempt to rattle Peter hadn't worked. It had backfired on him. Peter and the district attorney were pleased.

Maggie had to wait until the next day to testify, and she lay awake all night. She hated the bed she slept in, in that house. It reminded her of all the years she'd been so sick and thought she was dying, when that room was her entire world. Now, she felt claustrophobic in it.

They put her on the stand first thing in the morning. Peter was in the courtroom, as was Bill. And she walked to the stand with a modest limp. She sat down and was sworn in. She had walked past the defense table without looking at Michael, but she could see his form in her peripheral vision, and she could feel his eyes on her when she took the stand. She kept her gaze averted so she didn't have to see his face. She kept her eyes on the district attorney who stood in front of her.

He led her through her entire health history, her accident, her marriage to Michael, and all the illnesses and ill effects she had suffered over the years, and the alleged reasons for them, as told to her by Michael. And then he asked about her steady health improvement since Michael had been in custody and she was no longer being poisoned. It was easy for anyone in the courthouse to see that she appeared to be in good health. Her direct testimony took three hours until lunchtime. They recessed then, and after lunch she went back on the stand for cross-examination. The judge reminded her that she was still under oath, and she said she understood.

"Did you have headaches after your accident and after you were in a coma for five months?" was the question the defense attorney opened with.

"Yes, I did," she answered clearly. "For about a year."

"Did you have psychiatric problems? Anxiety? Hallucinations? Insomnia?"

"I was anxious sometimes, and I had trouble sleeping."

"Did you continue to suffer from those same complaints after you married Michael?"

"Sometimes."

"How did you handle them?"

"He medicated me."

"Did you ask him to?"

"Never. He insisted on it. He said it was good for me, and dangerous if I didn't." There was a ripple of people shifting in their seats in the courtroom.

"And did the medications he gave you help you?"

"They made me sleep, but they left me with hangovers and general weakness. They made me lethargic and dizzy."

"Do you know what medications he gave you?"

"He wouldn't tell me."

"Why did you take them? You're an intelligent woman. No one can 'make you' take medicine."

"He said I had to. He got very upset if I didn't. And he was my doctor and my husband. I didn't want to make him angry at me."

He switched tacks then. "Tell me about Peter McDowell. Did you sleep with him when you were fifteen?"

"No, I didn't."

"Why not?"

"I was a virgin, and I didn't want to."

"Were you a virgin when you slept with Michael? And please remember, Mrs. McDowell, you're under oath." His comment was meant to be insulting, but she didn't bristle.

"Yes, I was a virgin until I married Michael."

"That's not what he says," the defense attorney said smugly.

"Then he's lying," she said coolly.

"Did you have an affair with your brother-in-law when he came back to town last year?" He was clearly implying that this was a love triangle, and they had been trying to get rid of Michael so had framed him. The implication was clear.

"No, I didn't."

"Why not?"

"I loved my husband. I was faithful to him."

"Have you ever wanted to commit suicide?"

"No, I haven't."

"Have you ever taken anything that could cause it?"

"Never. Michael gave me all my medications."

"And you have no idea what they were?"

"That's correct."

"Did your husband take good care of you?"

"I thought so. Until I discovered that he was poisoning me." There was a sharp intake of breath in the courtroom. She looked calm and strong and believable.

"Did you ask him about it afterward? Did you ask him to explain it to you?" The attorney looked smug again, until she answered.

"I tried to. I wrote him many letters while he was in jail, asking him to call me, or write to me, or let me come to see him."

"And what did he say?"

"He never answered. Not a single one. From the day he was arrested, I never heard from him again, until the present. That was when I realized that he didn't love me, and it was true that he was poisoning me. Until then, I didn't believe what they were telling me and I thought it wasn't true. He never wanted to see me or talk to me again." Michael's attorney glanced at him after she answered. Michael was expressionless at the defense table. And it was obvious that the attorney had been surprised by her answer.

"Do you suffer now from any of the ailments that plagued you while you were married to Michael?" It was a long shot, but he risked it, and lost.

"None. They all disappeared within days, weeks, or months. I'm fine now. Except for the limp. He told me I had Parkinson's too, and would die from it. I didn't have it. It's one of the side effects of the poison he was feeding me. It looked like Parkinson's, but it wasn't. He kept me drugged all the time. I was a zombie."

"The witness is excused," the defense attorney said, and sat down next to Michael. He had expected her to be a basket case, from what Michael had told him. He said she would collapse on the witness stand, but she had been strong, intelligent, and coherent. She had destroyed their case more than any other witness. The district attorney was practically dancing when she came off the stand. And as she walked by him, she couldn't resist looking at Michael this time. She had to. Her eyes searched his face, and he looked right through her, as though he hadn't seen her, and had never known her. She felt as though a gust of freezing air had hit her face, and then she walked past him. His eyes were the most terrifying she had ever seen. The mask was off. He was everything Peter had said and Bill had feared.

On the final day of testimony, his attorney put Michael on the stand. He looked gentle and pleasant as he took the oath and sat down. He had his doctor face on, the one that had won him the title of saint in three counties for twenty years.

His attorney walked him through many of the same questions, about his career, his training, the fact that he'd been an anesthesiologist in Boston, and gave it up to join his father in his practice. The attorney asked about their marriage, Maggie's accident before that, and her health subsequently. Maggie had stayed in the courtroom to hear him and was sitting between Bill and Peter. And then the attorney asked him about Maggie's alleged affair with Peter.

"She had an affair with my brother when she was fifteen" was Michael's answer to the question.

"How do you know that?"

"He told me. We laughed about it. She was the school slut in those days." People in the courtroom looked uncomfortable as he said it, and Maggie felt sick. He was destroying her reputation for the hell of it, as a final act of vengeance, and for testifying against him.

"Did she have an affair with him again later, after you were married?"

"Yes, she did. I believe our first child was his." He said it with a wounded look.

"Did she admit it to you?"

"No, she didn't. And I didn't really want to know."

The district attorney stood up and objected then.

"Your honor, do we have to go through this again, about Mrs. McDowell's dating history at fifteen?"

"It's about the witness's credibility, your honor," the defense attorney insisted.

"Sustained," the judge said, looking annoyed. "Move on, counselor. We're dealing with more important matters here than who Mrs. McDowell slept with, or didn't, at fifteen."

He asked Michael about the medications he administered to her, and why he gave her tranquilizers and sleeping pills for many years.

"I had no choice. She suffered from severe psychiatric problems, even before I met her, and certainly after we were married. Much of the time, she was too frightened to leave our room, or she became violent. I had to sedate her. I didn't want to commit her to a psychiatric facility," he said, looking mournful. Maggie was sitting rigid in her chair next to Peter, shaking with rage, and Peter gave her a calming look. He could only imagine what she was feeling. It was Michael's last hurrah to hurt her, and he was having a field day with it. Maggie was afraid the jury would believe it.

"Did you ever put weed killer in your wife's food, or anything else she ingested?"

"Of course not. I'm a doctor. I'm under an

oath to do no harm," he said, looking virtuous and benign.

"Did your wife ever contact you after you were arrested? Write to you? Ask you to see her?"

"Never. I tried to contact her several times, but she wouldn't speak to me, or answer. I never received a single letter from her. I wanted to explain to her that it was all lies and I was being falsely accused, of all these charges." He glanced innocently at the jury as he said it.

"Do you know why she wouldn't speak to you?" his attorney asked him, as though he couldn't imagine a single reason.

"She was already sleeping with my brother, and had been for some time."

"Do you know that for a fact?"

"I was told by several people, even my own children. He lost all his money in the stock market crash, and I believe he came back to Ware to get hers. She's been obsessed with him all her life, and he knows that. He was taking advantage of her, and I believe he convinced her and my son to frame me."

"Do you have any proof of that, Mr. McDowell?"

"I don't, but I know her. She's a weak person, and very frightened, with deep psychiatric problems. She's easy prey for a man like my brother."

"Was she easy prey for you?"

"She was never my prey. I loved her," he said nobly.

After Michael's testimony, the district attorney asked Michael several more questions, and destroyed the credibility of almost everything he had said. But Maggie felt like she'd been dragged by the hair naked all over the courtroom. The defense asked him several questions about the geriatric patients, and even his own parents. And then finally, the defense rested. And both the DA and Michael's attorney made closing arguments. Both were eloquent and forceful. And after that the jury was instructed by the judge, and led out of the courtroom to begin their deliberations.

Michael was about to be returned into custody when he turned to where Maggie was sitting with their son and Peter.

"You were nothing!" he shouted at her. "You meant nothing to me! You never did! I felt sorry for you. You were pathetic," he said venomously, and then the deputies almost dragged him from the courtroom. And before they could, he turned to Peter, his eyes blazing at him. "You, with your high and mighty Wall Street life, while I stayed in this backwater to take care of our parents. I had as much right to that life as you did. I wanted to get out of here too, and be someone, but I stuck around and took care of them. You didn't!" he shouted at him. It had been all about jealousy and money and the life he'd wished he had. Maggie was shaking when Jack Nelson led her out of the courtroom, as the deputies dragged Michael away, still shouting at them. Jack took them back into their private room. Maggie looked like she was about to faint, as Peter stood near her.

"Listen to me," Peter said firmly, holding her arm to get her attention. "He's a very sick man. He's a murderer. What he says means nothing. He lies through his teeth." She nodded then, and sat down in a chair, fighting back tears. She had wasted twenty-three years of her life with him, and he had nearly killed her. And he had just told her that he never loved her. It wasn't even a crime of passion of some kind, it was cold-blooded attempted murder.

Jack Nelson left them alone after that, while the jury deliberated. The three of them were silent for a long time, and then Bill turned to Peter.

"Can I ask you something?" Peter could guess what it was.

"Sure," Peter said quietly. Maggie had started to get back a little color in her face.

"Am I your son?" Bill looked from Peter to his mother for confirmation, and they both shook their heads.

"I'm sorry to say you're not," Peter said kindly. "I wish you were. I'd be proud to be your father, and I wouldn't keep it a secret if I were."

"Shit!" Bill said with feeling, and all three of them laughed. "That would be the only piece of good news in this whole thing."

"Well, you can say you're my son any-time you want. Speaking of which," he turned to Maggie, "as often as we suppos-edly got laid, I'm damn sorry I missed it." Maggie smiled and then finally laughed at that too.

"I loved being called the school slut," she said miserably.

"You can't listen to anything he says. He

just wanted to hurt you," Peter said, and she nodded, and slipped her hand into his. It was easy to figure out that Michael had not only lied to everyone else, he had lied to his attorney, who had believed him.

An hour later, the district attorney came back to their conference room and told them that they might as well go home. The jury could be out for days and probably would be.

"We'll call you at home when they come back in."

Jack Nelson helped them out of the courthouse and past the reporters. He sent them home in a squad car again, as he had every day, and he patted Maggie's shoulder as she got in. He felt sorry for everything that had happened to her. And just like everyone else, Michael had lied to him too, and he'd believed him.

Maggie lay on the couch when they got back to the house, and fell asleep a little while later, while Peter and Bill watched basketball on TV. Bill had called Lisa to check in, but as they had since the trial began, they spared her the ugly details. She didn't need to know them. He was her father after all, and she had loved him. And she was only sixteen.

As Peter watched Maggie sleeping on the couch, he hoped the jury would return their verdict soon. This needed to end, for all their sakes. And as she slept, Bill and Peter exchanged a long tired look.

Chapter 24

The jury took three days to deliberate, and went over all the toxicology reports carefully, looking at the charts and descriptions about various medications and poisons. Particularly the paraquat that had been used on Maggie, and the succinylcholine he had used on the geriatric patients. They reread some of the testimony, and they voted unanimously.

They called Maggie at her house, and Jack sent a car for them. They walked into the courtroom, and the jury filed in a few minutes later. Michael was at the defense table, and the judge asked the defendant to rise.

The foreman of the jury stood in the jury box, and the judge asked if they had reached a verdict. He said they had, and the judge asked him how they had found the defendant. The judge then read off each charge, and the foreman spoke in a strong, clear voice on behalf of his fellow jurors.

"Guilty, your honor," he said, after each count of murder in the first degree. "We find the defendant guilty of eleven counts of murder in the first degree," which included his own parents. And then the judge asked him about the charge of the premeditated attempted murder of Margaret Higgins Mc-Dowell. "Guilty, your honor." There was shouting in the courtroom, as the judge rapped his gavel and then thanked the jurors. And a moment later, they left the court-room.

The judge set sentencing of the defendant for thirty days later, and Maggie already knew she didn't have to be there. She hadn't had the stomach to look at Michael after the verdict. He had stood silently through all the guilty charges. And there was no expression on his face. Maggie watched him walk out of the courtroom, with deputies on either side of him, and she felt absolutely nothing for him. He was a stranger to her. And Peter felt just as little for the man who was his twin, and had murdered their parents.

They left the courtroom with police protection, and sat staring at each other in her kitchen when they got home. Maggie couldn't think, couldn't move, couldn't eat, and didn't want to. Twenty-four years of her life had just ended. She had two wonderful children to show for it, but she knew now that her marriage had never existed for Michael, and it no longer existed for her either. And her children had lost their father. All she wanted to do now was pack and leave, and never see this house again, or anything to remind her of the life she had lived in it.

She went upstairs to pack, while Peter called the airlines for a flight to London the next day.

Before they left, on the following morning, Peter went to the cemetery to visit his parents' graves. He wanted to say goodbye to them and apologize for not being a better son, and not protecting them from Michael. Peter knew he wouldn't be back here again. And he thought they would understand it too. He hoped they would forgive him for what he hadn't been able to do for them.

He walked down the hill to the police car where Maggie and Bill were waiting for him. Jack Nelson had volunteered to drive them to Boston. He felt as though it was the least he could do to show his support.

None of them spoke on the ride to the airport. They were lost in their own thoughts, and there was nothing left to say. Justice had been done.

Jack hugged her when she got out of the car at Logan Airport, and he told her again how sorry he was. He shook hands with Peter and Bill, and then he left them, and they checked in. They had two hours until their flight to London, and Maggie couldn't wait to leave. She wanted to get as far away from here as she could.

They bought magazines, and stopped for something to eat. Bill was texting Lisa to tell her they were leaving Boston. They had talked late the night before about the verdict. She no longer believed their father innocent, so the verdict didn't come as a shock to her. It was a sad coming of age for her. And she was relieved that it was over for all of them. She could never feel the same way about her father again. It was a huge loss for her.

When Bill got up to get another cup of coffee, Peter looked at Maggie across the table. She had looked uncomfortable in her skin since the day before. Everything that had happened was so ugly.

"I just want you to hear something from me," Peter said gently. He looked at her, and he could see that she was numb. "This may be the wrong time to tell you, but I love you. I want to spend the rest of my life making up to you for what you went through. My brother is a monster, and you didn't deserve any of it. You may have meant nothing to him. But you mean everything to me." He was looking at her intently, and she could see that he meant it. She smiled and reached across the table for his hand.

"I love you too. I'm sorry we all had to go through it. It can't be any easier for you."

"I'm not the one who got poisoned," he said, as they stood up to walk to the gate and catch their flight. And with that, he put his arms around her and kissed her. It was over. Michael couldn't hurt either of them anymore. They stood in the airport and kissed as Bill saw them and smiled. He stood at a distance from them, and sent a text to his sister. He had promised he would if anything happened while they were away. She and Ryan had been hoping for this since Courchevel.

"The eagle has landed," he texted to his sister with a broad grin. She got it immediately, gave a long slow smile, and forwarded it instantly to Ryan in L.A. Ben was sitting next to him when he got it. They were eating breakfast before school, and Ryan laughed as he read it to him.

"What does that mean?" Ben asked him, looking puzzled. "What eagle?"

"I think Dad just kissed Maggie," Ryan explained.

"Awesome," Ben said with a grin. From Boston to London to L.A., the news was out and they approved.

Bill tapped them gently on the shoulder then. "Come on, you guys. Let's not miss our flight. You can do that on the plane."

"Right," Peter said, still holding Maggie. She was smiling broadly, as Peter looked at Bill and laughed, and the three of them walked through the terminal arm in arm to catch their plane. They had lived through it. They had survived. They had suffered enormous losses, and in the losses had been blessed with enormous gains.

About the Author

DANIELLE STEEL has been hailed as one of the world's most popular authors, with over 650 million copies of her novels sold. Her many international bestsellers include **Pegasus, A Perfect Life, Power Play, Winners, First Sight, Until the End of Time, The Sins of the Mother,** and other highly acclaimed novels. She is also the author of **His Bright Light,** the story of her son Nick Traina's life and death; **A Gift of Hope,** a memoir of her work with the homeless; and **Pure Joy,** about the dogs she and her family have loved.

Visit the Danielle Steel website at daniellesteel.com.